FRESH DISASTERS

BOOKS BY STUART WOODS

FICTION

Short Straw

Dark Harbor[†]

Iron Orchid[*]

Two-Dollar Bill[†]

The Prince of Beverly Hills

Reckless Abandon[†]

Capital Crimes[‡]

Dirty Work[†]

Blood Orchid[*]

The Short Forever[†]

Orchid Blues[*]

Cold Paradise[†]

L.A. Dead[†]

The Run[‡]

Worst Fears Realized[†]

Orchid Beach[*]

Swimming to Catalina[†]

Dead in the Water[†]

Dirt[†]

Choke

Imperfect Strangers

Heat

Dead Eyes

L.A. Times

Santa Fe Rules

New York Dead[†]

Palindrome

Grass Roots[‡]

White Cargo

Deep Lie[‡]

Under the Lake

Run Before the Wind[‡]

Chiefs[‡]

TRAVEL

A Romantic's Guide to the Country Inns of Britain and Ireland (1979)

MEMOIR

Blue Water, Green Skipper (1977)

[*]A Holly Barker Book   [†]A Stone Barrington Book   [‡]A Will Lee Book

FRESH DISASTERS

STUART WOODS

G. P. PUTNAM'S SONS | NEW YORK

ıllР

G. P. PUTNAM'S SONS
Publishers Since 1838
Published by the Penguin Group
Penguin Group (USA) Inc., 375 Hudson Street, New York, New York 10014, USA •
Penguin Group (Canada), 90 Eglinton Avenue East, Suite 700, Toronto, Ontario M4P 2Y3, Canada
(a division of Pearson Penguin Canada Inc.) • Penguin Books Ltd, 80 Strand, London WC2R 0RL,
England • Penguin Ireland, 25 St Stephen's Green, Dublin 2, Ireland (a division of
Penguin Books Ltd) • Penguin Group (Australia), 250 Camberwell Road, Camberwell, Victoria 3124,
Australia (a division of Pearson Australia Group Pty Ltd) • Penguin Books India Pvt Ltd,
11 Community Centre, Panchsheel Park, New Delhi–110 017, India • Penguin Group (NZ),
67 Apollo Drive, Mairangi Bay, Auckland 1311, New Zealand (a division of Pearson
New Zealand Ltd) • Penguin Books (South Africa) (Pty) Ltd, 24 Sturdee Avenue,
Rosebank, Johannesburg 2196, South Africa

Penguin Books Ltd, Registered Offices:
80 Strand, London WC2R 0RL, England

Library of Congress Cataloging-in-Publication Data

Woods, Stuart.
    Fresh disasters/Stuart Woods.
        p.   cm.
    ISBN 978-0-399-15410-2
    1. Barrington, Stone (Fictitious character)—Fiction.   2. Private investigators—New York (State)—
New York—Fiction.   3. New York (N.Y.)—Fiction.   I. Title.

PS3573.O642F74   2007   2006037329
813'.54—dc22

Printed in the United States of America
1   3   5   7   9   10   8   6   4   2

Book design by Stephanie Huntwork

This book is for

THERESA CRANE

E laine's, late.

Stone Barrington sat at his usual table with Dino Bacchetti and Bill Eggers. Dino was his old partner from when he had been on the NYPD, and Eggers was the managing partner of Woodman and Weld, the law firm for which Stone was of counsel, which is to say, he did the work that the firm did not wish to be seen to do, sometimes for clients the firm did not wish to be seen to represent. He did this work from a distance, at his home office in Turtle Bay.

Stone took his first sip of his second bourbon, while Dino and Eggers did likewise for their second Scotch.

"I'm hungry," Stone said. "How long since we ordered dinner?"

Eggers glanced at his watch. "Twenty minutes."

"I should have my green bean salad, hold the peppers, by now," Stone said.

"Look around," Dino said. "It's a busy night."

It was a busy night, Stone reflected, and then it got even busier. The front door opened, and in walked Herbert Q. Fisher with two hookers. Stone knew they were hookers, because renting was the only means by which Herbie Fisher could acquire company so attractive, not that they were all that attractive.

"Oh, shit," Stone said.

"Shit what?" Dino asked.

"It's Herbie Fisher." Stone looked away from the door, so as not to catch Herbie's eye. It didn't work.

Herbie stopped at Stone's table, picked up his hand and pumped it. "Hey, Stone, baby!" he yelled, forming his words carefully enough that he appeared drunk. "How's it hanging?"

"Hello, Herbie," Stone said. "How are you?" He immediately regretted the question.

"Well, I'm a lot better than okay," Herbie said. "I passed the bar today."

Stone squinted at him. "You're going to be a bartender?" Visions came to mind of customers clutching their throats and gagging.

"No, no—the *bar*. You and I are now brothers in the law."

"You're drunk, Herbie. Go away."

Herbie began searching for something in his inside coat pocket. "No, I'm not kidding. I've got it right here." He came up with a page from a newspaper and unfolded it to reveal a list of many names in small print. A circle was drawn around one of them. "See? Right here!" Herbie pointed helpfully.

Stone looked at the name. "This is a list of night students who got their GEDs, right?"

"No! Look up at the top of the page."

Stone followed Herbie's finger. "Candidates Successfully Completing the Bar Examination of the State of New York," read the title.

"It's a joke newspaper," Stone said.

"No, it's not!" Herbie said indignantly.

"You've never been to law school," Stone pointed out.

"I most certainly have," Herbie said, "for the past nineteen months, at the Oliver Wendell Holmes Internet College of Law. I graduated summa cum laude."

"Herbie, go away," Stone said.

"Oh, let me introduce you to my ladies," Herbie said, sweeping an arm toward the two hookers. "This is Suzette and Sammie.

Ladies, this is the distinguished attorney-at-law Mr. Stone Barrington. He and I have worked together in the past and, hopefully, will
be working together in the future."

"Herbie," Stone said, "you're hallucinating. The notion that
you graduated from any established law school and passed the
bar is insane, and the idea of working with you in any capa-
city is repellent. If you don't go away, I'll have a waiter throw
you out."

"Nice to see you, too, Stone," Herbie said with a wave. He took
the arms of his two companions and steered them toward a table in
Siberia, where a waiter was frantically beckoning.

"Who the hell was that?" Eggers asked.

"You remember that time when you wanted to catch a client's
husband *in flagrante delicto*, and you asked me to find a photographer, and Bob Cantor, who usually does that sort of work for me,
was out of town and recommended his nephew, and the nephew
fell through the skylight while taking the photograph?"

"Oh, yeah, I remember *that*."

"Well, *that* was Herbie Fisher."

"Holy shit, didn't you have that guy shot?"

"I wish."

"And now he's a member of the bar?"

"No, it's just one of Herbie's fantasies, probably cooked up to
impress the hookers."

"How do you know they're hookers?" Eggers asked.

Dino spoke up. "Just take a look," he said, nodding in the direction of Herbie's table.

One of the girls was sitting close to Herbie, exploring his ear with
her tongue, while the feet of the other, toes pointing downward,
could be seen to protrude from under the tablecloth. Herbie wore a
beatific expression.

"If Elaine sees that," Dino said, "she'll grab somebody's steak
knife and kill them all."

"Okay," Eggers said, "they're hookers. But that page of names he showed you was from the *Legal Review*, and they published the names today of those who passed the bar."

"Then somebody took the bar exam for him," Stone said.

"Probably the same guy who took G. W. Bush's exams at Yale and Harvard," Dino said.

Their first course arrived, and they dug in.

Elaine came over and sat down. "You ordered the porterhouse?" she said.

"Right," Dino replied.

"For three of you?"

"It's a big steak."

"It's a steak for two; you can carry home the leftovers, like always."

"Elaine," Stone said, "what's the difference if three of us finish the thing here?"

"The difference is one main course," she said. "Do the arithmetic."

Stone was about to argue with her when two very large men walked through the front door, looking around like wolves seeking out a wounded animal. "What's this?" Stone asked.

Dino glanced over his shoulder. "Wiseguys," he said. "So what?"

"They don't look like they're here for dinner," Stone replied. "At least, not for anything on the menu."

The two very large men walked the length of the restaurant, then homed in on Siberia, where the girl under the table had finished her work and had joined her companions in an upright position for a glass of wine. One of the men reached across the table, took Herbie by the lapels and lifted him over the table.

Stone was impressed that the lift was such that Herbie's feet had cleared the wineglasses. He watched as, braced between the two very large men, Herbie was escorted toward the front door, his feet not quite touching the floor.

"Dino," Elaine said.

"What?"

"Dino, you're a cop; do something," she said, nodding toward the three men.

"Elaine, I'm about to be in the middle of a steak."

"Listen, you want to fuck up my reputation here? I can't have that kind of stuff going on. Get your ass out there."

Dino heaved a sigh, got up from the table and walked out the front door, digging in his pocket for his badge.

"What's going on?" Eggers asked.

"Could be a collection under way," Stone replied.

"Or a hit," Elaine observed.

The door opened and Dino entered, supporting Herbie, who was dabbing at a bloody nose with a handkerchief. Dino walked him back to Siberia and sat him down at his table with the two hookers. Then he came back to Stone's table.

"What happened?" Eggers asked.

"Nothing," Dino replied. "I just saved his life, that's all."

Stone turned to Elaine. "Why do you allow people like Herbie in here?"

"He pays cash," Elaine replied.

T he three were picking over the remains of the porter-house when Eggers flagged down a waiter and pointed at the enormous bone. "Wrap that up for my wife's dog, will you?"

"Bill," Stone said, "your wife has a Yorkshire terrier; that bone will eat *him*."

"It'll keep him away from my shoes for a few days," Eggers replied, accepting the foil-wrapped gift from the waiter. "You pay three grand for a pair of custom-made shoes from Lobb's, and a four-pound canine perforates them."

Stone looked at Eggers in wonder. "You pay *three grand* for shoes?"

"That's a bargain; it's five grand if you go to Silvano Lattanzi."

"That's more than I paid for any of the first dozen cars I owned," Dino said. "If I were you, I'd insure the shoes."

"Hey, that could work," Eggers said. "I could claim against my household insurance. I mean, the deductible is only a grand."

"They'd probably make you shoot the dog," Stone said.

"That works for me," Eggers replied.

"Your wife would kill you in your sleep."

"You have a point."

Suddenly, Herbie and his two hookers materialized at their table. He was still dabbing at his nose, which had assumed the appearance of a small, battered eggplant. "Stone," he said.

Stone winced. "What, Herbie?"

"I want to sue those two guys, and I want you to represent me."

Dino burst out laughing.

"Herbie," Stone said, "you say you're a lawyer now; sue them yourself."

"Then I would have a fool for a client," Herbie replied, calling up the old legal maxim describing a lawyer who represents himself.

"I can't argue with that," Stone said, "but I will not, repeat *not*, represent you."

"I can pay."

"Herbie, the two guys who did that to your nose couldn't get you to pay."

"That's different," Herbie said. "Owing you would be a debt of honor."

"And that's different from the debt to the boss of those two guys how?"

"That debt involved sports; it's not the same thing."

"Try explaining that to Carmine Dattila," Dino said. "That's who those guys work for. Carmine would hollow you out and use you for an ashtray."

"No means *no,* Herbie," Stone said. "Good night."

Suddenly Eggers spoke up. "Mr. Fisher," he said, extending his hand, "I am William Eggers of the law firm of Woodman and Weld."

"Hey, how you doin'?" Herbie replied, pumping Eggers's hand.

"My firm would be happy to represent you in this matter; in fact, I would be pleased to handle the case personally."

Stone's jaw nearly hit the tabletop. "Bill, are you nuts, or are you just drunker than I thought?"

Eggers waved him away. "In fact, we would be pleased to represent you on a contingency basis."

"Bill," Dino said, "excuse me for interrupting, but I think you should know that Carmine Dattila is known by the sobriquet Dattila the Hun."

"Oh, Dino," Eggers said, shaking his head "don't you ever watch *60 Minutes*? The power those old guys once had has been much diminished."

"Nobody told Carmine," Dino replied.

Eggers whipped out a card and handed it to Herbie. "Mr. Fisher, please call me tomorrow morning around ten. I'll be out of the weekly partners' meeting by then."

Herbie read the card carefully, then produced one of his own.

Stone grabbed it: "Herbert Q. Fisher, Attorney at Law," it read, followed by a post office box and a cell-phone number. "Herbie," Stone said, "you only passed the bar today; when did you have these printed?"

"It was just in case," Herbie said defensively.

"And how come you were so sure you were going to pass the exam?"

Beads of sweat appeared on Herbie's brow. "I felt very confident that, given my education, it wouldn't be a problem."

"Who did you get to, Herbie? And how much did it cost you?"

"Well, if you'll excuse us, gentlemen," Herbie said with a little bow. "My ladies and I have an appointment elsewhere."

"Yeah," Dino muttered, "in the backseat of a cab."

Herbie swept his two companions out of the restaurant.

"Bill," Stone said, "what were you thinking?"

"Stone," Eggers replied, "you are obviously overlooking the public-relations effect of our handling a case against a . . ."

"Mafia chieftain, I believe the newspaper description goes."

"Yes, Mafia chieftain."

Dino spoke up. "Have you considered the public-relations effect of being found dead in a landfill?"

"Really, Dino, it's obvious that this Carmen . . . what's his name?"

"Carmine Dattila." Dino spelled it for him.

"It's obvious that Mr. Dattila has never been confronted in open court by a powerful law firm."

"Carmine Dattila has been confronted in open court a number of times by the United States Attorney for the Southern District of New York, who is a member of a fairly powerful law firm called the U.S. Department of Justice," Dino said. "And there ain't a mark on him."

"C'mon," Stone said, rising. "Let's get Clarence Darrow here into a cab before he decides to sue God."

3

Stone was drinking coffee at his desk the following morning when his secretary, Joan Robertson, appeared at the door.

"Got a minute?" Joan, a pretty June Allyson look-alike somewhere in her forties, ran Stone's office and Stone, as well.

"Sure, come on in. Bring coffee, if you like."

"Thanks, I've had mine," Joan said, sitting down. "Time to talk of unpleasant things."

"How unpleasant?"

"Not all that bad, really, just chronic."

"Tell me."

"Well, your monthly draw from Woodman and Weld just about covers my salary, the utilities and the copying machine, but only about half of what it costs you to live."

"And your point is?"

"We need a case now and then to pay, among other things, your monthly bill at Elaine's and to keep you in the black. You haven't, for instance, saved any money for the past three months."

"I'm aware of all that," Stone said. "More or less."

"Be more aware. Make rain."

"What do you want me to do, chase ambulances?"

"A nice personal-injury suit that lends itself to a quick settlement would do nicely."

"Maybe I could push somebody in front of a cab, then offer to represent him?"

"The problem is, Woodman and Weld has not been sending you much the past few months. Usually they're good for something fairly juicy now and then. That's how you support your preposterous lifestyle."

"Preposterous? What's preposterous about my lifestyle?"

"Well, let's see: You live alone in this large house . . ."

"I earn my living here, too," Stone pointed out.

"More or less. To continue, you have a country house in Connecticut; an armored, souped-up Mercedes in the garage; an airplane at Teterboro Airport; and a monthly bill at Elaine's that could feed a company of starving marines. All of it soaks up money. About the only thing you couldn't get along without is me."

"You're right, this is unpleasant."

"Look, you rarely use the house in Washington, Connecticut. Why don't you call Klemm Real Estate up there and put the place on the market? You bought it on a whim, and you've held onto it long enough to at least double your money."

"Yeah, but it's a good investment, better than the market, and anyway, I kind of like the idea of having a country place in Connecticut."

"Well, it's an awfully expensive way to get laid, Stone. Every time you take a woman up there for a few days, we get a thousand-dollar bill for drinks and dinners at the Mayflower Inn, and last time, you spent a couple of grand at a country auction, too. If it's not that, it's the annual Washington Antiques show. I don't even want to think about what you spent there."

Stone was growing very uncomfortable and was relieved to hear the phone ring.

Joan reached across the desk and picked up his phone. "Good morning, the Barrington Practice." She listened for a moment, pressed the Hold button and handed Stone the phone. "Bill Eggers for you. Maybe he's got some work for us?"

Stone took the phone and punched a button. "Good morning, Bill. How are you feeling today?"

"That's a cruel question," Eggers replied hoarsely.

"Was your wife's dog happy with the bone?"

"He ran when he saw it."

"And how did the partners' meeting greet your proposal to represent Herbie Fisher in a suit against Carmine Dattila?"

"Actually, they greeted it very well," Eggers said. "They immediately saw the public-relations benefit of going up against a mobster in a civil action."

"You astonish me," Stone said.

"What they didn't like was the idea of the managing partner personally representing Mr. Fisher."

"I can imagine," Stone chuckled. "Which poor schmuck did you stick with the case?"

"I'm actually on the phone with him now."

"Feel free to put me on hold while you break the news to him."

"That won't be necessary, since I'm speaking to him on this line."

Stone was confused for a moment, but then the full import of what Eggers was saying struck him like a wall of icy water. "Now wait a minute, Bill . . ."

"I'm afraid I can't wait, Stone. The case is yours, by unanimous vote of the partners."

"Bill, I begged you not to take this ridiculous case."

"Nevertheless," Eggers said, "there was a feeling among the partners that the firm has not been getting its money's worth from you lately, Stone."

"Well, God knows you haven't been throwing me any cases."

"Consider this one thrown."

"Bill, there's no money in this. Even if we managed to get a settlement, it would be limited to Herbie's medical expenses."

"But, if you went to trial, you could go for punitive damages."

"What, a few thousand dollars?"

"Stone, I think the partners would be happy without a large settlement if the case were to generate the kind of positive news stories that we think could be obtained by taking this case. Just think of yourself on the courthouse steps, after a day in court grilling Mr. Dattila. Think of a jury coming in with punitive damages of tens of thousands of dollars. You'd be all over the evening news, and so would Woodman and Weld. In fact, I'd be happy to come down to the courthouse and sit at your table for a few days, then share your moment on the courthouse steps."

"Bill, what have you guys been smoking over there? Whatever it is, it's illegal."

"Stone, let me put it to you bluntly. If you want to go on drawing the handsome monthly sum we pay you, and if you want to continue to have cases referred to you by our firm, then you're going to have to get on board with this case. The partners expect this of you."

"Oh, Jesus," Stone moaned. "Send me the case file, if there is one."

"I'll do better than that; I'll send you your client."

"You mean Herbie is at your office now?"

"Well, he was, but he's already on his way to you. He should be in your office shortly."

Stone glanced down the hallway and saw the front door open. "Oh, shit."

"I take it Mr. Fisher has arrived," Eggers said. "Do right by him, Stone. Make Woodman and Weld look good." He hung up.

Stone put the phone down.

"Stone," Joan said, "what's the matter?"

"Eggers has sent us a case."

"Oh, good."

"No." Stone nodded toward the hallway.

Joan followed his gaze. "Herbie Fisher? Yuck!"

"My sentiments exactly."

"What does he want?"

"He wants us to sue Carmine Dattila."

"Dattila the Hun?"

"One and the same."

"That's the case Eggers sent us?"

"That's the case."

"This is a bad joke. Make him go away."

"It is certainly a bad joke, but if we want to keep me of counsel to Woodman and Weld, I'm going to have to do this. Go and get your pad; I'll dictate a complaint."

Joan got up and left, squeezing past Herbie Fisher and managing not to touch him.

"Hey, Joanie," Herbie said.

"Yuck," Joan replied.

"Hey, Stone."

"Herbie," Stone said, "come in, sit down and shut up."

4

S tone gazed across his desk at Herbert Q. Fisher, Esquire. "You
  incredible fuckup," he said, as pleasantly as he could manage. Herbie had a plastic cup taped across his nose, and two
big black eyes. "You look like a demented raccoon."

"Stone," Herbie said, reprovingly, "I don't think Bill Eggers and
the partners at Woodman and Weld would like you to speak to a
client that way."

Stone resisted the urge to throw himself across the desk and
strangle Herbie. "Joan!" he yelled. "Come in here and bring the Polaroid camera!"

"Are we going to write a complaint?" Herbie asked.

"Stop pretending you're a lawyer," Stone replied.

Joan came into Stone's office. "We haven't had any film for the
Polaroid camera for two years," she said, "but I brought my phone."
She held up a cell phone.

"I don't want to make a call," Stone said. "I want to take pictures
of Herbie's injuries."

"There's a camera in my phone, Stone; there's one in yours, too."

"There is?"

Joan swiveled Herbie around in his chair and turned Stone's
desk lamp on his face. "Don't smile," she said, holding up the cell
phone.

Herbie smiled. "Cheese," he said, revealing a missing tooth.

Joan snapped several pictures, front and profile.

"Do you have any bruises on your body?" Stone asked.

"Oh, sure," Herbie said.

"Take off your shirt and stand against the wall."

Herbie slipped out of his jacket and shirt and stood up. He had half a dozen big bruises around his ribs and belly.

"Did they kick you in the balls?" Stone asked.

"Uh-uh," Joan said quickly. "That's where I draw the line."

"Never mind," Stone said. "Herbie, have you seen a doctor?"

"The girls made me go to the emergency room at Lenox Hill Hospital."

"Do you have a receipt for your bill?"

Herbie groped his jacket, then held up a credit card slip. "Here it is!" he said triumphantly.

Stone looked at it. "You have a working credit card?"

"Well, of course. Oh, I have to see a plastic surgeon to get my nose fixed."

"Joan, who's a good nose guy?"

"How should I know?" she asked indignantly.

"Who did your sister?"

"I presume you mean her nose. Steinberg."

"Make an appointment for Herbie with Steinberg, and make it clear to his secretary that we'll need a written description of his injuries, along with a statement of the cost to repair the damage. Tell him not to stint. And tell her not to bill us."

"I have to get my nose fixed pretty soon," Herbie said. "The ER doctor said it'll start to heal, and then it'll have to be rebroken."

"So, make an appointment and have the surgery," Stone said.

"That's going to cost."

"That's your problem, Herbie. As far as I'm concerned we'll have a stronger case if your nose looks bad at trial."

"But how am I going to attract women?"

"With the money you saved on plastic surgery; they won't charge you any more than they did before."

Herbie tucked in his shirttail and began tying his tie.

"Can we write the complaint together?"

"No. I require privacy when I compose complaints."

"Come on, Stone, let me work with you on this case."

"Your involvement in this case is going to be limited to your testimony in court, and that had better be good. Now go home and get some rest, and go see Steinberg as soon as possible; I need his report for the complaint."

"Oh, all right," Herbie said dejectedly. "And what are you going to do?"

"Research. Now go away. Speaking of research, what's your bookie's name?"

"Carlo."

"Carlo what?"

"Carlo the bookie."

"And how much do you owe him?"

"Twenty-four thousand, as of yesterday. The vig is ten percent a week."

"Good God! How did you ever get a bookie to let you owe twenty-four grand? Is this Carlo nuts?"

"They know I'm good for it," Herbie said, miffed.

"I guess that's why they didn't break your legs, too. No, they would have broken your legs if Dino hadn't shown up. You ought to write him a thank-you note; it's the polite thing to do. Joan! Get Herbie out of here!"

Joan came in with a slip of paper and handed it to Herbie. "Steinberg / tomorrow at 10:30."

Herbie stuffed the number into his pocket and shuffled out.

"I like the limp, Herbie," Stone yelled after him. "Cultivate it for the jury!"

Herbie vanished down the street.

"How do you get yourself into these things?" Joan asked.

"Look, I was having a quiet dinner at Elaine's with Eggers and Dino. Herbie turned up, and . . . Oh, the hell with it. I'm innocent! Now go pay some bills or something."

"With what?"

"I know you keep a secret cache for emergencies."

"It's not an emergency yet."

"Then don't pay anybody until they send somebody around to break your legs."

"Ho, ho, ho," she said, closing the door behind her.

Stone called Dino.

"Lieutenant Bacchetti."

"It's me. I need a Mob expert; you got a guy over there?"

"Wait a minute. Is this for Herbie's thing?"

"Yeah."

"Why are you involved in that?"

"Eggers was hung over this morning, but not enough to forget to weasel out of doing it himself."

"So he made you do it?"

"Can you think of any other reason why I'd be involved?"

"Joe Giraldi," Dino said. "He's one of my guys, and I lent him to the Mob task force. He could do a family tree. He hates those guys, and it makes him good at his work. Here's his number."

Stone wrote it down. "Then I bet he would enjoy testifying against them."

"He might, at that. I hope you don't think I'm going to testify."

"You sure as hell are. You're my only eyewitness; you saw everything." He paused. "Didn't you?"

"Maybe."

"What do you mean, 'maybe'?"

"What's in it for me?"

"You'll have Herbie Fisher's undying gratitude."

"I'd rather have his dying gratitude."

"Me, too, but I haven't figured out how to make that happen, yet."

"Oh, just pursue this case; it'll happen. Maybe you'll happen, too."

"I'm going to try and avoid that."

"Good idea. Maybe you better go see Eduardo."

Eduardo Bianchi was Dino's former father-in-law. He was Stone's former father-in-law, too, but that was complicated. "I hate to bug him with something this trivial."

"He likes you; he'll give you a good lunch."

"Maybe."

"What else you got?"

"Not much."

"Have a good time."

S tone dictated the complaint and told Joan to get it filed immediately, then he went through his accounts receivable, looking for who owed him. Hardly anybody, as it turned out, and
not very much. That took the rest of the morning. He ate a sandwich
at his desk and worried about money.

After lunch, he called Dino's Mob guy.

"Joe Giraldi," a voice said.

"Hi, Joe, I'm Stone Barrington; I used to be Dino Bacchetti's partner at the one nine."

"I know who you are," Giraldi replied. He didn't sound thrilled.

"Dino told me you know everything there is to know about the
Mob in New York."

"If I knew everything there was to know about the Mob in New
York, they'd all be doing time in Attica."

"Heh, heh," Stone said. "Well, the fact remains that you know a
hell of a lot more than I know, and that's what I'm looking for."

"For what? You writing a novel?"

"No, I'm filing a civil suit against Carmine Dattila and . . ." Stone
stopped talking. All he could hear was laughter from the other end
of the line. He waited for it to subside.

"That's rich!" Giraldi howled, trying to get control of himself.

"Hey, Charlie," he shouted to somebody in the room, "I got some schmuck lawyer on the phone says he's going to sue Carmine Dattila!" There were howls from what sounded like half a dozen other cops. Giraldi eventually got control of himself. "What are you suing him for, Barrington?"

"A couple of his people assaulted a client of mine while collecting a debt."

"Well, that's what they do," Giraldi chuckled. "Give your client some advice for me: Tell him to pay what he owes and not to bet with Mob bookies again. That'll solve his problem."

"I'm afraid it's a little late for that," Stone said. "He owes twenty-four grand."

"Sheesh!" Giraldi exhaled. "What do you want to know?"

"I've got a lot of questions about the structure of Dattila's family, who does what, that sort of thing."

"Well, my price for that sort of thing is a steak dinner."

"You're on. Elaine's at eight-thirty?"

"Nah, nah, nah. The Palm at seven-thirty. I get hungry early."

Stone sighed. "All right, but that's got to cover your testifying, too."

"I'd love to testify against Carmine for anything," Giraldi said, "in the unlikely event that it ever looks like you're getting to court. I predict that your client and your other witnesses will be inspecting the bottom of Sheepshead Bay well before the trial date. Carmine doesn't bother to buy off witnesses; it's cheaper to off them."

"The Palm at seven-thirty," Stone said and hung up. He buzzed Joan. "Please book me a table for two at the Palm at seven-thirty."

"You can't afford it," she said.

"Don't worry, it's research; I'll bill Woodman and Weld."

"Whatever you say. Oh, by the way, I can't find a process server who's willing to serve Carmine Dattila."

"What?"

"They all know his reputation."

"Double the fee."

"I tried that; the general response was, 'You don't have enough money.' Apparently, the last guy who tried to serve Mr. Dattila didn't make it home to dinner that night. Or any other night."

"Why don't you take off early tonight and drop off this summons?"

"Yeah, sure. I thought we already established that you can't afford to lose me. You're going to have to do it yourself, Stone."

"You think I'm afraid of some two-bit wiseguy?"

"I read in the *Post* that Mr. Dattila is worth at least a hundred million dollars, and if you have any sense at all, you're afraid of him."

"*You* read the *Post*?"

"The *New York Times* is not a full meal for everybody; some of us need dessert."

"Just book the table."

Stone arrived on time at the Palm to find Joe Giraldi waiting for him at the bar. He remembered the guy now; his desk had always been way across the squad room. "Good to see you again, Joe," he said, motioning the bartender for the cop's bill. He was about to leave a ten on the bar, when the bill arrived: fifteen bucks, not including tip. "Jesus, what are you drinking, Joe?"

"Johnnie Walker Black. Isn't that in your budget?"

"Sure, sure," Stone replied, leaving a twenty on the bar. Eggers would shit a brick, but that was okay with him. He steered Giraldi to their table. "Want another one?"

"Just to keep the flow of conversation going," he replied.

Stone ordered another Johnnie Walker Black and a Knob Creek, and they looked at the menu. Stone gulped. He hadn't been here in years, and inflation had taken its toll. He wondered if the waiter would speak to him if he ordered the hamburger steak, if they had a hamburger steak.

Giraldi didn't even look at the menu. "I'll have the Caesar salad and the Kobe strip," he said to the waiter. "Medium."

"I'll have the same salad and the regular, ordinary American strip," Stone said. "Medium rare." He closed the menu before he could see the price of Kobe beef, which, allegedly, came from Japanese cattle that had been massaged daily by geishas, or something.

"Would you like some wine?" the waiter asked. The question was directed at Giraldi.

"Yeah," Giraldi replied. "You got a Far Niente cabernet, right?"

"Yes, sir."

"What year?"

"The 2000."

"We'll have that, and decant it, will you?"

Stone knew that bottle was going to go for close to two hundred dollars. "You come here a lot, Joe?"

"Whenever somebody wants to hear about the Mafia." He sipped his Scotch. "Shoot."

"Okay," Stone said, taking a long draw on his Knob Creek, "my client was into a bookie called Carlo; you know him?"

"Yeah, his real name is John Quigley; he ain't even Italian, but he passes. For some reason, his clients are more willing to pay if they think he's Italian. He works out of a candy store on Second Avenue, downtown."

"Who's his boss?"

"A capo named Gianni Pardo, who's known as Johnny Pop."

"I can imagine why."

"Right."

"Who's *his* boss?"

"He reports to another capo, Santino Gianelli, known as Sammy Tools. He was a master burglar and safecracker before Carmine moved him up the ladder."

"Speaking of the ladder, who does Sammy Tools report to?"

"To Carmine or his consigliere, depending."

"Depending on what?"

"If it's to do with methods, to the consigliere; if it's money, to Carmine."

"Who's the consigliere?"

"Carmine's bastard son, Salvatore Stampano, known among the cognoscenti as Little Carmine."

Their dinner came and went, and Stone continued to plumb the depths of Joe Giraldi's mob knowledge. The check came, and Stone put two other cops' names on the credit card receipt, since the tab looked more like dinner for five or six.

At the door, Stone shook Giraldi's hand and thanked him. "Joe, you want to make five hundred bucks, quick?"

"How?"

"Serve Carmine Dattila for me."

Giraldi laughed heartily. "Listen, right now Carmine doesn't know who I am, and I want to keep it that way. I'll tell you where to find him, though."

"Where?"

"At the La Boheme coffeehouse on Mulberry Street. Carmine spends his days there, making decisions and issuing orders. We've tried a dozen times to bug it, but they always figure it out. There's an office upstairs we've never been able to get into."

"Thanks, Joe." Stone trudged home, dreading his next move. He was going to have to serve Carmine Dattila himself.

6

The following day Stone met Dino at P. J. Clarke's for lunch. The place was mobbed with advertising guys, lawyers and secretaries, but they had held a table for Dino.

"I hear you met with Joe Giraldi," Dino said. They sat down and ordered cheeseburgers.

"'Met with' doesn't cover it; the meeting cost me dinner at the Palm, and Giraldi ordered the Kobe beef."

Dino couldn't suppress a chuckle. "That's my Giraldi," he said. "He wouldn't take a nickel from anybody, but his knowledge trades high. But what's the difference? You're going to stick Eggers with the bill."

"Yeah, and I put your name on it, too, and another one, too, to try and justify the expenditure."

"Giraldi gave you what you need, didn't he?"

"Yeah, and he agreed to testify, too."

"Did you really offer him five hundred to serve Dattila?"

"Yes. I would have gone to a thousand, but I got the impression it wouldn't have worked."

"Carmine has never been sued. You know why?"

"Because nobody will serve him?"

"You got it."

"How about you?"

"Stone, detective lieutenants of the NYPD do not do process serving."

"Not even for a thousand bucks?"

Dino looked hurt. "You wound me."

"Will you go with me for backup?"

"Neither do we sell backup services to process servers."

"Will you drive me down there and wait?"

"In whose car?"

"I guess mine; you won't use a squad car?"

"Good guess."

"After lunch?"

"Why not? Somebody needs to bring the body back."

A couple of years before, Stone had wandered into the Mercedes dealership on Park Avenue with a fat check in his pocket and a yen for some German engineering. He had driven away in a lightly armored E55 sedan that had been ordered by a man who had feared for his life, but the car had arrived a couple of days late. The deal was with the widow, with the salesman taking a cut. It had saved Stone's life only once, but that had made it a bargain.

Now they made their way into Little Italy, with Dino at the wheel, and Dino, Stone reflected, always drove as if he had just stolen the car.

Dino screeched to a halt directly in front of the La Boheme coffee-house, a dingy storefront with a cracked front window. "Are you carrying?" he asked Stone.

"You bet your ass," Stone said.

"Gimme," Dino said, holding out his hand.

"You want me to go in there naked?"

"You're going to end up naked anyway, and it will inspire trust if they don't find hardware when they frisk you."

Stone tugged the little Tussey custom .45 from its holster and handed it to Dino. "I'm going to want that back," he said.

"If you still need it," Dino replied, admiring the beautiful weapon. "What does it weigh?"

"Twenty-one ounces."

"Nice," Dino replied.

"I said, I'm going to want it back; don't get too comfortable with it."

"What, you want to be buried with it?"

Stone opened the car door. "You're a ray of sunshine, you know that?"

"I'm a realist."

"I'll be back shortly."

"I'll keep the engine running."

Stone grabbed the envelope containing the summons and got out of the car. He turned and rapped on the window with his signet ring, and Dino pressed the button. "What does Dattila look like?"

"Oh, I forgot," Dino said, reaching into an inside pocket and coming up with a photograph. "That's him in the middle," he said, "except he's thirty years older."

Stone looked at the shot of half a dozen men in double-breasted suits, looking tough for the camera. The man in the middle was small, balding, and he wasn't bothering to look tough. It made him look toughest of all. "Okay," he said, pocketing the photo.

He walked across the street and into the La Boheme coffeehouse. As he closed the door, the room—half full of men, no women—went silent. Stone looked around and spotted at a large table at the rear of the room Carmine Dattila, older, grayer, balder and heavier than in his photograph. He started toward the table.

A large young man got up from a front table and impeded Stone's progress. "Something we can do for you?" he asked, pleasantly enough.

"I have business with Mr. Dattila," Stone said. "My name is Barrington."

"Come again?"

"Barrington." Stone spelled it for him.

The man quickly frisked Stone, and, feeling the empty holster, unbuttoned his jacket and had a look at it. "Where is what was in there?" the man asked.

"In my car," Stone replied. "I didn't feel the need to come armed when visiting with Mr. Dattila."

"Wait here," the man said, pointing at the floor, as if Stone didn't know where it was. He walked back to the rear table, spoke for a moment with Dattila, then returned. "What is your business with Mr. Dattila?" he asked.

"I'm an attorney; I want to speak with Mr. Dattila on behalf of a client, Mr. Herbert Fisher."

The man walked to the rear, imparted this information, then returned. "Mr. Dattila don't know you or your client."

"Please tell Mr. Dattila it could save him a great deal of money if he talks to me."

The man returned to the rear, spoke to Dattila, then came back. "Follow me," he said. He led the way to the rear, then stopped at the table. "Mr. Dattila," he said, "this is Mr. Barrington." He stepped a yard away but kept his eyes on Stone.

Carmine Dattila gazed up at Stone through small eyes under bushy eyebrows. He reached into his shirt pocket, produced a stopwatch, punched it and laid it on the table. "You got thirty seconds," he said.

"Oh, I won't need that long." Stone reached inside the envelope in his hand, drew out the summons and handed it to Dattila. "You've been served." He turned to go.

"And how is this supposed to save me money?" Dattila asked, looking baffled.

"It could save you a lot, if you settle, instead of going to trial." He laid his business card on the table. "Have your attorney get in touch with me, and we'll talk." He turned and headed for the door, careful not to walk too quickly.

He heard heavy footsteps behind him and before he could turn, somebody spun him around, and a fist crashed into his jaw. Stone flew backward through the plate-glass door onto the sidewalk. As if in sympathy, the cracked front window shattered, too.

The man threw the summons at Stone, then stepped through the shattered door, ready to aim a kick.

Suddenly, Dino was standing over Stone, a badge in his hand. "Police!" he said. "Back off." The man grudgingly took a step backward, and Dino helped Stone to his feet. "You okay?" he asked quietly.

"Fine," Stone said, though he felt dizzy from the punch and the fall to the pavement. He bent over, picked up the summons and threw it into his assailant's face. "Tell Mr. Dattila he's been served, and the service was duly witnessed by Lieutenant Bacchetti of the NYPD. Also tell him I'll see him in court." He turned and began walking toward the car.

"I'm wearing a vest," Dino said. "Are you?"

"Nope," Stone said, straightening his tie. He got into the car, while Dino walked around to the driver's side.

Dino put the car in gear. "Here they come," he said.

Stone glanced over his shoulder and saw men spilling out of the La Boheme coffeehouse.

"Dino," Stone said, brushing broken glass off his jacket, "now would be a good time for you to drive the way you usually drive."

Dino stood on it.

7

Stone dropped Dino at the 19th Precinct. "Elaine's, later?"

"Sure," Dino said.

Stone drove home, put the car in the garage and went into his office. He sat down at his desk, and Joan came in. "Uh-oh," she said, then disappeared toward the kitchen. She came back with some ice cubes wrapped in a dish towel and pressed it against his jaw.

"I'm glad you're alive, but I guess you didn't exactly come away unscathed."

"You could say that," Stone said, taking the ice pack from her and holding it to his face.

"The swelling is conspicuous," she said.

"I noticed."

"I guess the other guy is pretty messed up, huh?"

"Not a mark on him," Stone replied, "but their front door is in many pieces."

"You busted their front door?"

"In a manner of speaking."

"Did Mr. Dattila get served?"

"He did."

"You think he'll respond?"

"Probably not, but then I'll get a summary judgment, and I'll take his fucking coffeehouse."

"Good luck on that," Joan said. "I take it Eggers is expecting some ink from this episode?"

"Apparently."

"Maybe I'd better do something about that."

"Do what?"

"I know somebody who knows somebody on Page Six at the *Post.*" Page Six wasn't on page six; it was just the name of the biggest gossip column in town.

"I'm not sure how Eggers would respond to having Woodman and Weld on Page Six."

"Well, we're not going to get it in the *Wall Street Journal,*" Joan said.

"You have a point. Go ahead and speak to your friend; Page Six is what Eggers deserves." He worked his jaw back and forth; it was sore.

The phone rang, and Joan picked it up. "The Barrington Practice. Yes, he's right here." She handed Stone the phone. "A client." She walked back toward her office.

"Stone Barrington."

"Hi, it's Herbert Q. Fisher."

Stone couldn't suppress a groan.

"I hear you're having trouble getting Dattila served."

"Where did you hear that?" Stone demanded, annoyed.

"I got my sources."

"Well, Mr. Dattila was duly served an hour ago."

"You think he'll respond?"

"I'm not clairvoyant, Herbie; we'll just have to wait and see."

"If he doesn't, we'll take everything he's got."

"Herbie, it was tough enough serving Dattila; think how hard it would be to take property from him, under *any* circumstances."

"But we'd have the power of the court on our side."

"So far in Mr. Dattila's life experience, the courts haven't laid a glove on him. Now go away, Herbie; I've got work to do."

"I'll check with you tomorrow."

"Don't bother; I'll call you when Dattila sends us a check." He hung up and buzzed Joan.

"Yes?"

"I'm sort of sore and tired; I'm going to go upstairs and take a nap."

"But you never take naps."

"Today is the exception." He hung up and walked to the elevator. He didn't feel like climbing stairs.

S tone woke up in his darkened bedroom and looked at the bedside clock: nearly eight. He rolled out of bed and into a shower.

At eight-thirty he walked into Elaine's, feeling somewhat more human. The Knob Creek was on the table as soon as he sat down.

"You're looking a little rough," Frank, one of the two headwaiters, said. "What happened to your face?"

"I bumped into something."

"It's turning a funny color."

"It is?" Stone got up, went into the men's room and checked the mirror. It was, indeed, turning a funny color. He went back to his table, where Dino had arrived and was taking a sip of Stone's drink.

"I don't know how you drink that bourbon stuff," he said, making a face.

"It's the patriotic thing to do," Stone explained, "instead of drinking that foreign gunk you're so partial to. Bourbon is our only national whiskey these days. Do you know why it's called Knob Creek?"

"I give up."

"Knob Creek is the birthplace and boyhood home of Abraham Lincoln. You see how patriotic that is?"

"How do you know this stuff?"

"I am a student of American history. Also, it's on a little tag that comes with the bottle."

"Your face is turning blue," Dino said.

"Don't change the subject."

"Maybe you ought to get it X-rayed."

"It's not broken, just bruised."

"That was a pretty big guy who hit you."

"Yeah, but look what I did to his door."

"Well, you really cleaned that door's clock, but I still think you ought to get your face X-rayed."

"Dino, when I start relying on you for medical advice, I'll already be dead."

"And I'll be there to say I told you so."

"I know, I know." Stone flexed his neck and shoulders.

"What's the matter?"

"I'm sore from hitting the pavement," Stone said. "I think I need a massage; you know a masseuse?"

"Well, I heard about this place down on First Avenue."

"Not *that* kind of masseuse."

"I'll check my Rolodex when I get back to my desk."

"Thanks, pal." Stone looked up to see a very beautiful woman enter the restaurant. Frank caught his eye and laughed. A moment later, he seated the woman at the table next to Stone's.

"Good evening," she said as she sat down.

"Good evening," Stone responded. He turned back to his bourbon, again flexing his shoulders and neck.

"You look a little stiff," the woman said. "You should have a massage."

"You know, I was just telling my friend here that very thing when you walked in."

She opened her purse and produced a card, handing it to him. It read:

MARILYN

MASSAGE IN YOUR HOME OR OFFICE

Stone smiled. "This is providential. If you're alone, would you like to join us?"

"Thank you, yes," she said, rising.

Stone held a chair for her. "My name is Stone Barrington; this is my friend, Dino Bacchetti."

"I'm Marilyn," she said.

"Marilyn what?"

"Just Marilyn; it's easier that way."

"May I get you a drink?"

"I'd love an appletini," she said.

Stone ordered the drink.

"Now," she said, after her first sip. "Let's get business out of the way." She produced a notebook. "I'm free tomorrow morning at ten," she said.

"By an odd coincidence, so am I," Stone replied. He handed her his card.

"Will it upset anyone at your office if you are naked on a table?" she asked.

"Not in the least," Stone replied, handing her a menu.

M arilyn had ordered and was on her second appletini. "So, what do you gentlemen do?" she asked.

"I'm an attorney," Stone said, "and Dino isn't a gentleman."

She laughed. "I'm sure that isn't true," she said soothingly to Dino.

"Of course not," Dino replied. "I'm a police officer. Stone used to be, but since he retired he thinks he's a gentleman."

"I make no such claims," Stone said. "That was Marilyn's characterization."

"You look awfully young to be retired," she said to Stone.

"He was retired by popular demand," Dino said.

"You were kicked off the police force?" Marilyn asked, looking shocked.

"I took a bullet in the knee; it was a medical retirement."

"How long were you a policeman?"

"Fourteen years. It was long enough."

"And what kind of law do you practice?"

"The shady kind," Dino interjected.

"I resent that," Stone said.

"You go right ahead."

"I'm sure that's not true," Marilyn said. "You strike me as an ethical person."

"You are an excellent judge of character," Stone said, patting her hand.

"I am," she agreed. "I rely on first impressions."

"You must be disappointed a lot," Dino said.

"Not at all." She turned back to Stone. "And what sort of cases are you working on right now."

Dino burst out laughing. "Tell her, Stone." He turned to Marilyn. "You're going to love this."

"It's a personal-injury suit," Stone said, glaring at Dino.

She reached over and touched his swollen jaw. "Were you the person injured?"

"Not initially."

"I don't understand."

"Stone served a summons on a nefarious character today, and another nefarious character took a swing at him. And connected," Dino said.

"And how did you respond?" she asked Stone.

"Stone hurt the guy's front door," Dino explained, "while flying through it."

"And how did you respond?" she asked.

"My response was curtailed by the number of nefarious characters who were present."

"We both beat a hasty retreat," Dino said.

"Oh? You were there, too, and you didn't come to the aid of your friend?"

"I came to his aid with my badge and gun, and by driving the getaway car."

"Discretion was the better part of valor," Stone said.

"That's Shakespeare," Dino explained. "Stone quotes people a lot."

"Not a lot," Stone said defensively.

"Just all the time."

"Well, it's a very nice quote," Marilyn said, "and it sums up your reaction very succinctly."

Stone nodded. "That's why I used it. Dino would just have said, in his inimitable way, 'We got the fuck out of there.'"

"And," Dino said, "that would have summed up our reaction very succinctly."

"You two are a sketch," Marilyn said. "Did you used to be married?"

"We were partners when I was a cop," Stone said. "It's pretty much the same thing, except for the absence of sex."

"What makes you think that's different from marriage?" Dino asked.

"Dino is recently divorced," Stone explained.

"Oooh," Marilyn said, patting Dino's hand.

"Your sympathy is misplaced," Stone said. "Dino is a happier man these days, not that you can tell."

"Then my congratulations," Marilyn said. "What about you, Stone? Are you divorced?"

"No," Stone said. "Never married."

Dino staged a coughing fit.

"Well, for a couple of days, once; it was sort of annulled."

Dinner arrived.

"I'm interested in your personal-injury case," Marilyn said. "Who is the defendant?"

"A gentleman downtown."

"What does he do?"

"Let's just say he's in a rather old-fashioned Italian business."

"Like a deli?"

"More like a coffeehouse, among other things."

"And how did he injure your client?"

"He hired two other gentlemen to beat him up."

"Well, that wasn't very nice."

"That's why I'm suing him."

"What did he have against your client?"

"There was a gambling debt involved."

"I think I'm beginning to get the picture," Marilyn said.

"You're very quick," Dino interjected.

"Poker?" Marilyn asked.

"Sports," Stone said.

"Like horse sports?"

"Very probably, though I wouldn't exclude professional athletics."

"Isn't a lawsuit, ah, nontraditional in such a case?"

"You might say that."

"You might say it's never been done before," Dino said.

"Wouldn't calling the police be a better idea?"

"The police have failed in their duty where this defendant is concerned," Stone said.

"Shame on you," Marilyn said to Dino.

"It didn't happen in my precinct," Dino said. "Anyway, these things are usually settled privately, without resort to the courts."

"By 'settled privately,'" Stone said, "Dino means the plaintiffs are usually too badly injured to complain and are further discouraged from legal action by threats to their existence."

"This does not sound like a very nice man you're suing," Marilyn said.

"I think that sums him up in a nutshell," Stone replied. "He is not the sort of man most people want to tangle with."

"Then why are you tangling with him? Are you so very brave?"

"It's a long story," Stone said.

Marilyn turned to Dino. "People say that when they don't want to talk about something."

"You *are* quick," Dino replied.

There was a muffled ringing noise, and Marilyn dug a cell phone out of her purse. "Excuse me," she said. "Hello? It's difficult to say at the moment. If you insist. All right. Half an hour." She closed the phone. "I'm afraid you gentlemen are going to have to excuse me," she said. "I have kind of an emergency."

"A massage emergency?" Dino asked.

"It's a long story."

Dino turned and glanced at Stone. "People say that when they don't want to talk about something."

Marilyn laughed. "You *are* quick, Dino. Stone, I'll see you tomorrow morning at ten."

"I'll look forward to it."

"I can't wait to get my hands on you." She gave a little wave and hurried away.

"Ask her if she makes calls at police stations," Dino said.

9

S tone slept a little later than usual. At nine Joan buzzed him.

"*Mmmf,*" Stone said.

"Rough night?"

"No, I have a masseuse coming at ten, so it's hardly worth getting out of bed."

"A Mr. Bernard Finger called and left a message before I got in. Do you know him?"

"He's a lawyer. I met him once, at the courthouse; he was defending a drug dealer. It's probably about the Dattila thing."

"So, Mr. Dattila is responding?"

"I'm not going to count on it. I'll call him back later; don't want to look too anxious."

"Right."

"Will you send the lady up when she arrives? Her name is Marilyn."

"Wilco."

"I love it when you talk pilot." He hung up, turned over and went back to sleep. The phone buzzed again; Stone picked it up. "What?"

"It's ten forty-five, and she hasn't shown."

"Ah, okay. I'll deal with it." He rolled out of bed, went to his dressing room, rummaged through the contents of his pockets dumped on the dresser top the night before and found Marilyn's card. He went back, sat on the bed and dialed her number. There came back a loud squawk and a mechanical voice: "The number you have dialed is not in service; please check the number and dial again."

He must have dialed a wrong digit, he thought, and he dialed again; same result. Very peculiar. By the time he had showered, shaved and dressed it seemed very, very peculiar. He went down to his office and called Bernard Finger.

"Stone Barrington!" Finger shouted into the phone, as if they were long-lost friends. Finger was a large, voluble man.

"Good morning, Mr. Finger. You rang?"

"Call me Bernie!" Finger shouted. "Everybody does! And I'll call you Stoney!"

"Over my dead body," Stone replied.

"Ha! My client can arrange that!" He dissolved in loud guffaws.

"And your client is . . . ?"

"You've met him, Stone. Is that better?"

"Yes, thank you. What can I do for you, Bernie?"

"I represent a certain party downtown who was baffled yesterday to have you walk into his place of business and hand him a summons! He wants to know what this is all about!"

"Didn't you read the complaint, Bernie?"

"Well, not exactly; it didn't really survive the day!"

"I'll send you a copy."

"Just give me a quick run-through, and I'll read it later!"

"My client lost a considerable sum of money, betting with one of your client's employees. When he failed to pay fast enough, two of your client's other employees dragged him from a public eating establishment, causing him great humiliation and embarrassment, then proceeded to beat him on the sidewalk, until they were interrupted by a police officer."

"Did the cop arrest them?"

"No."

"Well, then it couldn't have been too serious, could it?"

"I assure you, my client takes it very seriously, since he now faces plastic surgery to his face, and he is looking forward to meeting your client in court."

Finger's tone changed, and he spoke more quietly. "Well, Stone, I have to presume you know who you're dealing with here."

"Bernard Finger, Esquire, I presume."

"Heh, heh. Well I'm sure you understand that my client is not accustomed to being hauled into court on civil matters."

"Only landlords are accustomed to that," Stone replied. "I suggest you explain to your client that this is, indeed, a civil matter, which means that he will be required to testify, and he won't be able to clam up the way he does when he's addressed by the U.S. attorney. Tell him that I will look forward to questioning him about his various sources of income and his business practices, and I am certain that various members of the federal legal establishment will be present in the courtroom to hear his answers and to learn if he perjures himself. I would also expect a trial to be attended by many members of the media."

"Well, Stone, that ain't never going to happen."

"Then I will see your client in civil jail while he ruminates on his response to my client's lawsuit."

"You don't understand."

"No, Bernie, your client doesn't understand, and I hardly need remind you that it is your duty to explain it all to him, a prospect that I do not envy you. By the way, yet another of your client's employees attacked and injured me in the La Boheme coffeehouse yesterday, and I am contemplating legal recourse. Finally, you should tell your client that I anticipate an extralegal response to this suit, either against my client or myself, and that I welcome such actions, since they will only strengthen my position and make him further liable for a criminal action against him."

"Stone, you sound very tense, you know. You should have a massage, or something. Good morning." Bernard Finger hung up.

Stone called Dino.

"Bacchetti."

"It's Stone."

"Morning."

"Guess who I just had a call from."

Dino sighed. "Just tell me."

"Bernard Finger."

"The man himself?"

"None other. He represents Carmine Dattila."

"Big surprise, not that he represents Carmine, but that he bothered to call you."

"Guess who else represents Dattila."

"You got me again."

"The lovely Marilyn, from last night."

"You're kidding me."

"She didn't show for our appointment this morning, and the phone number on her card is a phony. Then, after my conversation with Finger, he says, slyly, that I sound tense and I should have a massage. I think the preponderance of the evidence points to a pecuniary relationship, at the very least, between Marilyn and Carmine."

"So you think he sent her to Elaine's to pump you about your lawsuit?"

"What else?"

"That sounds more like something Bernie Finger would do."

"You have a point," Stone said.

"I frequently do."

"Listen, why don't you put some of your little-used police skills to work and find out who she is?"

"So what am I going to go on? Beautiful blonde with phony phone number? I don't think our computers could handle that."

"I guess not."

"And besides, it's not as though she committed a crime. I don't think it's a felony to offer massage and not show up."

"It ought to be," Stone said.

"In a more perfect world."

"I was looking forward to that massage."

"And I was looking forward to hearing about it."

"I hope I run into her again," Stone said.

"What are you going to do, slug her? Besides, she looks like she could take care of herself. Pretty big girl."

"Parts of her."

"That's probably what Carmine wants you to do, so he can have her beat you up."

"Good-bye, Dino."

"Have a nice day."

10

S tone sat and stared at his desktop. His back was still stiff and sore; he had really wanted that massage. He buzzed Joan.

"Yes?"

"Do you know a really good masseuse who makes house calls?"

"What is this sudden obsession with massage?"

"It came with the sudden contact of my back with a sidewalk."

"No, I don't know anybody."

"I'll bet your sister who knows the cosmetic surgeon knows somebody."

"You should have been a detective. I'll call her. When do you want it?"

"At the earliest possible moment, if not sooner."

Five minutes later, Joan buzzed him. "Two P.M.," she said. "Her name is Celia."

"Is she beautiful?"

"You requested availability, not beauty."

"Is she good?"

"You didn't request good, either, but seeing that she's available on such short notice, I wouldn't be too optimistic about her skills."

"Joan, just being around you fills me with hope." He hung up and went to the kitchen to make himself a ham-and-Swiss on whole grain with mayo and honey mustard. Since he planned to spend the early part of the afternoon semiconscious anyway, he treated himself to a cold Heineken, as well.

At two o'clock sharp the phone buzzed in Stone's bedroom. "She's here," Joan said. "Shall I send her up?"

"Please do. Is she beautiful?" But Joan had already hung up. A moment later he heard the elevator door open, and he rose to greet the masseuse. The sight of her caused a sharp intake of breath.

She was more than just beautiful; she was a giant of a woman, at least six-two, his own height. As he shook her hand and introduced himself, he measured: He hoped she was wearing heels, because he came up to about her eyebrows.

"I'm Celia Cox," she said.

"How do you do, Celia. Thank you for coming on such short notice. I had an appointment with someone else, but she didn't show up."

"That's very unprofessional," she said. "Is right here good for my table?" She pointed to the foot of the bed.

"Perfect," he said. "May I ask how tall you are?"

"Six-three," she said. "The shortest of three sisters."

The mind boggled. "You carry your height beautifully," he said.

"Thank you. That's the kindest thing anyone has ever said to me about my size."

He could not begin to guess her weight, but whatever it was, it was perfect. And all of her went very well with the long chestnut hair that spilled around her shoulders. When she pulled her hair back into a ponytail and secured it, he thought her nose and her jawline were perfect, too. And her eyes were a deep green.

She spread her sheets over the table, affixed the face cradle and patted the leather top. "You hop up here, face down, while I wash my hands. Bathroom in here?" She pointed.

"Yes, help yourself." Stone tossed his robe onto the bed and crawled under the top sheet, settling his face into the cradle.

She returned after a moment. "Any special problems I should know about?"

"Yes, I suffered a fall onto my back on the sidewalk yesterday, and I'm pretty sore and stiff."

"Do you suspect any skeletal problems?"

"No, I don't think so; just muscular."

He heard her squirt something, then rub her hands briskly together. "I apologize if my hands are cold," she said, placing them on his back gently.

"They feel very good," he said.

"I'm going to go over your back and shoulders lightly, and I want you to tell me if what I do makes you hurt in any particular place." She did so. "How was that?" she asked.

"Wonderful."

"May I go deeper, do you think?"

"Yes, please."

She went deeper and covered everything from his neck to his heels. "Okay," she said, holding up a sheet, "you can turn over on your back now. Do you need any help?"

"No, I'm fine," he said, turning over.

She began massaging an arm. "Who was the masseuse who stood you up?" she asked.

Stone nodded at the bedside table. "Her card is over there," he said. "Her phone number didn't work."

Celia went and got the card. "I know her," she said. "Her name is Marilyn Martin; we both used to work at the same day spa." She began working on his arm again. "Last I heard, she wasn't working anymore, she'd moved into an apartment that some lawyer is paying for, guy with a funny name."

"Wouldn't be Bernard Finger, would it?"

"That's it! Do you know him?"

"Only slightly. He's the opposition in a personal-injury suit I'm working on."

"Flashy kind of guy. I saw them in a restaurant once; she was wearing a lot of jewelry. So was he, come to think of it." She began working on his other arm. "I think he's married."

"That's kind of sore," Stone said. "I must have fallen more on that side."

"I'll spend a little extra time on it. Are you in a rush?"

"God, no. You can take all afternoon, if you want to."

She laughed. "I don't have that much time, I'm afraid; I was able to come to you only because one of my regular clients was ill."

"Can we set up a regular time?" he asked.

"My schedule is full, but I could call you when I have a cancellation."

"Yes, please."

She worked silently on the arm and shoulder, then she moved to the top of the table and began massaging his neck, then his face and scalp. She finished slowly. "There," she said. "Is that better?"

"Oh, yes," Stone sighed. "I could go to sleep."

"That's a good idea," she said, "but lie on your back, with a pillow under your knees."

Stone sat up. "I have an electric bed that can elevate my knees," he said.

"Good idea." She took his hand, led him to the bed and tucked him in.

"Celia," he said, then he hesitated.

"Yes, I would," she said.

"Would what?"

"Would like to have dinner with you sometime."

"How did you know I was going to ask you?"

"It was pretty obvious when you turned over onto your back," she said.

"Tonight?"

"Tomorrow night would be better."

"Great. Shall I pick you up at say, eight?"

"It would be better if we met."

"Do you know Elaine's?"

"I've heard of it, but I don't know where it is."

"On Second Avenue, between Eighty-eighth and Eighty-ninth. At eight-thirty?"

"Perfect," she said, laying a card on the bedside table. "My cell number is there, should you need to reach me. How should I dress?"

"You can wear anything from jeans to a ball gown at Elaine's; I'd suggest fairly casual."

"I can do that," she said.

"Just one thing: You don't work for Bernard Finger, do you?"

"No, I certainly don't."

"Joan will have a check for you downstairs."

She put her cool hand on his forehead for a moment. "There," she said, "sleep."

He followed her instructions to the letter.

II

As Stone left his house that evening to look for a cab to Elaine's, a black Lincoln that was double-parked a couple of doors up the street started to move slowly. He looked over his shoulder, as if looking for a cab, which he was, and checked out the car. Darkened windows. He suddenly regretted that he was not armed.

He walked down to Third Avenue and hailed a cab, and fifteen minutes later he was sipping his first Knob Creek. Dino arrived five minutes later, simultaneously with his first Scotch, via waiter.

"You're looking very fresh and relaxed," Dino said.

"I am exactly that," Stone replied. "I found a replacement for Marilyn this afternoon, and the woman is an angel."

"I want to meet her," Dino said.

"Come around this time tomorrow evening and have a drink with us, but don't stick around for dinner, even if I invite you to, which I won't."

"What's she like?"

"That'll be a surprise; you're not going to believe what you see."

"I take it that's a favorable assessment of her charms."

"You may infer that. Oh, and she knows Marilyn—they used to work at the same day spa—and she tells me that Marilyn has retired from the business and moved into an apartment paid for by a married lawyer, who is . . ."

"Bernie Finger."

"You're so smart."

"That's a cheesy thing to do, send his girlfriend around to spy on you."

"I'm going to make him pay for that before all this is over."

"And how will you do that?"

"I don't know, but I'll think of something." Stone looked up to see two large men in shiny clothes walk into the restaurant and be seated across the room. "Dino, was there a black Lincoln parked out front when you came in?"

"There's a black Lincoln parked outside every restaurant in New York," Dino said.

"Including this one?"

"Yeah, it's there."

"I think it belongs to the two gorillas over there," Stone said, deliberately pointing with his arm outstretched at the pair.

They feigned looking at the menu and sipped their drinks.

Stone waved Gianni over. "What are the two apes over there drinking?"

Gianni gave them a glance. "Chivas Regal."

"What's the worst Scotch you stock?"

"We've got something called Great Scot. We use it to discourage those who've had too much to drink. It tastes like paint thinner, with iodine."

"Send them one on me, and make sure you tell them it's from me."

Gianni headed for the bar.

"You think Carmine is having you followed?"

"Carmine or Bernie. I think they're trying to intimidate me."

"Is it working?"

"Not yet." Stone watched as the drinks were delivered to their table and Gianni delivered the message. The two tried to look baffled but raised their glasses in thanks to Stone and drank. Both looked stricken, and one of them waved Gianni back. A brief conversation took place: What the hell was this Scotch? Gianni explains that Stone specified it. They glower at Stone.

"Message received," Dino said. "I have to tell you, I think it's a faulty strategy to deliberately annoy people who are already considering beating you up."

"I don't think they've been told to do that yet, or they would have done it as soon as I left the house this evening."

"They followed you from your house?"

"Yep."

"I hope you locked up tight."

"I always lock up tight."

"Did you set the alarm?"

"Yep."

"You forget to do that a lot."

"Dino, I set the alarm, all right?"

"Whatever you say." He sounded doubtful.

Stone got out his cell phone, dialed a number and, when it answered, punched in several numbers.

"What was that all about?"

"I was setting the alarm."

"You can do that with your cell phone?"

"It's a new feature I just got."

"That's a good idea for somebody who's always forgetting to set the alarm."

"I don't think Dattila would have my house broken into. Would he?"

"Stone, if those two guys are Dattila's and if they haven't already beaten you up after tasting that Scotch, then this is a war of nerves. And if that's what it is, then turning over your house would be exactly the sort of thing Dattila would do. It's all about driving you nuts."

"Order me the spinach salad, chopped, and the spaghetti carbonara," Stone said, rising. "And loan me your backup gun. I'll be back shortly."

Dino passed him a small automatic under a napkin, and Stone slipped it into a pocket. He went outside to get a cab, then he saw the black Lincoln. He went over and tapped on the driver's window, and it slid down.

"Yeah?" a thick voice asked.

"You're driving the two guys inside?"

"Yeah."

"My name's Barrington; they said you could run me down to Turtle Bay and back. I'm a friend of Carmine's. Only take a couple of minutes."

"Okay," the man said.

Stone heard the electric locks click, and he got into the backseat. When they reached his house, Stone had a quick look around inside to be sure nothing had gone amiss during the time the alarm had not been set, then he went up to his dressing room, opened the safe and took out the little Tussey .45 and a holster. Shortly he was back at Elaine's. Stone opened the door. "Thanks very much," he said to the driver.

"Don't mention it."

"Oh, I almost forgot: The two guys said they wouldn't need you anymore this evening."

"Great," the man said. "The game's still on, I think."

"Good night," Stone said with a cheery wave. "Enjoy the game." He went back inside and sat down, slipping Dino his backup piece under the table. The spinach salad appeared before him.

"You checked the house?"

"Yeah, everything was fine."

"Did you set the alarm when you left?"

"Shit," Stone said, getting out his cell phone and going through the procedure again.

"You always forget to do that," Dino said.

"Dino, if you say that again I'm going to dump this salad over your head."

"Good thing you got that cell phone feature; it'll be invaluable."

Stone sighed deeply and began eating his salad.

At the end of the evening, Stone and Dino walked out to look for a cab home. A moment later, the two gorillas appeared at the curb, looking around, mystified. One of them got on his cell phone, apparently looking for his driver.

"Have a nice evening, fellas," Stone said as he got into a cab.

12

Stone was working his way through his mid-morning when Joan buzzed. "Bernard Finger on one."

Stone picked up the phone. "Stone Barrington."

"It's Bernie Finger, Stone! Didn't your girl tell you?"

"You'd better hope she's not still on the line, Bernie, because if she heard you refer to her as my girl, she'd do terrible things to you."

"Whatever," Finger said. "You free for lunch?"

"To what end?"

"I thought we'd have a little chat and see if we can sort this thing out."

"All right."

"Twelve-thirty at the Four Seasons grill room?"

"All right."

"And Stone, they require a tie and jacket."

Stone was going to skewer him with an acid remark for that, but Finger had already hung up.

Bernard Finger, Stone was surprised to see, had claim to a well-placed plot in the hottest power-lunch real estate in the United States of America. While being escorted to the table, Stone did a mini sweep of the room and turned up half a dozen business moguls, plus Barbara Walters; Morton Janklow, the literary agent and attorney; and Henry Kissinger. And that was just a mini sweep.

Finger didn't bother to rise to greet him, a sign that he considered his guest inferior in status, but offered a hand attached to a wrist wearing a gold Rolex with many diamonds in its bezel. So, Bernie was left-handed. "How you doin', Stone?" he asked, as if he didn't really care.

Stone shook the hand by grabbing the fingers, preventing a grip. "Just fine, thanks." He sat down.

"I've already ordered," Finger said. "Important meeting. What'll you have?"

"A small salad and the Dover sole," Stone said to the waiter. "And a glass of sauvignon blanc."

"You know," Finger said, leaning forward and resting his elbows on the table, giving Stone a close view of thousands of dollars of hair plugs embedded in his scalp, "I hear around town you're a fairly smart guy. How'd you let yourself get involved in this ridiculous thing?"

"Oh, well, let's see," Stone said, screwing up his face for thought and staring at the ceiling. "Egregious violence perpetrated in a public place upon an innocent by a man with deep pockets. That clears my bar for case acceptance." He looked at Finger and smiled. "I'll bet it clears your bar, too, Bernie."

"But Stone, didn't you consider who you're suing?"

"Bernie, it's not like Carmine Dattila is the archbishop of New York; he's a cheap hood—all right, an expensive hood—who makes his way in the world by preying on those weaker than he. He's a piece of dog shit in the gutter, Bernie, and I have to wonder what kind of lawyer would represent him in a public courtroom."

Finger went all pink, but his response was cut off by a tray of a dozen fat oysters set before him. He ate four of them, emptying them from the shell into his mouth, before he managed a reply. "All right, let's just stay away from personal abuse here."

"Stop insulting my intelligence, and I'll stop insulting your client list."

Finger ate four more oysters. "Look, let's cut to the chase; I want to make a proposal!"

Stone dug into his salad. "So, propose."

"What we've got here is your stubborn client and my stubborn client. Carmine is never, repeat *never*, going to cough up a thin dime of his own money to buy your client off."

"That's okay," Stone said. "When I win in court, and I will, I'll just attach everything connected with him—lock, stock and coffeehouse. I'm sure I can wring a nice piece of change out of his visible assets."

"You think Carmine has assets? Jesus, Stone, not even his fucking pinkie ring is in his own name; even his *clothes*, for legal purposes, are borrowed. You're talking about drilling a dry well, and that's going to cost you a lot of time, and time, as any lawyer knows, is money."

Stone's Dover sole arrived and was expertly boned by the captain and placed before him. He took a bite and savored the flavor and the texture. "Speak, Bernie."

"How's about this. I've got a nice little personal-injury suit in my firm right now—my newest associate is handling it—and it's going to settle for half a million, maybe six hundred thousand, before very long. How about I toss you the case; you settle it, take your cut and give Mr. Fisher whatever you think he'll take, then pocket the rest. It's quick, clean, and requires no outlay for my client or even, for that matter, his knowledge. Your client makes out, you make out, my client doesn't get mad and I make it up on the next case!"

Stone took another bite of the sole, chewed, swallowed, then took a sip of his wine. "Bernie, I do not possess the mathematical skills to count the number of ways that that is unethical, immoral, illegal and just a *terrible* idea. If you're so afraid of your client that you won't or can't persuade him to do the right thing, then just write me a check for, say, half a million on your firm's account, and make it back from Dattila in fees. Then everybody's happy, unless Dattila figures out what you did, but you're too smart to let that happen."

Finger downed his last four oysters, stood up and threw down his napkin. "All right, you son of a bitch, I tried. Now I'm going to show you how law is practiced."

"Is that what you were doing last night, with the two gorillas? Practicing law? Oh, by the way, did they ever find their car?"

Finger went pink again. "You'll see," he said, and turned to leave.

"And Bernie . . ."

"Yeah?"

"If you try and stick me with the check, I'll embarrass you before the whole room."

Finger turned and did his very best impression of a man, in high dudgeon, storming out of a restaurant. Half the eyes in the place followed him, then swiveled back to Stone, who was calmly enjoying his Dover sole.

13

S tone had been sipping bourbon at Elaine's for ten minutes
when Celia Cox swept into the place. She was wearing a long
wool coat, which was open at the front, to reveal a short silk
dress that displayed an acre of cleavage and miles of leg. The sound
of heads swiveling and eyeballs snapping could be heard in the sudden silence, which lasted for about a second and a half before the
hubbub resumed.

Stone rose to greet her, but not far enough. She was wearing four-
inch heels, which made her tall enough to play in the NBA game
on the TV. He stood on his tiptoes, kissed her on the cheek and took
her coat.

"Where's the ladies'?" she asked.

Stone pointed to the rear door. "Turn right there, then it's the
second door on your left."

"Be right back."

Stone sat down to applause from a bunch of guys a couple of
tables down. He tried not to blush.

Dino walked in and took his usual seat. "So, where's the broad?"

"In the ladies'," Stone said. "Remember, you get one drink, then
you vanish in a puff of smoke." He was looking forward to this
introduction.

"Sure, sure." Dino's Scotch arrived. He took a sip and spat.

"It's the Great Scot," Stone said. "I ordered it special for you, so you would get the message." He signaled to a waiter, who brought Dino's usual Johnnie Walker Black and removed the offending glass.

"That was a shitty thing to do to a guy," Dino said, swishing the Johnnie Black around in his mouth to dissolve the last remnants of the Great Scot.

Celia returned from the ladies' and Stone and Dino stood. "Celia Cox, Dino Bacchetti, an old friend."

She reached down to shake his hand. Dino came up exactly to her nipples. "How do you do?" she asked, amused.

"Hello," Dino managed, awestruck.

"Dino's joining us for just this one drink," Stone said.

"Oh, what a shame," Celia said. "Can't you stay for dinner, Dino?"

"Well, I . . ."

Stone kicked him under the table.

Dino winced. "I'm meeting somebody, business."

"What a pity."

"Isn't it," Stone said, unable not to smile. "What would you like to drink?" he asked Celia.

"Do they have any decent bourbon in this joint?" she asked sweetly.

"Waiter, bring the lady a Knob Creek. On the rocks?"

"Perfect," she said.

"So nice to meet a woman who drinks bourbon," Stone said.

"I'm a southern girl from a small town in Georgia called Delano, where they consider Scotch un-American."

Menus arrived. "Only two," Stone said to the waiter. "Dino has to be someplace."

"I think that's my cue to scram," Dino said, rising. "So nice to meet you, Celia. I hope to see a lot more of you."

"That's my line," Stone said. "Good night, Dino."

The waiter escorted Dino to another table and held the chair for him.

"You were rude to your friend," Celia said.

"We do that a lot," Stone replied, "but only because I didn't want to share you."

"Thank you for not saying there's enough of me to go around; I've heard all the tall jokes."

Elaine came over and sat down, and Stone introduced the two women. "You're taller sitting down than I am standing up," Elaine said.

Celia laughed. "I take it back, Stone, I hadn't heard that one."

Elaine peered at Celia's glass. "What are you drinking?" she asked.

"Bourbon," Celia replied.

Elaine spotted a friend coming into the restaurant and stood up. "I'll look forward to the wedding invitation," she said. "Stone has found his dream girl."

Celia laughed again, a pleasing sight and sound. "So," she said, "go ahead and ask me how I became a masseuse."

"I'm sure you have the answer ready," Stone said.

"It was the only way I could earn two hundred dollars an hour without turning tricks. And I'm too smart to be a Las Vegas showgirl."

"Perfect answer," Stone said.

"The truth is, I lived in Santa Fe for a while, and they have a lot of massage schools. I had to find something more financially rewarding than waiting tables, so I took the training."

"And the training took."

"So you're a lawyer? Why?"

"It was the only way I could earn five hundred dollars an hour without turning tricks. And I'm too smart to be a cop, which is what I used to be before I got so smart. Dino was my partner in those days."

"Did you ever hear anything from Marilyn?"

"No, but I had lunch with Bernard Finger today, if you can call watching him slurp down a dozen oysters and hearing a stupid proposal for a settlement lunch."

"He's kind of gross, isn't he?"

"I think that sums him up very well."

"I met him once when he came to pick up Marilyn at the day spa. He's been very generous, though; he bought her that apartment. You know the skinny modern building on Park Avenue in the sixties?"

"The one with one apartment per floor?"

"Yes. He bought her the penthouse in that building."

"What do you want to bet the deed is in Bernie's name?"

"I wouldn't take that bet, and Marilyn isn't smart enough to insist on having it in her name. He tells her they're going to be married as soon as he can get a divorce."

"I'll bet he tells her that."

She laughed. "Marilyn says he loves to make love out on their terrace."

"Right out in the open?"

"Yes, and there are taller buildings all around them."

"Then they must enjoy exhibitionism."

"I guess. I'm hungry."

"What would you like?"

"You made me think of oysters," she said.

"It'll be more fun watching you eat them than watching Bernie." They ordered.

T wo hours later they stood on the curb, looking for a taxi.

"Can I tempt you back to my house?"

"I've already seen your etchings," she said, "along with everything else. It'll have to wait until next time."

"Is tomorrow too soon for next time?"

"Yes. Call me and we'll figure it out." A cab stopped.

"I'll drop you at home," Stone said.

"That would be inconvenient," she said, getting into the cab.

"Where do you live?" Stone asked, but she had already closed the door, and the cab was moving.

Stone watched her drive away, regretting her reluctance to come home with him. He'd have to work on that.

14

The next morning, Joan buzzed Stone. "It's Herbert Fisher," she said.

"Tell him to get lost."

"He insists on talking to you. Says it's urgent; his life is in danger."

"God, I hope so," Stone said, punching at the flashing light. "I told you not to call me, Herbie."

"Stone, you gotta help me," Herbie panted. "They're trying to kill me."

Stone sighed. "Okay, Herbie, who's trying to kill you?"

"My bookie, I think. Last night when I came home there were two guys in a black Lincoln waiting for me. I had to run like hell for nearly a mile before I lost them in an alley."

"Where did you spend the night?"

"At my girlfriend's."

"*You* have a girlfriend, Herbie?"

"Sure, doesn't everybody?"

"Then what were you doing with those two hookers at Elaine's?"

"Oh, that was a celebration."

That did not compute. "Are you at your girlfriend's now, Herbie?"

"No, I'm in a candy store. She made me leave when she left for work."

"She's afraid to leave you in her apartment?"

"Well, we had this little problem once, with some money."

"You stole money from her?"

"I borrowed it, but she noticed before I could pay her back."

"I'm surprised she let you in the door last night."

"Well, she won't tonight, and I need someplace to hide from those guys."

"Try one of your hookers."

"Stone, can I stay at your house? You've got a lot of room."

Stone thought fast. If he merely said no, Herbie would be on his doorstep in half an hour. "My house is the first place they'd look for you, Herbie; you wouldn't be safe."

"Oh, yeah, I guess you're right. So where can I go?"

"Call your Uncle Bob."

"Well, there's kind of a problem there, too."

"It seems there's a problem with everybody who knows you, Herbie. Think of somebody who doesn't know you well, and go there."

"There isn't anybody like that, Stone. You've gotta help me; I'm homeless!"

"That's it, Herbie! Go to a homeless shelter! And don't call me again." Stone hung up.

Joan came into his office and laid a newspaper on his desk. "You'd better take a look at Page Six," she said.

Stone picked up the *Post.* "Is this the thing you got in the paper?"

"Nope." She tapped a finger on a boxed part of the page.

TWO LAWYERS IN BROUHAHA AT FOUR SEASONS

Well-known attorneys Bernard Finger and Stone Barrington had a not-too-pleasant lunch in the Grill Room yesterday. According to Finger, Barrington invited him to lunch and proposed some unethical conduct. When Finger refused and walked out in a huff, Barrington then told the management to charge the very expensive meal to Finger.

Barrington says it's all a lie. (Not really. We were unable to contact him, but that's what he would have said.)

Stone was speechless for a moment. When he recovered himself he told Joan to take some dictation. "The only true statement in your blurb about Bernie Finger and me is that it's all a lie. Even if I didn't say so."

"That's it?"

"Fax it to them now."

"You think they'll print it?"

"I don't know; what else can I do?"

"I know somebody who'll kill Bernie Finger for five thousand dollars."

"No you don't."

"*I* would kill him for five thousand dollars."

"I can't afford it. Just fax the statement to Page Six, will you?"

Joan left, and Stone called Bob Cantor. Cantor was an ex-cop who was expert in all things technical, especially surveillance, and who often did work for Stone.

"Cantor."

"Bob, it's Stone."

"Hey, Stone, what's up?"

"First of all, your insane nephew says people are trying to kill him, and he wants to come and stay at my house."

"I wouldn't advise that. Last time I put him up I had to get my 500 mm Hasselblad lens out of hock."

"Don't worry."

"The kid is kind of rich, you know."

"*What?*"

"Kind of. His mother died and left him the house in Brooklyn, free and clear. He rents four apartments, which gives him a nice income, and he lives in the super's apartment."

"That little shit. He owes a bookie twenty-four grand and won't pay. He could have borrowed from a bank on the house."

"No, he couldn't."

"Why not?"

"Because I'm his trustee, and I won't let him do that, and he knows it. Did you want to talk about something besides Herbie? I'm getting nauseous."

"Yeah, I've got a job for you."

"Shoot."

"There's a building on Park Avenue in the sixties, new, very skinny, one apartment to a floor."

"I know the one."

"Good. Here's what I want you to do." He gave Cantor full instructions, then hung up.

Joan came into his office, grinning. "That's wonderful!" she said. "I love it."

"You were listening to my phone conversation?"

"You betcha."

"Didn't you ever hear of the Constitution of the United States?"

"Vaguely."

"It says you can't do that; I have a right to privacy."

"Not from me, you don't; I know everything about you."

"Not everything."

"What I don't know isn't worth knowing," she said, and sauntered back to her office.

Stone dug out Celia's number and called her.

"Hello?"

"Hi, it's Stone."

"Thank you for last evening," she said. "I enjoyed myself."

"So did I. Let's do it again."

"When?"

"Tonight?"

"Tomorrow night."

"Great. Where do you want to meet?"

"Does your house have a kitchen?"

"Of course, a very nice one."

"Let's meet there; I'll cook dinner for you."

"You talked me into it."

"Seven?"

"Perfect. Can I shop for anything for you?"

"I'll bring everything but the wine."

"I've already got that."

"Bye."

"Bye." Stone hung up feeling better.

15

Bob Cantor packed his car and left his Brooklyn apartment.
Stone Barrington, he reflected, was his favorite client, not
because he gave him the most work but because the work
was always interesting. Cantor had kicked open his share of bedroom doors, but this was a new wrinkle, and he was looking forward to it.

He drove into Manhattan and up the FDR Drive, then got off at
Sixty-third Street and drove toward Park Avenue. He parked in a
very expensive garage just off Park, took his large equipment case,
the one with the wheels, and his tripod from the trunk, then walked
down Park until he reached the building in question. It was a steel-
and-glass tower of around fifteen stories, very slim and elegant, and
he could only guess at what the apartments cost. He stood to one
side of the building and looked up.

What he saw was an array of tall buildings, but the one that
interested him most was directly across the street, a prewar co-op
with a limestone facade and the usual awning. A doorman stood out
front, rocking on his heels, waiting to open a taxi door for somebody. Cantor crossed the street and approached the doorman.

"Good morning," he said.

"Morning, sir," the doorman, a paunchy man in his fifties,
replied. "Can I be of service?"

"Is the super around?"

"No, he's in the hospital; had his tonsils out. Ain't that something, a guy his age having his tonsils out?" He laughed in a way that made Cantor think the guy didn't like his boss much.

"That's a good one," Cantor chuckled. "How would you like to make five hundred bucks?"

The doorman stopped rocking on his heels and eyed him warily. "We're not allowed to murder the building's occupants."

"No violence involved. I just want to take some photographs up and down Park Avenue from the top of your building. There's probably part of the roof devoted to equipment, that's separate from the penthouse property, isn't there? You know, air conditioning, satellite dishes, that sort of thing."

"Yes, there is."

"Good view of Park from that spot?"

The doorman nodded. "A *very* good view." He looked at Cantor for a moment, then took a deep breath.

Cantor cut him off. "Five hundred is the max. I'll need to be up there until dark, probably, and if I don't get what I need, I'll have to come back tomorrow, and in that case, it's another two hundred."

"You're not a cat burglar?"

"I'm a retired cop." Cantor flashed his badge.

"Name?"

"That's all you need to know."

Another doorman appeared from inside. "I'll take the outside for a while, Tim."

"Okay," the doorman replied. "I've got to run this guy up to the utility area, anyway." He took a clump of keys from the doorman's station in the lobby and motioned with his head for Cantor to follow. They rode up in the elevator to the sixteenth floor in silence, then got off. "I don't want to know what this is about, do I?"

Cantor shook his head. "Why would you? It doesn't involve any of the people who live in your building."

The doorman led him to a door marked "Staff Only," unlocked it, then led him up a flight of stairs to another door, marked "Utilities." He unlocked that and held it open for Cantor. "This what you're looking for?"

Cantor walked through a forest of antennae and steel boxes to the parapet and looked up and down Park Avenue, noting especially his view of the building across the street and the angle to the penthouse terrace. "This will do," he said.

The doorman made a motion with his fingers, and Cantor took five folded hundred-dollar bills from a pocket and handed them to him.

"The doors will lock themselves when you come downstairs," the doorman said, "and the elevator won't stop until it gets to the ground floor. If you need to piss, there's a drainpipe over there." He nodded at the corner. "Don't leave no trash, and if you see any of the building tenants, try not to look like a criminal."

"Got it," Cantor said. "And thanks very much." The two men shook hands, and the doorman left. Cantor walked back to the parapet and surveyed the penthouse apartment across the street and two stories below him. "Fucking perfect," he said aloud. He set up his tripod and began unpacking equipment.

He affixed a very long lens to the electronic camera and sighted the terrace, then he screwed on a Polaroid filter, in case he wanted to shoot through the sliding glass doors. When he was satisfied that he was ready for anything, he set a portable radio beside him, already tuned to a classical station, then he opened a folding camp stool, sat down and took a sandwich and a Diet Coke from his case. It was a nice day, and an al fresco lunch was just the thing. He stayed there all afternoon, occasionally stretching his legs but always with an eye on the penthouse across the street.

At five-thirty sharp, Bernard Finger left his office in the Seagram Building on Park Avenue at Fifty-second Street and stepped into his waiting limo. The driver closed the door and got in while Finger settled himself in the custom leather backseat. He pressed a button, and the window between himself and the driver lowered a foot. "You know where," he said, then he raised the window and picked up the telephone beside him, pressing a speed-dial number.

"Hello?" She sounded cheerful.

"Hello, dearest," Finger said. "How was your day?"

"It was okay; I did a little shopping."

This was not the time to call her on her shopping addiction. "Dearest, I'm headed to a client meeting out of the office, and then I'm going to have to take him to dinner, so you'll have to count me out for this evening. I'm sorry."

There was a long, deadly silence. "Bernie," she said, finally, "you're fucking somebody." It wasn't a question.

"You're absolutely right, dearest; I'm fucking the guy who's suing my client. It's what I do."

"You're out three or four nights a week, Bernie, and I know you too well not to think that you're following your dick somewhere."

"I'm just following the money, dearest, which is what keeps you in such style, isn't it? If I were home for dinner every night, you'd have to close half a dozen charge accounts." She thought in shopping terms; she'd understand that.

She sighed. "All right, but you remember that we have the theater tomorrow night. It's a benefit performance for Beatrice's charity, and there's dinner to follow. That means black tie and in the car at seven thirty."

"I've already cleared the decks for that, dearest; I won't disappoint you." He certainly wouldn't; that would create a marital nuclear event, whose shock wave would break windows in New Jersey. "I'll try not to wake you when I come home."

"You do that." She hung up without saying good-bye.

He replaced the phone in its cradle, poured himself a short single-malt Scotch and tossed it down. He wanted his blood flowing freely by the time the elevator reached the penthouse and the lovely Marilyn.

16

Bob Cantor snapped to attention. He had been half dozing, but a movement on the terrace below had caught his eye. One of the sliding glass doors had opened, and now a tall blonde, wearing a floor-length robe that appeared to be silk, swept onto the terrace. He recognized her immediately. It was Marilyn, the masseuse.

Marilyn set down a drink on a little table next to a double-width chaise longue, made a motion with her shoulders and the robe fell in a puddle at her feet, revealing a lithe, naked body with high-hung breasts. She pulled something from her hair and shook it loose.

Cantor grabbed the camera and sighted through the long lens. The low afternoon sunlight washed over her pale body, turning it gold, as he focused and fired off a couple of shots. He checked the screen on the back of the camera to be sure he had it right. He had it right. The girl was now rubbing some sort of lotion on her body, and Cantor was getting an erection.

Suddenly, Cantor's erection wilted. Bernard Finger stepped out onto the terrace with a drink in his hand. He was stark naked, and it was not a pretty sight. Marilyn did not leap up to meet him but patted the other side of the chaise. Finger sat down, they clinked glasses and began to chat.

Marilyn was doing more than chatting. She had her hand in Finger's lap and was kneading his genitals. Cantor clicked away. The lens was the perfect length; he might as well have been sitting next to them.

Marilyn rolled over and buried her face in Finger's crotch, and his face took on an ecstatic grimace, which Cantor preserved in digital code. Then they changed positions, and Finger was doing the work in her lap. He was on his knees, his buttocks pointing to the sky. Cantor was almost as ecstatic as Finger. He continued photographing until both Marilyn and Finger had collapsed in a tangle of love.

Cantor took out a small laptop computer and the little portable color printer he traveled with, and, minutes later, he had a sheet of postage-stamp–sized prints, half a dozen enlargements and everything on a CD. He pulled out his cell phone and pressed a speed-dial number.

Up at the *Post* on the floor where the Page Six staff worked, a phone rang and a young man picked it up. "Page Six."

"You know who this is, Henry?"

"Yeah, I know who it is."

"I want you to do two things: I want you to go down to your cashier and draw ten grand in hundreds and fifties, then I want you to meet me at the bar across the street. You've got an hour, and if you don't bring the money, I go elsewhere."

"What could be that hot?"

"If you don't think it's hot enough, you don't have to give me the ten grand. I'm not going to hit you over the head and take it."

"Give me a hint."

"How's this for a hint: *in flagrante delicto*?"

"Who is?"

"Trust me, you're going to love it." The caller hung up.

Cantor removed the lens from the camera, packed his equipment and took the elevator to the lobby, giving Tim, the doorman, a little salute as he passed. Half an hour later, he was in a back booth of a dark bar, nursing a dirty martini with two olives. Presently, Henry entered the bar, waited for his eyes to become accustomed to the light, or lack of it, then headed for the booth. He was carrying a small, zippered canvas envelope that bulged just a bit.

"Okay," he said, "let's have it."

"First, I want complete confidentiality," Cantor said. "I don't want even your editors to know where this came from."

"Guaranteed," Henry said. "The paper loves it when we go to jail for not revealing sources. It makes them look brave, and they get a chance to run editorials about First Amendment issues."

Cantor laid an eight-by-ten photograph on the table and switched on a penlight.

"Beautiful girl!" Henry enthused. "Who's the guy with his head up her twat?"

Cantor laid another photo on the table and illuminated it.

"Holy shit!" Henry spat. "Is that Bernie Finger?"

"None other." Cantor spread out more photos and held up the CD. "Many more where that came from."

Henry was not actually salivating yet, but Cantor was afraid his prints were going to get wet. He scooped them up and put them, along with the CD, back into his briefcase. "There's a backstory, too, a juicy one, but first, the ten grand."

"First, the photos, the CD and the backstory," Henry said.

Cantor snapped the briefcase shut. "You're going to have to excuse me, Henry; I have another appointment in five minutes."

"All right, all right," Henry said, holding up his hands in surrender. He unzipped the leather bag, showed the money to Cantor, then rezipped it and handed it over.

Cantor unzipped it, riffled through the bills, then put the money into his briefcase and handed over the prints and the CD.

"Now, the backstory," Henry said.

Cantor grinned. "Bernie Finger is, as you no doubt know, a 'happily' married man" [he made quotation marks with his fingers], "but he's been promising the girl, a masseuse named Marilyn, that he's getting a divorce any minute. To prove his undying love, he bought her the Park Avenue penthouse, or at least, that's what he told her. I am reliably informed that the deed is in his name, not hers."

"Good stuff," Henry admitted, looking through the photos again. "I'm not sure we can actually print these, but we could certainly use them as evidence in defending a slander suit."

"Come on, Henry. A little black tape in strategic places would do the trick. But hey, they're your photos; do with them as you will."

"The timing is good," Henry said. "We've just had a little back and forth in the column between Bernie and Stone Barrington."

"Who?"

"Another lawyer."

"Never heard of him, but let me know if you want him photographed doing the nasty." Cantor slid out of the booth, offered a quick handshake and was on his way.

B ack in his car, Cantor hit another speed-dial number.
"Stone Barrington."

"The deed is done," Cantor said.

"Which deed?"

"All the deeds. And the rag paid so well that I'm not even going to charge you expenses."

"You're such a nice man," Stone said.

"Well, we all know that. Listen, I haven't heard from my nephew for a couple of days, and that's unusual. He normally calls every day, wanting money."

"Oh," Stone said, "he called me and said he was being chased by some of his bookie's leg breakers and needed to go to ground somewhere. I suggested a homeless shelter."

"That doesn't sound like the boy's style."

"Who cares about his style? He stayed one night with a girlfriend, then she kicked him out. He says he has nowhere else to go, said you weren't talking to him, either."

"That's kind of true," Cantor said. "Kind of true is as close as he ever gets to the truth. Let me know if you hear from him, will you? I promised his mother on her deathbed I'd look after him."

"I hope I don't, but if I do, I will. Any idea when the *Post* will publish?"

"Could be as early as tomorrow," Cantor replied. "Henry will have to clear it up the ladder, but he's hot to trot. Bye-bye." He punched off the cell phone and drove home happily with the ten thousand in his briefcase.

17

J oan brought in the *Post* just before lunch. "Story, but no pics," she said, handing the paper to Stone, opened at Page Six.
Stone read the piece:

ATTORNEY NESTLES WITH MISTRESS IN LOVE NEST,
BUT DEED TO NEST IN WRONG NAME

Ace lawyer Bernard Finger has been shacking up in a Park Avenue penthouse with his honey, Marilyn the Masseuse, for weeks, unbeknownst to his wife. (Note to Missus: New York is NOT a no-fault divorce state, so go for it!) The lovely Marilyn thinks the lovely nest is hers, but somehow the deed got registered in Bernie's name. Wonder how that happened?

"Cute," Stone said, "but why no photos?"
"I expect they're afraid of a suit from ol' Bernie," Joan replied.
"They need have no fear with those pictures in their possession. No, something else is going on here."

A t the *Post*, Henry Stead was sitting at his desk when he spotted the process server, a short, plump man in a wash-and-wear suit. Henry waved at him cheerfully. "Over here, Arnie! I'll accept service!"

Arnie waddled over to the desk and ignored Henry's out-stretched hand, holding the summons close to his chest. "How come you're so anxious to get sued?" he asked suspiciously.

"Arnie, you of all people are in a position to know that we get sued all the time."

"Well, yeah, but I've never seen anybody here look so happy about it."

"It breaks up the day, Arnie. Gimme the summons."

Arnie handed it over with some reluctance. "This goes against my experience of these things," he said. "Ordinarily I have to chase people around if they know what I'm doing."

"Gimme the clipboard, Arnie," Henry said, extending a hand.

Arnie handed over a clipboard holding a sheet of paper with space for a dozen signatures. "Sign on line six," he said.

Henry signed with a flourish. "That's it, Arnie; your work is done. I'm sure that up in heaven an angel just got his wings." He picked up a little bell on his desk and tinkled it. A copy boy sprinted toward him. "False alarm, Terry," Henry said. "That was a heavenly bell."

Terry came to a screeching halt. "Don't pitch me no balks," he said sullenly, turning away.

"That was an oxymoron, Terry," Henry called after him.

With a last, untrusting glance, Arnie turned and trudged toward the elevators.

Henry ripped open the envelope and read the document. "Bingo!!!" he yelled, and everybody in the room turned and stared at him as he sprinted toward his boss's office. He ran into the room without knocking, startling a man who had just taken a big bite of a corned beef and chopped liver sandwich on rye with Russian dressing. "Bernie Finger came through like a champ!" Henry yelled, holding up the summons so his boss could read it without getting chopped liver on it.

The editor made a monumental effort to swallow, but required a slug of celery tonic to choke down the mass. He wiped his mouth with two napkins. "Okay," he said, when he was finally able to speak, "run the pictures. In color."

Henry skipped back to his desk, happy in his work.

S tone was tidying up the kitchen when the doorbell rang. He picked up a phone. "Yes?"

"It's Celia."

Stone pressed the button that unlocked the front door. "Straight through the house and down the back stairs," he said.

"I'm on my way."

Stone made a quick check of the kitchen bar, which held a collection of liquor bottles, the ice bucket and a wine dispenser with two bottles of chilled white and two of red. He went to the stairway to meet her.

She came down the stairs in a fur coat, carrying two large grocery bags. He took them from her, set them on the kitchen counter, helped her off with her coat and hung it on a peg. She accepted a hello kiss.

"I'm sorry I didn't meet you at the door, but it would have taken me twice as long before I could offer you a drink."

"Do you have any champagne?" she asked.

"A rhetorical question," he said, going to the fridge and removing a chilly bottle of Veuve Cliquot Grande Dame and working on the cork. "Can you grab a couple of flutes from over there?" he asked, nodding toward the china and crystal cabinet.

She was able to reach the top shelf with no difficulty and brought back the flutes.

Stone filled them, then filled them again when the bubbles had subsided. They raised their glasses and drank.

"That's lovely," she said. "I like it even better than Dom Perignon."

"So do I," Stone said. "Why didn't you have the groceries delivered? I hate to think of you humping those bags around."

"One bag was delivered; it was sitting on your doorstep, waiting for some homeless person to make his day. The other bag contains some of my preparations." She set down her drink and began unpacking a sealed Tupperware container.

"And what is that?" he asked, peering through the cloudy plastic.

"That is boned chicken thighs, marinating in port as they have been for twenty-four hours."

"I can't wait," he said.

"It'll be on the table in forty minutes," she said. "Starting from when we finish this glass of champagne."

"I take it we should drink a red?"

"A full-bodied red, preferably a cabernet."

"I have just the thing," Stone said, going to the bar and bringing back a bottle. "I brought it up from the cellar in anticipation of your request."

She peered at the label. "Phelps Insignia '94; that should do nicely."

"Can I help you do anything?"

She downed the rest of her champagne. "You can best help by keeping my glass full and otherwise staying out of my way."

Stone refilled their glasses and sat down on a bar stool. "Proceed," he said, retrieving a decanter for the wine.

And she did.

Forty minutes later they were dining on something she called *poulet au porto,* chicken in port with sliced green apples, saffron rice and *haricot verts.*

"God, this is good!" Stone enthused. "I can't remember when anyone cooked for me, and I can't remember ever eating anything as wonderful as this."

"You say all the right things," she replied. "You keep doing that."

"I intend to."

"You get to do the dishes," she said, putting a last bite into her mouth and taking a sip of the wine.

"My housekeeper gets to do that in the morning," Stone said.

"Does she serve breakfast in bed?" Celia asked.

"She does, on request."

Celia smiled at him. "Good," she said. "But first, we have to find the bed."

Stone showed her where it was.

The night passed in a fog of champagne and mad love, with mouths employed voraciously and plenty of good, straight sex: sitting, standing, kneeling and reclining. Stone woke, exhausted, with a hand on his penis, and to his alarm, it was responding yet again.

"This time I'll die," he said.

"There are worse ways to go," she replied, then used her tongue to help her hand. She threw a leg over him and settled down, guiding him in.

Stone emitted a pitifully gratified noise.

"Why didn't they print the pictures?" she asked offhandedly.

"Huh?"

"I saw the mention of Bernie and Marilyn on Page Six, but they didn't use the photographs. Why?"

Stone stopped helping, but Celia continued to slowly move up and down on him. "What?"

"Oh, come on, Stone. Don't be coy. When I told you about the penthouse exhibitionism I expected you to use the information, but didn't you give the *Post* the pictures your man took?"

"You flabbergast me," Stone said.

"It doesn't seem to be affecting your erection," she said, giggling.

"How on earth do you know . . . what you think you know?"

"Didn't you used to be a detective?"

"Yes, but . . ."

"Then figure it out."

Stone thought for a minute. "Okay, you got me. I can't figure it out."

"I'm living, temporarily, in the building directly across the street from Marilyn, and the doorman, Tim, is my buddy. He saw the piece in the *Post*, too, and he told me about the man with all the cameras on the roof."

"I'm relieved to hear that," Stone said, "because I had begun to think that you were some sort of psychic."

"Oh, I'm pretty psychic, too; how do you think I knew you would use the information I gave you?"

Stone began to help with the sex again. "I think I'm just going to stop thinking, at least when you're around."

"Well, you've been thinking with your cock all night, and that's all right with me. You don't need a brain to make me happy in bed."

"Then you've come to the right place," Stone said.

"You didn't answer my question."

"There was a question?"

"Why didn't they use the photographs?"

"I was thinking about that—this was before we got into bed together—and I think they're playing it very smart."

"Hang on a minute." She began moving faster and making little noises, then she came all in a rush, followed closely by Stone.

She rolled off him and lay on her back, panting. "Okay, you can have your brain back now. How is the *Post* playing it smart?"

Stone took a few deep breaths and handed her the box of tissues from the bedside table. "This is how I figure it: Bernie doesn't know they have the pictures; he thinks they're operating on nothing more than a rumor. So they run what he thinks is a rumor the first day, then Bernie sues them immediately, denies everything, claims slander. They wait for the suit to be filed, then the next day—that's today—they run the pictures, thus blowing Bernie's lawsuit out of the water and making him look even more like the ass he is. You could call that humiliating him, legally, and Bernie prides himself on knowing how to manipulate the law, so he's hoist with his own petard."

"What's a petard?"

"Some sort of medieval weapon, I think, but the phrase means, if I'm right, that the *Post* will pretty much fuck Bernie with his own dick."

"How very appropriate," Celia said, laughing.

"Just what is your interest in all this?" Stone asked. "Do you have an axe to grind?"

"You might say that," she replied. "Right after Bernie had started seeing Marilyn, when we were both working at the day spa, he made a big pass at me. She never even knew that, but somehow she got the idea that *I* was interested in *him*, and she took delight in telling me all the details of their affair, as if she were making me jealous. I got really tired of it, but she wouldn't stop, even when I asked her to. I quit the job, just to get away from her."

"God, I hope I never make you angry with me," Stone said.

"That would be unwise, indeed. Where's the breakfast in bed you promised me?"

"Celia, it's . . ." he checked the bedside clock ". . . six oh five in the morning, and my housekeeper doesn't arrive until eight. And I can't even make a fist, let alone cook, in my present condition."

"What you need is a hot bath," she said, getting out of bed. A moment later, water could be heard running in the bathroom.

Twenty minutes later, Celia sat in the big tub, holding a limp Stone in her arms. "There, there," she said, stroking his hair.

"This is wonderful," he sighed.

"Of course it is. And when we're done here, I'm going to give you the best massage you ever had in your life."

"I think I'm going to have to take the day off," Stone said.

She laughed. "I wish I could join you, but I have appointments today."

"So you live in that building on Park? You've been very mysterious about it."

"Not mysterious, just careful."

"Why careful?"

"I'm afraid I have a crazy ex-boyfriend on my hands."

"Tell me about it."

"Not much to tell. I lived with him in a big loft downtown for a couple of years. It was fine for a while, but then he got into drugs and started becoming violent."

"He was violent with *you*? He *is* crazy."

"You'd think my size would have intimidated him just a little, wouldn't you? He was only about six feet, and I think that always annoyed him. I took it at first, and then I started hitting him back."

"Didn't that stop him?"

"No, he started using weapons—his belt, once a whip, if you can believe it."

"And how did you respond to that?"

"I picked up one of his small sculptures—he's a sculptor—and coldcocked him with it. Then, while he was still unconscious, I packed up and got the hell out of there. A friend lent me the apartment on Park, but Devlin, the sculptor, is looking for me, and he's furious, so mutual friends tell me."

"What do you think will happen if he finds you?"

"I think he'll kill me." She paused. "If he can."

"Then I think you ought to start taking this seriously," Stone said.

"Oh, I am taking it seriously."

"Have you applied for a protective court order?"

"If I did that, the court would bar him from coming within a hundred yards of me, or something, right?"

"More or less."

"The problem is, he'd have to be told where I'm living, so he could stay a hundred yards away."

"You have a point. So what do you intend to do?"

"I'm thinking of killing him," she said.

19

S tone lay on the bed while Celia kneaded his body.

"So, what do you think of my idea of killing Devlin?" she asked.

"Morally repugnant."

"Forget morality for a minute. How should I go about it?"

"You shouldn't go about it, even forgetting morality."

"If I have no morals, then why shouldn't I?"

"How are your nerves?"

"Pretty cool."

"Could you stand an investigation by a team of police detectives into every aspect of your private life, maybe lasting for years? Could you stand being portrayed in the newspapers as the likely suspect, even if it couldn't be proven? Could you stand the loss of your business when your clients learned that you were a suspected murderer?"

"Who knows, it might even improve my business."

"I don't think you'd like your new customers."

"Don't you think I could plan the perfect crime?"

"Did you ever watch the old TV series *Columbo,* with Peter Falk?"

"Sure. I bet I saw all of them."

"Well, every week, Columbo solved a murder that was supposed to be the perfect crime. The series was a weekly lesson in how many ways there are to screw up when you're trying to commit the perfect crime. And that was before DNA and fiber analysis, and all that stuff."

"What would be my chances of getting away with it?"

"Have you ever met any homicide detectives?"

"One or two, I guess, at parties."

"They looked pretty ordinary, didn't they?"

"*Very* ordinary."

"Your usual homicide detective is a guy in a suit who looks like a businessman or a high school teacher or an insurance salesman. Of course, there are those who look like bums, but my point is, they share one thing in common."

"What?"

"They're smart. They get assigned to homicides because they're the best detectives. They also have a lot of experience at solving murders. Sometimes they get it wrong, and sometimes they don't solve it at all, but year in and year out the NYPD solves close to two-thirds of all homicides. Now, you may think that gives you a one-in-three shot at getting away with it, but it also gives you a two-out-of-three shot at getting caught."

She slapped him on the ass. "Turn over."

He turned over. "Most murders are committed by someone the victim knows—family member, lover, next-door neighbor. Most of the unsolved murders are committed by someone the victim doesn't know—mugger, rapist, like that. If Devlin is murdered by someone who knows him, like, say, you, then your chances of getting caught go way up, just because you're known to know him. In fact, because you lived together and were lovers and had a sometimes violent relationship, you would instantly be the chief suspect in the eyes of the police."

"Okay, suppose I got caught and sent to trial. Wouldn't I have a good chance of getting off when the jury learned that he had been violent toward me for a long time?"

"You really want to take a chance on the opinions of twelve ordinary citizens?"

"Maybe."

"Okay, let's say you go down to Devlin's studio, pick up another one of his small sculptures and coldcock him. One blow might not do the trick; you might have to hit him until his brains are on the floor, and in that case, you'd better show signs of his trying to kill you—bruises on your neck, maybe even his fingerprints on your throat, something like that. And even if he is smaller than you, you'd be taking a chance on whether you could win the fight."

"Suppose I wait until he attacks me, then shoot him."

"Again, you might lose; he might take the gun away from you and shoot you. Also, the cops are going to want to know where you got the gun, if you had a license for it and why you took it to his studio. You could go to prison for just possessing the gun."

She massaged his scalp and his face. "You make it sound awfully difficult."

"It's not just difficult, it's very nearly impossible to kill somebody you know and just walk away." She began rubbing the back of his neck. "And if I thought you really had it in you to murder somebody, I don't think I'd want your hands where they are right now; they're too close to my throat."

"Suppose I hire someone to kill him and I'm in, say, San Francisco on the day."

"Your chances of getting away with the actual killing go way up, but now you've got another person in the picture who might be a very great liability. Do you know any contract killers?"

"No, but I bet I could find one."

"Okay. You walk into a bar in a not-so-hot neighborhood, strike up a conversation with some guy who looks like he'd do anything for money, and you make the deal and give him half. He could just start drinking at another bar and keep your money; in fact, if he's smart, that's exactly what he'd do. But let's say he goes through with the deal, commits a clean murder, leaves no evidence, collects the rest of his fee and goes away. All of this is unlikely, of course, because he'd probably make mistakes that would get him caught, and then, to get a light sentence, he gives you to the D.A. on a platter. The D.A. will find witnesses in the bar who saw the two of you together; you're the kind of girl who's not easily forgotten. Or suppose, a year or two down the line, your hit man gets arrested for some other crime, something petty, like burglary. He doesn't want to do time, so he does a deal where he gets immunity for Devlin and you get the death penalty. In short, you can't rely on a person who will kill for money."

She laughed and dropped his head. "All right, I won't kill him. What should I do?"

"Unless you want to leave town or spend the next few years as a kind of fugitive in your own city, you have to confront him. Legally, I mean. Would you like for me to visit him and tell him what you can do to him in court? That might cool his ardor."

"What a good idea!" she enthused. She kissed him lightly on the penis. "Now, how about that breakfast in bed?"

20

S
tone made it through breakfast without having to perform again, which was just as well, because he was nearly too sore to walk properly. He saw Celia to the front door, and she took an invitation from her purse and handed it to him.

"Devlin has a show opening tomorrow night at this gallery in SoHo. It might be a good time to speak to him."

"I'll see what I can do," Stone said. "How about lunch at La Goulue, Sixty-fifth and Madison at one o'clock the day after?"

"See you there," she said, planting a serious kiss on his kisser.

Stone disengaged with reluctance and limped to his office.

Joan came in, bearing the *Post*. "I won't ask why you're late," she said. "I saw her leave from my window."

"Thanks for not asking," Stone said, accepting the newspaper, which was open to Page Six. Four excellent photographs of Bernie Finger and Marilyn the Masseuse adorned the upper quarter of the page, and tiny strips of black covered only their most private parts. "Wow," Stone breathed, as he read the story, which made mincemeat of Bernie's slander suit.

The phone rang, and Joan picked it up. "The Barrington Practice," she said in her best secretarial tones, then she listened and covered the phone with her hand. "It's Henry Stead, from Page Six."

Stone had had one previous conversation with Stead a few months before. He pressed the speakerphone button. "Good morning, Mr. Stead."

"Good morning, Mr. Barrington. I trust you've seen Page Six today."

"Mr. Stead, I know this will come as a crushing disappointment, but I am not a regular peruser of either your newspaper or your page."

"And yet you managed a timely riposte to Bernie Finger's account of your luncheon at the Four Seasons."

"My secretary's taste in newspapers is not so lofty as mine, and, from time to time, she may share some tidbit with me, particularly if it takes my name in vain. Today, so far, she seems to actually be doing her work, so she has shared nothing. Care to give me the short version?"

"Well, yesterday we ran a mention of Bernie's current extramarital affair. Bernie, of course, sued us immediately, so today we ran the corroborating photographs, featuring a naked Bernie on a penthouse terrace with an equally naked masseuse named Marilyn. Tomorrow, we expect to report that Mrs. Finger has filed for divorce. In fact, I believe the story is already set in type."

"And however did you get Bernie to pose for these pictures? I've met him only once, at the aforementioned luncheon, but he certainly didn't seem built for nude photos."

"Oh, your good friend Mr. Cantor supplied the photographs."

"I'm afraid the only Mr. Cantor with whom I am acquainted is Eddie, of the banjo eyes, and I believe he is far too dead to supply you with nudies of Bernie Finger."

Stead managed an appreciative chuckle. "Mr. Barrington, this page appreciates your contributions to our output, and as long as we can maintain this friendly relationship, you will have our gratitude, expressed in our treatment of you in these pages."

"Mr. Stead, while I am always appreciative of kind treatment, I cannot offer a quid pro quo, not being the gossipy sort, but I wish you well in your endeavors, particularly with regard to Bernie Finger. I bid you good morning." He disconnected.

"Nicely done," Joan said. "Tell me, did you ever feel even a twinge of conscience about this? I wasn't really sure you'd go through with it."

"A twinge, yes, for about half a minute. Then I remembered Bernie's attempt to sabotage my reputation with his altered-state account of our lunch, and I started to feel really good about screwing him, which is how I still feel."

"And how about torpedoing his marriage? Do you expect to reap any karma for that?"

"Well, Bernie's ego, not his marriage, was my objective, but although I have done Bernie an ill turn, I'm sure that is more than made up for in good karma by the service I have done Mrs. Finger, who will presently be rid of Bernie and very rich. I predict she will remarry within the year."

The phone rang again, and Joan picked it up. "The Barrington Practice." She listened and handed Stone the phone. "Bob Cantor." She returned to her office.

"Good morning, Bob," Stone said.

"Morning, Stone."

"I've just had Page Six on the phone, and Henry Stead made a half-hearted attempt to make me admit that I know you."

"Which you repulsed?"

"In emphatic fashion. What's up?"

"I still haven't heard from Herbie, and now I'm really worried. He's never gone this long without asking for money."

"Have you made inquiries?"

"Yeah. I know I'm supposed to be a detective, but I'm damned if I can catch his scent."

"Have you been to his home?"

"Not yet, but I guess I'd better go over there. I have a key."

"Give me the address, and I'll meet you," Stone said. He scribbled it down. "Give me half an hour. I'll meet you out front." He hung up and buzzed Joan.

"Yes?"

"I'm going to run out to Brooklyn; Herbie Fisher is missing and Bob is concerned."

"I thought it was awfully quiet around here," Joan said.

S tone hailed a cab and gave the driver the address. It was weird, he reflected, how Herbie's sudden absence could leave a hole in his day. He couldn't say he missed the idiot, but still . . .

Bob Cantor was standing on the sidewalk in front of a handsome brownstone in a gentrified neighborhood. "This way," he said, opening the iron gate and taking the stairs that led to the basement. "He lives in the super's apartment."

Cantor let them in with his key and scooped up a pile of mail on the floor outside the apartment. He opened the front door.

"Let's do this like a crime scene," Stone said.

"I'm way ahead of you," Cantor said, handing Stone a pair of latex gloves. He led the way from the foyer into the living room. The room had been tossed—no, more than tossed, trashed. A bookcase holding an elaborate stereo system lay facedown on the floor, its contents smashed. Every piece of upholstered furniture had been slashed to the springs, and the drawers of a small desk were scattered here and there. An inspection of the single bedroom revealed the same treatment, and even the bathroom had been thoroughly turned over.

"What do you think they were looking for?" Stone asked.

"Money, what else?"

"And why would anybody think Herbie has money?"

"Well, he's always telling anybody who'll listen that he does. I guess somebody believed it."

"I suppose so."

"You think this is Carmine Dattila's work?"

"Who else?"

"Well, I'm sure he's not the only person Herbie owes money," Stone said.

"Maybe not, but Dattila is probably the only lender with a personal army to do work like this."

The two men stood in the apartment with but one thought between them.

"You think Herbie is still alive?" Cantor asked.

"I think that depends on whether Herbie can convince them that he has some hope of paying," Stone said. "It's time to call the Brooklyn cop shop."

21

Stone sat on the arm of a formerly overstuffed chair in Herbie Fisher's apartment and watched the two detectives pick their way around the apartment.

"Well, so far," Detective One said, "this is vandalism, as I see it."

Detective Two nodded in agreement.

"It's kidnapping, possibly a homicide, with burglary," Stone said.

Detective Two shook his head. "I don't see anything missing."

Stone sighed. "If you could see it, it wouldn't be missing."

"Huh?"

"Herbie had money here; you see any money?"

"Well, no, but how do we know there ever was any money here?"

"We have only the kidnap victim's word for that, but it's a start, don't you agree?"

Cantor broke in. "Look, guys, my nephew has been missing for three days, and when we enter the apartment, we find this." He waved an arm around.

"What can I tell you?" Detective One said.

"I'll bet you could tell me a lot if the kidnapped person was a beautiful twenty-one-year-old model. I'll bet your crime scene people would be all over this."

"Here's another thing," Detective Two said. "You've disturbed this crime scene; it's no longer any good."

Stone and Cantor both held up both hands to show their latex gloves.

"We're both retired from the job," Cantor said. "You think we don't know at least as much as you two assholes about crime scenes?"

"Now, speaking to us disrespectfully is not going to get you extra service," Detective One said, sounding hurt.

"When I speak of you disrespectfully, it will be in the newspapers," Stone said, "which is my next stop if you don't get your ass in gear and put out a bulletin on Herbie. As we explained to you, he owes one of Carmine Dattila's bookies a lot of money, so you already have a suspect."

"Yeah, but that Dattila guy works out of Manhattan," Detective Two said.

"He works wherever the fuck he wants to work," Cantor pointed out, "and the kidnapping and burglary happened in Brooklyn, in, of all places, *your* precinct. And in just a minute, I'm going to be speaking to *your* captain."

"While I'm speaking to the *New York Post*," Stone added.

"Awright, awright," Detective One said. "I'll make out a report and get Mr. Fisher's description circulated."

Stone's cell phone rang, and he flipped it open. "Yes?"

"It's Joan. You have a new client waiting, so you should get your ass back here in a hurry. This one smells of money."

"What new client? Eggers hasn't said anything about sending anybody over."

"Mrs. Bernard Finger."

"I'll be right there," Stone said. He closed the phone. "Bob, you'll have to take it from here; I've got a fire to build."

Cantor nodded.

Stone ran out of the building, searching for a cab.

J oan met him at the outer door to his office. "She's *very* upset; I did
the best I could to calm her."

"Good girl," Stone said, kissing her on the top of her head. He
strode into his office and found Mrs. Bernard Finger sitting on his
sofa, sipping a cup of tea and munching on a cookie, looking not at
all upset. She appeared to be in her early forties, very well main-
tained and pretty much a knockout in her age group and maybe a
couple of younger ones, Stone thought.

"Mrs. Finger," he said, extending a hand, "I'm Stone Barrington.
I'm so sorry to have kept you waiting."

"Call me Bernice," she said, shaking his hand. "I expect you
know why I'm here."

"Why don't you tell me," Stone said. "Tell me everything." He
sat down on the sofa and listened intently to every word she said,
nodding sympathetically. He knew most of it, but when she patted
a briefcase on the sofa beside her, he *really* began to listen.

"It's all in here," she said. "Everything."

"May I have a look?" Stone asked.

She unsnapped the briefcase and spun it around. Inside were
a number of file folders. "I think you will find this helpful."

Stone picked up the folders. There were four, and they were a
collective two inches thick. "May I take a moment to familiarize myself?" he asked.

"Take your time," Bernice said. "I've got the rest of the day."

Stone opened the first file and found himself staring at a series of
financial statements going back over ten years. The most recent was
dated a month before, and in toto the statements gave a very good
picture of Bernie Finger's climb from a net worth of four million
dollars ten years before to a current net worth of thirty-eight million dollars. The beauty part, Stone thought, was that Bernie was
at least fifty percent liquid. He went through the other folders,

which contained brokerage account statements; bank statements; and copies of deeds for his Fifth Avenue co-op, the house in the Hamptons, a ski lodge in Telluride and, wonder of wonders, the new penthouse on Park Avenue where he had stashed Marilyn the Masseuse. Stone cleared his throat. "And Bernice, may I ask how you came by these documents?"

"Of course," she said. "They were in the safe."

"In the safe, where?"

"In our study—we share it—in our apartment."

"And you had the combination to the safe?"

"We each have a safe. He didn't know that I knew he kept the combination taped to the side of a desk drawer."

"How long have you been married to Bernie, Bernice?"

"Seven years."

"And were you married before that?"

"No, I was a businesswoman. I founded a cosmetics company, small but growing fast. Bernie made me sell it when we got married. He did the deal for me, and I never thought I got enough for it."

"Bernice, I'm going to need a copy of your financial statement as well."

"I don't own anything separate from Bernie," she said. "I put all my money into our joint accounts when we got married."

"And how much did you get for your cosmetics company?"

"Six and a half million dollars."

"And did you have any other assets in your own name at the time of the marriage?"

"I had a co-op on Park, paid for. Bernie sold both our apartments, and we bought the co-op on Fifth."

"And how much of the money used for that purchase was yours?"

"Half: two million dollars."

"And that was seven years ago?"

"Yes."

Stone referred to the most recent financial statement in the folder. Bernie had valued the apartment at a little over six million dollars. "How big an apartment is it?"

"Six bedrooms, living, dining, library, study, kitchen, butler's pantry, two maids' rooms."

Bernie had seriously undervalued his real estate for some reason, and lying on a financial statement was a felony. "Bernice," he said, "who recommended me to you as an attorney?"

"Bernie did," she said.

"What?"

"He talks in his sleep. He was bitching about you, calling you all sorts of names."

"In his sleep?"

"Yes, that's what he does when he's nervous about the opposition. So, I figured, if Bernie is nervous about you, you're my man."

"Bernice," Stone said, "I would be very pleased to represent you in this action." He explained his fees.

"Can you take a percentage, instead of a fee?"

"Of course. If you'd prefer it I can do it on a contingency basis." He certainly could! "I'd need a retainer, to apply against the contingency on the final settlement."

"How do you think we'll do in court?"

"Bernice, with a little luck, I don't think we'll ever see the inside of a courtroom. I would expect this to settle, and fairly quickly."

"Stone," she said, "are you telling me I've got Bernie by the balls?"

"Bernice," he replied, "that's a very good assessment of your position. And his."

"Then let's do it."

Stone pressed a button on the phone. "Joan, will you please print out a copy of our standard contingency agreement and bring it in, please?"

"Yes, Mr. Barrington," she replied meekly.

Bernice reached into her handbag, brought out a check and handed it over. "Will this do for a retainer?" she asked.

It was written on her and her husband's joint checking account and was made out for a hundred thousand dollars. "That's very generous, Bernice," he replied, handing it to Joan as she walked in with the agreement. He explained the terms of the contingency agreement, while she nodded along, then she signed the document and Joan took it away to notarize.

Stone turned back to Bernice. "Have you thought about what you want in the way of a settlement?"

"I want the money I got in the sale of my business, the Fifth Avenue apartment, and the house in the Hamptons. He can have Telluride and the love nest on Park Avenue. And I want half of everything else."

"I don't think that's unreasonable," Stone said.

"And the everything else includes the bank account in the Cayman Islands."

Stone's eyebrows went up. "Do you have copies of the statements?"

"They're in the bank file," she said. "Oh, and you should know that Bernie didn't pay taxes on what's in that account."

Stone's heart leapt. "That's good to know," he said.

She rose to go, and he walked her to the front door. "I'll call Bernie and arrange a settlement conference," he said, shaking her hand and closing the door behind her. He walked back to Joan's office. "You hotfoot it to the bank and get that check cleared before Bernie finds out she wrote it, and I'll dictate a complaint as soon as you get back. I want him served first thing tomorrow morning."

S tone walked into Elaine's and sat down. Dino was already there with his usual Scotch, and Stone's Knob Creek arrived immediately.

"You look like you had a good day," Dino said.

"Why do you say that?" Stone asked, sipping the bourbon.

"Well, you have a smile plastered on your face, and you don't seem to be able to make it go away."

"Dino, *nothing* could make it go away."

"All right, tell me."

"Well, first of all, the lovely Celia and I had a very good evening together, which lasted until after breakfast."

Dino sighed. "I don't suppose you'll give me details."

"A gentleman doesn't tell."

"What else?"

"Second, Herbie Fisher has disappeared."

"That *is* good news."

"It gets better: He may be dead."

"Carmine Dattila?"

"The primary suspect. Herbie hasn't shown or called Bob Cantor for three days, and his apartment has been ransacked."

"Didn't you say that Herbie owes Carmine's bookie twenty-four grand?"

"And counting."

"Well, it doesn't make sense that Carmine would off him; he'll never get his money that way."

"Maybe he's mad enough, what with the lawsuit, that he just wants Herbie to go away. God knows, I can sympathize."

Dino shook his head. "Guys like Carmine don't kill money. He would be more likely to get the money, then kill Herbie. Maybe that's what he's doing right now, torturing Herbie in a cellar somewhere, trying to get the money out of him."

"Well, I would certainly not want Herbie or anybody else to be tortured, even if he did bring it on himself by betting with bookies, failing to pay, then suing Carmine."

"But you don't mind if Carmine offs him?"

"I'd off him myself, if I thought I could get away with it."

"Well, the thought of Herbie dead isn't enough to make you this happy. What else?"

Stone fished an envelope out of his pocket. "Read this," he said. "Bernie Finger is going to be served with it tomorrow morning, but I thought you'd enjoy seeing it first."

Dino opened the envelope and read the complaint. "Holy shit!" he said. "Bernie Finger's wife has hired *you*?"

"Can you believe the luck?"

"I saw the pictures in the *Post* today," Dino said. "I thought Bob Cantor's fingerprints were all over them."

"You think so?"

"I think more than that. I think you put Bob up to it."

"I would never cop to that," Stone said.

"Well, it is a little extreme for you, but there was that thing that Bernie said on Page Six about your lunch at the Four Seasons."

"The guy offers me what amounts to a bribe to settle Herbie's case, leaves in a huff when I call him on it, then lies about it to the *Post*. That kind of thing could hurt a lawyer's reputation. In fact, that was his intention. A piece like that in the papers could cost me a lot of business."

"I guess he was trying to tell you not to fuck with him and his client."

"Exactly. You know how reluctant I was to get involved in this suit, but now I'm going to nail Dattila to the wall."

"And screw Bernie Finger at the same time?"

"Well, a little."

"Handling his wife's divorce isn't going to make him happy."

"Listen, God sent me that case. You know how Bernice Finger chose me? She heard Bernie cursing me in his sleep. How about that for a recommendation!"

Dino laughed. "That's good; that's really good."

Stone looked at the front door. "No," he said, nodding toward the door, "*that*'s good."

Dino swiveled his head in time to see Bernard Finger and Marilyn the Masseuse being led to a table up front.

Stone grabbed the complaint from Dino's fingers and stuffed it back into the envelope. "I'll be right back," he said, rising.

He walked toward the front of the restaurant. Finger didn't see him coming, but Marilyn did, and her face fell. Finger turned around to look for the problem and found it immediately.

"Oh, hi, Stone," he said. "I was going to call you in the morning to set up depositions in your case against Carmine Dattila. Why don't we do Mr. Dattila and Mr. Fisher back to back in my office, day after tomorrow at two?"

"I'd be very happy to depose Mr. Dattila, Bernie," Stone said, "but as you probably know, my client is momentarily indisposed."

"Well, in that case, I guess we'll just have to postpone depositions until Mr. Fisher is feeling more disposed," Finger said, smirking.

"I hope, for your sake, that Mr. Fisher is found alive and well," Stone said, "because if he isn't, you're going to be reading a lot about him and his lawsuit in the papers, and Dattila doesn't like seeing his name in the papers, does he?"

"You've got no case, Stone," Finger said. "Learn to live with it. It's sad, I know, since that's probably the only work you've got at the moment."

"No, Bernie, it isn't my only case," Stone said, taking the envelope from his pocket. "I have a brand-new one." He laid the document on the table.

Finger removed the document from the envelope, and as soon as he read the first sentence his face fell.

"You've been served, Bernie. Call me tomorrow, and we'll arrange a settlement conference." Stone sauntered back to his own table and sat down, pointedly not looking in Finger's direction.

"You served him?" Dino asked.

"I did. What's he doing?"

"He's still reading, and he doesn't look happy. Now he's turning to Marilyn and saying something, and she's wearing a huge smile and kissing him."

"Well, I'm sorry to make Marilyn so happy, but if that's the price of making Bernie unhappy, then so be it."

"Uh-oh, here comes Bernie."

Stone looked up to see Finger approaching, clutching the complaint.

"Can we meet tomorrow morning in my office at eleven?" Bernie asked, his face expressionless.

"Perfect, Bernie."

"I'll make short work of this."

"That will be easy, if you accept Bernice's terms. And Bernie," Stone said, "remember: A lawyer who represents himself has a fool for a client, so bring somebody. Oh, and congratulations to you and Marilyn on your engagement. I wish you every happiness."

Finger turned around and stalked back to his table.

Stone waved for another round of drinks, and when they came he raised his glass to Dino. "You know, yesterday I was having trouble paying the bills, but today I've got a hundred grand of Bernie Finger's money in the bank, and when I'm through with him, he'll never know what hit him."

"I'll drink to that," Dino said, raising his own glass.

S tone arrived at Bernie Finger's office fifteen minutes late, just to annoy him. As he waited for the receptionist to announce him he looked around Finger's waiting room. Everything was tasteful but with an extra coat of gloss, which pretty much described Bernard Finger, Esquire, Stone thought.

A shapely young woman materialized before him. "Mr. Barrington? Will you please come with me?"

Stone resisted the riposte and, with pleasure, followed the young woman. He was led to a large conference room, where Bernie Finger and a younger man awaited. The huge table was completely bare.

"Morning, Stone," Finger said, as if they were just meeting for coffee. "Would you like something? Coffee? Tea?"

"Thanks, no; I've already had coffee this morning." He set his briefcase on the table.

"Allow me to introduce my colleague, Samuel Teich," Finger said, waving a hand at the man next to him.

The table was too wide for Stone to reach across and shake hands, so he just waved. "Hi, there."

"Sam is one of our bright young men around here," Finger said, "and, following your advice from last evening, he's going to represent me."

Stone regarded Sam Teich for a moment. He was on the small side, with thick, black, close-cropped hair and dark eyes under heavy eyebrows. Stone thought he could pass for either an Arab terrorist or a Mossad agent. He didn't doubt that young Mr. Teich was bright, perhaps even brighter than advertised, and he was happy that Finger had come so well armed.

"All right, Mr. Barrington," Teich said, "let's get to it. What does Mrs. Finger want?"

"It's very simple, Mr. Teich," Stone replied evenly. "She wants the Fifth Avenue apartment and the house in the Hamptons. Bernie can have Park Avenue and Telluride. She also wants the six and a half million dollars from the sale of her company, plus interest at eight percent a year, and half of the rest of Bernie's assets. Oh, and all her legal costs."

Sam Teich permitted himself a tiny smile. "Oh, and is that all?"

Finger spoke up. "Not half my blood?"

Teich quieted his client with a raised hand. "Mr. Barrington, unless you can make a reasonable proposal, I'm afraid we're going to have to see you in court, and then Mrs. Finger will have to see her personal life laid bare. I don't expect she's told you about her personal life, has she?"

"Mr. Teich . . ."

"Please . . . call me Sam."

"Sam. My dear Sam. I think it might be helpful if I run down our court case for you, just to give you some idea of what you'll be facing. We have a woman who gave up her career to marry Bernie and sold her business far too cheaply on Bernie's advice, just to make him happy; we have a seven-year marriage, dare I say it?—the best years of Bernice's life?—with a man who took her money, then committed flagrant adultery for years; a man who actually bought an expensive penthouse for his current paramour, though the deed remains in his name; a man whose net worth has appreciated from four million dollars to thirty-eight million dollars during the marriage, and that figure does not take into account the undervaluing of his assets on his financial statement or the large sum in his Cayman bank account—an account, incidentally, unknown to the Internal Revenue Service—on which no taxes have been paid. Finally, Mrs. Finger has had to endure the shame and humiliation of seeing her husband's nude photographs with his lover in a gossip column, seen by everyone she knows, something every woman on the jury—and it will be a jury trial—will find disgusting in the extreme."

"Are you finished?" Finger asked.

"No, Bernie, not quite. I should tell you that everything I have just mentioned can be substantiated with your own files, to which Bernice has legal and proper access, and of which she has availed herself." Stone opened his briefcase and slid a handful of file folders across the table. "Of course, if we go to trial, there's just no telling what my investigators will come up with when they start pawing through your law firm's files and, of course, your personal life. I don't think that will play very well with your firm's clients, Bernie, particularly with those clients on the criminal side of your practice, when they start reading their names in the newspapers." Stone snapped shut his briefcase. "And you and I both know that any court is very likely to give Bernice half of everything, even without Bernie's outrageous adulterous behavior." He stood up. "I think that about does it for now, Sam. Have a chat with your client and get back to me." He turned and began walking toward the conference room door.

"Just a moment," Teich said.

Stone turned and looked at him.

"Would you mind waiting outside for a few minutes while I confer with my client?"

Stone noticed that Finger had turned a peculiar shade of red. "Not at all, Sam. Take your time." He walked outside, took a seat in the waiting room, picked up a copy of the *Times,* turned to the Arts section and started working on the crossword puzzle. He was a little more than halfway through when the conference room door opened and Sam Teich walked toward him, a sheet of paper in his hand. Stone stood to meet him.

Teich handed him the paper, on which there was a handwritten list. "Is this everything you asked for?"

Stone read the list carefully. "Everything except one hundred percent of Mrs. Finger's legal costs," he said.

"And what do you estimate those will be?"

"Thirty percent of her settlement."

A tiny grimace of pain crossed Teich's face. "She signed a contingency agreement? How did you get her to do that?"

"It was her expressed wish, with no suggestion from me."

"We'll give you everything on the list and ten percent. It's not as though you'll have put in a lot of hours."

"Fifteen percent, if we have a signed agreement before the end of the business day."

Teich sighed. "Done. Send me your draft."

"It won't be a draft," Stone said, "it'll be final, and it will include a provision for hidden assets that may be uncovered at some later date."

"Bernie will sign an agreement for the real estate and half of the assets contained in the file you showed us," Teich said.

"And half what's in the Caymans account. I'll want to see a bank statement."

"It's not the kind of account that produces a monthly statement, and for legal reasons, Bernie does not want any document to exist that mentions a balance. We'll add a million dollars to the settlement to cover the Caymans account and any assets not mentioned in the files."

"Oh, then there are unnamed assets?"

"All right, two million."

"Five million."

"Three million, and no more."

"Bernie signs the agreement first."

"All right. We have an agreement." Teich offered his hand.

Stone shook it. "It's a pleasure doing business with you, Sam; you gave Bernie good advice."

"I know," Teich said, then he turned and walked back into the conference room.

Stone left the law firm in a rosy daze of elation. He forced himself to breathe normally as he hailed a cab and went back to his own office.

"So?" Joan said, as he walked into the office.

"Come in and bring your pad," Stone said. "I want to get this thing wrapped up today."

He called Bernice Finger and gave her the news.

"He agreed to *everything*?" she asked incredulously.

"Everything, plus your legal costs. I cut my contingency from thirty to fifteen percent."

"If he agreed so quickly, he must be hiding a *lot* of money," she said. "We should ask for more."

"I got you three million to cover any hidden assets."

"Wow!" she said softly.

"It's a good deal, Bernice, and without the pain of a trial. I'll have it ready for your signature by the end of the day."

"I'll sign it," she said.

Stone hung up with his heart pounding.

Joan came into the office. "What did you get for her?"

"The earth, sun and moon," Stone said, hardly able to believe it himself. Bernie's net worth was going to run to at least forty million dollars, and he was going to get fifteen percent of half of it. That was . . . he did the arithmetic . . . good God, three million dollars! Stone's mind spun out of control; he started thinking about one of those new, very light jet airplanes.

24

Stone had a dinner date with the lovely, rangy Celia, but first he had promised her he would perform a chore. He got out of the cab in front of the SoHo gallery and peered through the window at the very good crowd that had assembled to see the artist's work. A very large sign in the window read:

DEVLIN DALTRY

"Wait for me," Stone said to the cabbie. "I won't be long. He walked into the gallery, grabbed a glass of champagne from a passing tray and looked around for the artist. He located him at the center of a small group of women who were at least as fascinated with him as with his sculpture, so Stone passed a little time peering at the lumps of marble and steel arrayed on pedestals throughout the large room. They were uniformly uninteresting, Stone thought, the product of an empty mind.

Shortly, he spotted Devlin Daltry, slim and dressed entirely in black and momentarily alone, so he set his champagne glass down on a pedestal next to a lump titled "Doubt," walked quickly over to the man and offered his hand. "How do you do, Mr. Daltry," he said, squeezing his hand, and with his other taking him by the arm and steering him out of the hearing of others.

Daltry followed, because he had to. "What's going on?" he asked.

"My name is Stone Barrington, and I am the attorney representing your former friend, Celia."

"I don't have to talk to you," Daltry said, attempting and failing to free himself from Stone's clutches.

"That's right, you don't," Stone replied. "But you have to listen for just a moment, or I'll break your hand." He squeezed it for emphasis.

Daltry winced. "All right, get it over with."

"I've come here to tell you that your relationship with Celia is over from this moment and that, should you attempt to see her or even contact her ever again, I will see that a world of legal and financial problems falls on you from a great height and makes your life not worth living. This will be in addition to the criminal penalties that will follow, and follow you they will, right into Rikers Island. And finally—and this is entirely personal, not legal—after all that is done, I will find a quiet moment with you alone and leave you in a condition that will prevent you from making any more of these awful little things you dare to call 'sculptures.' Is all that perfectly clear?" He squeezed Daltry's hand again for emphasis.

"Yes," Daltry grunted.

"I hope I won't find it necessary to see you again." Stone released the sculptor from his grip, walked out of the gallery and got into his waiting cab. "Sixty-fifth and Madison," he said.

He walked into La Goulue, one of his favorite non-Elaine's restaurants, twenty minutes later to find Celia waiting for him at his usual table, sipping a glass of wine. He gave a kiss to Suzanne, who ran the place, then slid into his seat. "Sorry to be late," he said. "It's a long trip from SoHo."

"You went to the opening?" she asked.

"I did," he replied, waving at a waiter and making drinking motions. "His stuff is awful, soulless."

"I can't disagree. Did the two of you talk?"

"I did all the talking," Stone said, "but he seemed to get the message."

She looked doubtful. "Devlin is not very good at getting the message. I'm afraid I haven't been completely truthful with you."

Stone took a sip of his drink and wondered what was coming next. "I'm listening," he said.

"I mean, it's not that I've lied to you; it's just that there's more to Devlin than I've mentioned."

"Tell me about him."

"He's wilder than he looks."

"How do you mean, 'wilder'?"

"He's capable of attacking men twice his size and of doing damage."

"And has he found attacking men twice his size a profitable activity?"

"He hits unexpectedly, then runs, and he can run very fast."

"I'll keep that in mind," Stone said, taking another sip. "Anything else?"

"He's also capable of hiring people to do his dirty work for him. A couple of weeks ago, I was followed out of a restaurant I used to frequent by two men, and it was obvious what they had on their minds. Fortunately, I made it into a cab before they got to me, and I lost them. This is why I don't want Devlin to know where I'm living. These days, I make it a rule not to go anywhere I usually go. I've even dropped two clients that he knew about, because I was afraid I'd come out of their buildings and find Devlin or those two men waiting for me."

"I think that's very wise," Stone said. "Our next move is to get a temporary restraining order against him."

"I told you before, that won't stop him."

"It often doesn't stop the aggressor, but violating it has legal consequences up to and including jail time, depending on how pissed off the judge is."

"All right, if you think that's best."

"I do. Tell me, can you take a couple of weeks off work without going broke?"

"I suppose so. Why?"

"I think it's best if we get you out of town for a little while, during which time we can let this business play out." He took a slim leather notebook from his pocket, placed it on the table and gave her a pen. "Give me Devlin's address and phone number."

She wrote it down.

"What sort of daily schedule does he keep?"

"He works in his loft, so he's usually there during the day. In the evenings he goes out, often to a bar called Crackers and a restaurant called Emile's, both downtown."

"Anyplace else he frequents?"

"Wherever I am. When he knew where to find me, he used to devote a good part of his day to tracking me down, then following me around, just to let me know he was still after me. It was unnerving, because I never knew when he might cause a scene in some public place or even attack me."

"That's good to know about," Stone said. "I'll put it in your petition for the TRO."

"Will I have to appear in court?"

"No, I can represent you."

"Oh, good. I don't want to see Devlin, even in court."

The waiter brought menus, and they devoted themselves to choosing among the dishes.

S tone signed the check. "Ready?"

"Would you do me a favor?" she asked.

"Sure."

"Would you take a look outside and make sure he's not out there?"

"If it would make you feel better."

"It would."

"I'll be right back." Stone slid out of the banquette, walked to the front door and went outside. He looked up and down Madison Avenue. Traffic was light. A car was double-parked in front of the building next door, and two bored-looking men sat in the front seat.

Stone hailed a cab. "Start your meter. I'll be right back," he said to the driver. He went back inside and got Celia. "There are two men waiting in a car outside, and there's no back way out of here, so we're just going to have to brazen it out the front way."

"Whatever you say."

He led her outside and got her quickly into the cab. "Take your next left, then left again on Fifth Avenue," he said to the driver. He positioned himself so that he could see the rearview mirror.

The car with the two men followed.

25

C elia looked over her shoulder. "It's the same two men," she said.

Stone dug in his pocket and handed the cabbie a hundred-dollar bill. "Do you think you can lose the car with the two guys behind us?"

The cabbie glanced in his rearview mirror, then grabbed the hundred. "I'll do my best," he said.

They were on Fifth Avenue now. "Turn right onto Central Park South, then turn into the park at Sixth Avenue," Stone said.

The cabbie raced up Central Park South, but there was a red light at the corner of Sixth Avenue.

"Run it," Stone said, "and turn into the park."

"The park's closed," the cabbie said, pointing. "There's a sign."

"We could use a cop right now. Do it, and I'll square it with the cops."

The cabbie ran the light and turned into Central Park. The car behind them followed.

"Is there a tire iron in the trunk?" Stone asked.

"There's a tire iron right here," the cabbie said, reaching down to the floor and handing Stone the steel tool.

"Brake hard and pull over here," Stone said. "I'm getting out of the car, and if I whistle loudly, get the hell out of here and find a cop."

The cabbie stood on the brakes and ran the cab up onto the curb. The car behind followed, nearly rear-ending the cab. Stone got out and, clutching the tire iron, advanced on the car. He yanked the driver's door open, grabbed the driver and pulled him into the street.

The man's companion got out the passenger door and leveled a snub-nosed revolver at Stone. "Freeze, police!" he yelled.

Stone flashed his own badge. "Yeah? If you're on the job, what are you doing harassing an innocent woman for money?"

The driver of the car struggled to his feet. "You just assaulted a police officer, pal."

Stone put away his badge and took out his cell phone, punching a speed-dial button.

"Bacchetti," Dino said. "This better be good."

"Lieutenant? This is Stone Barrington. I've got two deadbeat cops here who are moonlighting as muscle for a probable felon, and . . ." He stopped. The two men were back in their car, backing up very fast, then spinning a hundred and eighty degrees and heading the wrong way up the park drive. "Never mind, Dino," Stone said.

"What the hell is going on?"

"I was being followed by two off-duty cops who're working for a former friend of Celia's trying to give her a hard time."

"Did you get their names?"

"No, but I will next time."

"You all right?"

"I'm fine. I'll talk to you tomorrow." Stone hung up, got back in the cab and gave the driver Celia's temporary Park Avenue address.

"Are they gone for good?" Celia asked.

"I doubt it, but they're gone for now." They made their way back to Park Avenue, and the cab stopped. "I want you to go pack enough stuff for a week, jeans and like that; you won't need a cocktail dress. I'm going to go get my car, and I'll be back here in half an hour. I want you downstairs with your luggage, waiting, all right?"

"Where are we going?"

"I'll explain when we're on the way."

"All right." She got out of the cab and ran for the door.

"You did good," Stone said to the cabbie, then gave him his address.

"That was kind of fun," the cabbie said. "Who were the two guys?"

"A couple of bad cops working for a bad guy."

"I hope they didn't get my cab number."

"Don't worry, they weren't interested in you."

S tone left Joan a note, saying he'd be back in a day or two, and not to tell anyone but Dino where he'd gone, then he got into his car, drove out of the garage and uptown. He didn't need to pack a bag. He watched for tails all the way.

The doorman at Celia's building walked her out of the building and put her luggage in the trunk. She got into the passenger seat. "All right, where are we going?"

"You can't call anybody," Stone said.

"I'll have some appointments to break in the morning."

"I have a little house in Washington, Connecticut, where you'll be safe. It'll take us an hour and forty-five minutes to get there."

"How long am I going to have to stay there?"

"Until I can get your TRO and do some assessing of the threat."

"I know the threat; you don't have to assess it."

"Have you ever had any help in dealing with Devlin?"

"No, I've managed it myself up until now."

"Then we don't know how Devlin will react to opposition, do we? The very fact that the law will be involved may be enough to ward him off."

"Don't count on it."

"One thing that surprises me is how quickly he got those two cops on my tail. I had a cab waiting when I talked to him, so they must have been at the opening, and I can't figure out what two cops were doing at that opening. Does he ever have bodyguards?"

"He has on a couple of occasions that I know about, when he was having disagreements with people: his landlord, once, and a gallery owner another time."

"Good to know. Why don't you put the seat back and get some sleep?"

"That's not a bad idea," she said, pressing the Recline button.

Stone drove on into the night.

26

Stone woke with sunlight streaming into the bedroom and the phone ringing. Telemarketer, he thought; nobody knew he was here. He let the machine get it.

Celia never cracked an eye; she snored on, lightly. Stone got up, went downstairs and found a can of coffee in the freezer. Ten minutes later, Celia came down the stairs, almost dressed, in a robe that he kept for guests.

"Good morning," she said, yawning. "Where are we again?" They had fallen into bed on arrival, both exhausted.

"In Washington, Connecticut, a village in the upper left-hand corner of the state."

"I've never been to Connecticut. You got anything for breakfast?"

Stone looked at the kitchen clock: eleven-ten A.M. "Nope, we'll have to pick up some things. I'll buy you lunch, though."

"Have I got time for a shower?"

"Sure. We'll go to the Mayflower."

"The moving company?"

"The country inn, maybe the best in the United States."

"I'd better look nice, then." She took her coffee and headed upstairs.

Stone noticed the message light blinking on the kitchen phone, and he pressed the button.

"Mr. Barrington, this is Seth Hardaway. I noticed you were missing a few shingles after that storm last week, so I replaced them and a section of gutter. I'll fax the bill to New York."

Next message: "Stone, it's Joan. I don't know if you're there, but your cell is off. Call me; Herbie Fisher has surfaced."

Stone erased the messages and called home.

"The Barrington Practice."

"Good guess," Stone said.

"Well, it is your only other home, not counting Maine."

"Only because I'm not rich enough yet. When the Finger divorce is over, maybe I'll think about something in Santa Fe."

"Dream on."

"Did Bernice sign the document?"

"She did, and so did her soon-to-be ex-husband."

"Thank God," Stone sighed. "That's a load off my mind."

"When do we get a load into your bank account?"

"What's the matter, isn't the hundred-grand retainer enough to satisfy you?"

"After taxes, you've got eight grand and change left."

"Where's the rest?"

"You want me to read you the list of bills I paid, starting with the insurance premiums on both houses, the car and the airplane?"

"No thanks. You said Herbie has surfaced?"

"He's sitting in your office."

"Well, get him out of there, before he sets it on fire!"

"Talk to him first."

"Put him on."

There was a short silence, then: "Stone? Is it really you?" He sounded like a little boy just home from summer camp.

"Where have you been, Herbie?"

"In an attic downtown somewhere."

"Tell me."

"Those two guys grabbed me on the street, near my house."

"What were you doing near your house? I told you to stay away from there."

"All I wanted was some clean underwear."

"Was it worth it?"

"I never got it. In fact, I've been wearing the same underwear for four days."

"I didn't need to know that, Herbie. What did they do to you?"

"They slapped me around a lot and threatened to do stuff with pliers."

"Did you get any names?"

"Cheech and Gus. And an old guy named Carmen."

"Do you, by any chance, mean Carmine?"

"Yeah, that's it, with a 'mine.'"

"What was he doing there?"

"He just came into the room for a minute this morning, looked at me and said, 'Kill him as slow as possible.'"

"He actually said that?"

"Right before I jumped through the window."

"You jumped out an attic window?"

"I jumped *through* an attic window, glass and all. You would have, too, if somebody had said to kill you slow."

Herbie had a point. "Have you talked to your uncle?"

"Not yet."

"Put Joan back on the phone."

"Now what?" she asked.

"Let Herbie take a shower in the little bathroom off the kitchen, and tell Helene to throw his clothes into the washing machine and give him something to eat. Then give him two hundred dollars and call Bob Cantor and tell him to come get his nephew. I want Herbie out of there in two hours, and tell him it's very, very dangerous for him to be in my house."

"Gotcha," Joan said.

"Any other calls?"

"No."

"Call Sam Teich at Bernie Finger's office and tell him we want an accounting today and a check in three days. Fax me anything he sends you. Call Bernice and tell her we're ironing out the final details, and give her my cell number and the number here, if she needs to have her hand held."

"Okay. When are you coming home?"

"Probably tomorrow. I'm stashing Celia up here to keep her former boyfriend away from her. If he should call me, tell him I'll see him in court."

"Okay. See ya." Joan hung up.

Stone finished his coffee, showered and shaved and drove Celia to the Mayflower.

"Wow," she said, as they drove up the driveway. "This is really beautiful." She was impressed with the dining room, too.

They ordered lunch. "I'm going to have to go back to the city tomorrow morning," he said. "We'll get you some groceries this afternoon; if you need any more, you can charge them to my account at the market, and I'll rent you some kind of car from the guy at the gas station. You might drive around the county a little, take a look around. I'll give you a map."

"What if Devlin finds me here?"

"Have you ever fired a gun?"

"Sure, I grew up with guns. My daddy was a handgun freak, so I've fired just about everything."

"I'll leave you with one, but you are not, repeat *not*, to kill anyone, even if you think it's absolutely necessary. Fire into the floor to scare him. I live a quiet life when I'm here, and I don't want to get to be known as the owner of the house where the guy got blown away by the giant girl."

"I understand," she said. "But what if Devlin does find me?"

"That's very unlikely, but worse come to worst, I've got a house on an island in Maine that my cousin left me, and I can guarantee you he won't find you there."

"Maine sounds nice."

"It's a little early in the year for Maine; you can still freeze your ass off up there, but the house is comfortable."

"How would I get there?"

"I have an airplane. I'll fly you, if necessary, but believe me, Devlin is *not* going to find you in Washington, Connecticut."

"What if I run into somebody I know?"

"Tell them you're up here doing some antiquing, and you're going back to the city almost immediately. Then go back to my house, lock yourself in and call me."

"You think of everything," she said, smiling sweetly. "I'm going to have to think of something to do for you."

The thought made Stone squirm in his seat.

27

S tone drove back to the city early the following morning, trying to remember every detail of what he and Celia had done
to each other for much of the night, right into the dawn. Occasionally, he had to slap himself to stay awake through the drive.
Once, he stopped for coffee.

Back at home, he pulled the car into the garage, let himself
into the house and went to his office. Joan heard him and came
down the hall.

"I hope the lovely Celia is safe and sound."

"She is, indeed, but I would be neither safe nor sound if I had
spent another night there."

"You do look a little peaked," she said. "Nothing much to do
today. Sam Teich says he'll have an accounting to you by close of
business, which probably means tomorrow morning, and he needs
five days to liquidate assets and produce a check, unless you want
to just divide some of the assets, like the stocks. He says to give him
a call tomorrow and let him know how you want to handle it."

Stone shook his head, "Frankly, I can't believe how cooperative
Bernie is being."

"I bet it's not Bernie, but Sam, who is doing the cooperating. I bet
Bernie is screaming bloody murder."

"You're probably right. I assume Bob Cantor came and took his nephew away."

Joan looked at the floor. "Well, there was a teensy problem with that."

Stone's eyes narrowed. "What do you mean by a 'teensy'?"

"Well, Bob is actually in Atlanta for a couple of days, and he doesn't want Herbie in his house while he's gone, for fear that Herbie will hock everything and bet on the ponies."

"So, where is Herbie?"

"In the third-floor guest room."

"*My* third-floor guest room?"

"He's so sweet; I couldn't just throw him into the street and let Dattila's thugs get him again."

"You're fired."

"Okay, but who's going to do everything for you?"

"All right, you're hired back, but how could you leave that little creep alone in my house? He's probably hocked everything I own."

"No, he hasn't; I locked him in when I left last night, so he couldn't get any of your stuff out of the house. Anyway, he seems to sleep most of the time."

"Did you drug him?"

"I would have, but he didn't seem to need it. He's probably exhausted after his ordeal in the attic."

"Did he have any cuts on his body?"

"Not on the parts of his body I saw, but I didn't do a full inspection."

"He's lying, the little bastard! He said he jumped clean through a glass window and fell from an attic, and yet he doesn't have a mark on him!"

A voice came from the doorway. "I've got a nick right here, on my elbow, that I used to break the window." Herbie was standing there in one of Stone's Sea Island cotton nightshirts.

"Take off the nightshirt," Stone commanded.

"Huh? Right in front of the lady?"

"She's not that much of a lady, so take it off."

Herbie lifted the nightshirt over his head. There was some bruising around his ribs.

"Turn around," Stone said.

"Please," Joan echoed.

There were bruises on his back, too.

"All right, so you got pounded a little; how come no cuts from the glass and the fall?"

"Well, the window was actually open, and it was only a short fall to the canvas."

"Canvas?"

"They had a big piece of canvas draped over some stuff, and it broke my fall. I sprained my ankle, though, when I went over the fence and landed on the sidewalk."

"How did you get here?"

"I sprinted down the block, ignoring the intense pain from my ankle, went into a subway station, jumped the turnstile and here I am! Can I put the nightshirt on again?"

"No. Go get your clothes on and give the nightshirt to Helene, in the kitchen. You're leaving here immediately."

"But where am I going to go?" Herbie wailed.

"How many times do I have to tell you that I don't *care* where you go?"

Herbie turned to leave the room.

"Wait a minute," Stone said.

"Huh?"

"Put on the nightshirt to save Joan's modesty. Joan, get me Bernie Finger."

Joan picked up the phone on Stone's desk and dialed. "He's on the line," she said.

Stone picked up the phone. "Bernie? Let's do the depositions today. Three o'clock at your place?"

"I thought your client was unavailable," Finger said.

"He's just become available," Stone replied. "Didn't your client tell you that Herbie made good his escape from the attic where Carmine had him imprisoned and beaten?"

"Of course he didn't tell me any such thing."

"All right, three o'clock at your office. Tell Sam I'll pick up the accounting while I'm there."

"I'm under strict instructions from my attorney not to discuss that with you."

"Just give him the message." Stone hung up and pointed at Herbie. "Does he have any clothes at all?" he asked Joan.

"Helene should have them washed and ironed by now."

"Herbie, get dressed; we have a three-o'clock appointment."

Herbie looked at the clock on Stone's desk. "Can I watch the soaps until then?"

"Please, but do it in the kitchen. And give Helene that nightshirt and tell her to disinfect it."

"Sure, Stone," Herbie said happily, as he padded off to the kitchen.

"Is he driving Helene crazy?" Stone asked Joan.

"No, she thinks he's sweet, too."

"You're both crazy or hormonal or something."

"Careful, you're treading a thin line, on one side of which is the kind of sexism that could result in a lawsuit." She went back to her office.

Stone's phone rang, and Dino's cell number came up on the caller ID screen. Stone answered. "Morning, Dino."

"Good morning. What was that thing the other night about bad cops?"

"Oh, I don't know. Two bozos with badges were tailing Celia until I rousted them. I didn't get any names or badge numbers."

"Next time I.D. them, and I'll put the fear of God into them."

"Thanks, I'll remember that."

"So, is Celia safe from her ex-boyfriend?"

"For the moment. I stashed her in the Connecticut house."

"That should do it. Those downtown artsy-fartsy types can't breathe in Connecticut; the air isn't dirty enough."

"I hope you're right; I don't want to have to move her to Maine."

"Dinner tonight?"

"See you then." Stone hung up and began making a list of questions for Carmine Dattila.

28

Stone and Herbie got off the elevator at Bernie Finger's office. Herbie elbowed him.

"Stop that," Stone said.

"Look over there," Herbie said, nodding.

Stone looked. Two large men were occupying a sofa meant for four; they were the two who had dragged Herbie from Elaine's the night all this had started. He walked past them to the reception desk, gave his name and was directed to the conference room.

"Are they the guys who held you in the attic?" Stone asked.

"Yeah," Herbie replied, tugging at Stone's sleeve and nodding again. Carmine Dattila was getting off the elevator. "And that's the guy who told them to kill me slow."

"You wait here," Stone said. "I'll call you when we're ready."

"Are you kidding? With those two guys? They'll kill me while you're gone."

"Just a minute," Stone said. He went to the reception desk. "I'm here for two depositions, and I need a private room where one of the witnesses can wait."

"First door on your right," the woman said. "That's an empty office."

Stone walked back toward Herbie, noting that the two large men were deep in conversation with Carmine Dattila and ignoring them.

He escorted Herbie to the empty office. "You wait in this room, and don't leave for anything," he said.

"But what if I have to go to the john?"

"You're just going to have to hold it, unless you want to have another conversation with Tweedledum and Tweedledee out there."

"Their names are Cheech and Gus," Herbie replied. "I forget which is which."

"Do you want to die, Herbie?"

"No."

"Then don't leave this office until I come for you."

"Aw, okay."

"If you're gone when I come back, your lawsuit will be dismissed, and Cheech and Gus will find you and kill you slow."

"I'm not going anywhere," Herbie said testily.

"There's a TV; you can watch the soap operas."

"Yeah, great!"

Stone left and went back to the conference room. Bernard Finger, Carmine Dattila and a court stenographer were waiting for him. "Good morning," he said to the assembled group, then took a seat.

"Are you ready to begin?" Finger asked.

"Yes." He turned to the stenographer. "Please swear the witness."

"I don't think that will be necessary," Finger said.

"Swear him, and if you haven't already explained to him that the laws of perjury apply, please do so now."

"He understands."

The stenographer produced a bible and swore in Dattila.

Stone elicited his name and address and made sure the stenographer got it down right. "What is your occupation, Mr. Dattila?"

"I manage a coffee shop."

"Do you also own the coffee shop?"

"No."

"Do you own the building in which the coffee shop operates?"

"No."

"Do you own a corporation that owns these properties or do you own them through a third party?"

"Objection," Finger said. "Mr. Dattila declines to answer on the grounds of possible self-incrimination." He turned to the stenographer. "In the future, I'll just say 'Fifth' when objecting on those grounds."

"It's not a crime to own a building or a coffee shop, Mr. Dattila."

"The objection stands."

"Mr. Dattila, do you also directly or through other parties operate a gambling enterprise?"

"Fifth!" Finger said. "You surprise me, Stone."

"Mr. Dattila, does anyone owe you money?"

Dattila looked at Finger.

"You may answer," Finger said.

"Maybe."

"Where do you keep the record of who owes you money?" Stone asked.

Dattila silently tapped his head with a forefinger.

"Let the record show that the witness tapped his forehead. Do you have a written record of those who owe you money?"

"No," Dattila replied.

"How much money does Herbert Fisher owe you?"

"Who?"

"Herbert Fisher, the plaintiff in this lawsuit. How much does he owe you?"

"Fifth!" Finger said.

"That was a little slow, Mr. Finger. This is material information, and you can't object to it."

"I'm not sure," Dattila said.

"Does the figure twenty-four thousand dollars ring a bell?"

"Could be, maybe."

"What means have you employed to collect Mr. Fisher's debt?"

"I might have had a friend ask him, you know, nice."

"Does *nice* include having him dragged out of a restaurant and beaten on the sidewalk?"

"Objection," Finger said. "Irrelevant."

"It's perfectly relevant, as it's part of the basis of our suit."

"Maybe somebody insisted a little," Dattila said, "without my personal knowledge."

"Mr. Dattila, after repeated, unsuccessful attempts to collect the debt from Mr. Fisher, what steps did you take?"

"I don't understand the question."

"Did you order two of your employees, namely Cheech and Gus, who are sitting outside in the reception room, to kidnap and torture Mr. Fisher?"

"Me?" Dattila looked shocked.

"Answer the question, Mr. Dattila."

"I wouldn't never do nothing like that."

"Did you enter the room where Cheech and Gus were torturing Mr. Fisher and order them to, quote, 'kill him slow'?"

"I'm afraid you've got me mixed up with some other guy." Dattila turned to Finger. "Can I go now?"

Finger turned to Stone. "I don't think you're getting anywhere here."

"I'll make the charge of perjury at an appropriate time," Stone said. "No further questions, until I get him on the witness stand in court."

"Then I think we're done here," Finger said. "I'll call you, Carmine." The two men shook hands, and Dattila left.

"My witness is ready," Stone said. "Wait here, and I'll get him."

"Oh, I don't think that will be necessary," Finger said. "I'm not going to sit here and listen to a lot of lies."

"You mean, like the lies we just heard from your client?"

"Good day, Stone. I'll see you in court."

"You certainly will." Stone got up and walked through the reception area to the empty office where he had deposited his client.

Herbie was gone. He checked the men's room: not there, either. He went back to the receptionist. "Excuse me, have you seen my client, the young man I put in the empty office?"

"Oh, he left about five minutes later," the woman replied.

"What about the two large men who were waiting on the sofa over there?"

"They left right after your client did," she replied, then went back to her *People* magazine.

Back on the street, Stone looked up and down the block. Herbie, Cheech and Gus were nowhere in sight. He was crossing Third Avenue, with the light, when the car struck him.

29

Like a film clip on a loop, the scene played over and over against the inside of Stone's eyelids. He felt some sort of blow, then flew through the air, looking down at the top of a dark blue car. When he was about even with the rear bumper, the scene repeated. "Stop it, goddammit!" he yelled.

"Well, you're awake," a low woman's voice said.

Stone opened his eyes and saw a ceiling of acoustic tiles and fluorescent light fixtures. He lifted his head, but a soft hand on his forehead pressed it back down.

"Just relax. Do you know where you are?"

He had caught a glimpse of a pretty girl in a green garment with a stethoscope around her neck. "Hospital, maybe? Just a wild guess."

She laughed and pressed a button, raising the head of the bed. "Right the first time," she said. "Do you remember anything?"

"Flying over a dark blue car," he replied. "That's it. I left a law firm's office, and I was flying over a dark blue car. Over and over."

"Just once, I think. You feel up to talking to the police?"

Stone lifted the sheet and examined himself. "Two questions first: One, am I hurt? Two, why am I naked? Have you had your way with me?"

"That's three questions. You have a hairline fracture of the left wrist, which will require a temporary cast for a week, and a bad bruise on your left leg, probably from the bumper of the car, but no fracture. You were very lucky. You are naked, because I and others removed your clothing. It's a nice suit; you're lucky we didn't have to cut it off. And I haven't had my way with you—not yet, anyway."

"Well, that's disappointing. Okay, I'll talk to the police."

Dino appeared at his side. "Anything to meet a pretty doctor," he said.

"I'm fine, thanks."

"Who cares?"

Joan appeared on the other side of the bed. "You scared the hell out of me."

"That's it, make it about you. And I'm lying here, injured."

She laughed. "Don't start faking; we've already talked to the doctor."

Stone looked at the pretty girl. "You're a doctor?"

"I am. You want to see my license to practice?"

"Later, maybe. You told these people everything before you told me?"

She strapped a blue plastic cast to his left wrist and secured it with Velcro straps. "You were unconscious at the time. Oh, did I mention the bruise on your head, under your hair, and the concussion?"

Stone grinned at Joan. "See, I told you I was injured."

"Tell me what you remember," Dino said.

"I saw a dark blue car, from above, as I was flying through the air. Or maybe that was a dream."

"What kind of car?"

"I'm not good at identifying automobiles from above."

"Well, you're right. A guy abandoned a dark blue Ford Taurus a block and a half from where you were hit, then he ran like hell. It's being processed."

"Anybody get a description of the guy?"

"Young, old; tall, short; fat, skinny."

"The usual eyewitness testimony."

"Right. I suppose there are forty or fifty people who would like to run you down with a car, but can you think of anybody in particular?"

"Let's see: Carmine Dattila, Bernie Finger, Bernie Finger's girlfriend, who should feel grateful to me, anybody who works for Carmine Dattila."

"That's a start. Anybody else?"

"Yeah, a guy named Devlin . . . I can't think of his last name; must be the concussion. He's Celia's former boyfriend, and she told me to watch out for him."

"She should have told you to look both ways before crossing the street."

"Daltry. Devlin Daltry. Lives downtown somewhere. Call Celia at my Connecticut house, she'll give you the address. Tell your guys to beat him with rubber hoses when they question him."

"We don't beat people with rubber hoses anymore."

"All right, beat him with whatever you're using these days."

"We don't beat people at all."

"Well, what kind of police work is that? What is the world coming to?"

The doctor spoke up. "Does he always talk this much?"

"Always," Dino said. "Can't shut him up. Is he ready to leave?"

"Normally, with a concussion, we'd want to keep him overnight, but he's alert and responsive, so you can take him home—*if* he goes to bed immediately and stays there until lunchtime tomorrow."

"I'll see to that," Joan said.

"I'll get his clothes," the doctor said.

"I think you should dress me, since you so sneakily undressed me."

"I'm going to send in a big black guy named Roger to handle that," she said, handing a card and a slip of paper to Joan. "Here's a prescription for a painkiller and a sleeping pill. Call me if he misbehaves, and I'll stop by and hit him over the head again."

"I'll fill your prescription and deal with the bill," Joan said.

Stone grabbed the doctor's card from her hand. "Gimme that."

Roger appeared with Stone's clothes.

"I'll leave you two alone," Dino said. "Don't be long; my car's waiting outside."

"I thought she was kidding about you," Stone said to Roger.

"The doc don't kid," Roger said, tossing Stone's clothes into his lap. "Get dressed; we need the bed."

30

S tone awoke from a drug-induced sleep, tried to turn over, then emitted a girlish shriek. Every muscle and bone in his body seemed to be making an angry protest. He struggled into a sitting position, grabbed the pill bottle on the bedside table and tossed down a painkiller with half a glass of water. He steadied himself for a moment, then navigated his way into the bathroom, taking short steps, peed, and shuffled back onto the bed.

He managed to reach the phone and page Joan.

"Good morning," she said cheerily. "Did you sleep well?"

"That wasn't sleep, it was a coma," he replied. "And stop sounding so chirpy."

"Oooh, it's going to be one of those days, is it?"

"I hurt all over."

"The doctor said you would."

"She didn't say that to me."

"She said it to me, when you couldn't hear her. Apparently, she made a quick assessment of your character and decided it would be better if you didn't know."

"I always want to know what's happening to me."

"She said you could faint or go into convulsions if you move around too much."

"I didn't want to know that."

"Only joking. She said just to stay in bed until lunchtime, at least."

"What time is it?"

"Lunchtime, in the land of the living."

"Will you ask Helene to bring me something to eat, please?"

"What would you like?"

"I don't care. Anything."

"A sandwich?"

"No, I can't eat a sandwich with one hand."

"Did you lose a hand?"

"I have this blue plastic thing on my wrist."

"Does it interfere with the movement of your fingers?"

Stone wiggled his fingers. "Apparently not."

"Then you can handle a sandwich?"

"Tell her scrambled eggs and bacon. And an English muffin with marmalade. And orange juice and coffee."

"Well, at least your appetite has survived." She hung up.

Stone gingerly rearranged himself in bed and waited for the painkiller to kick in. His first inkling that it was working was when the pounding in his head began to subside. A moment later, he woke up with a tray on his belly.

"Eat," Helene commanded. She was a compact woman with a thick Greek accent who had done for him for years.

Stone pressed the remote control, and the bed sat him up and raised his feet. "Good morning, Helene," he said.

"Eat," she said again. "You feel better." She marched out of the room.

Stone ate hungrily. The various pains in his body were gradually replaced by a cozy warmth, and he was able to move more freely.

Dino walked into the room, unannounced. "You're alive."

"Why do you sound surprised?"

"How did you feel when you woke up?"

"I hurt all over, but I took a pill."

"How do you feel now?"

"Warm and fuzzy."

"Must be a good drug. We hauled in Devlin Daltry and had a chat with him."

"Did you beat him to a pulp?"

"Sure we did, and we dumped the body in the East River."

"Did he have anything to say before he died?"

"He had an alibi, backed up by two retired cops."

"The ones who chased me into Central Park, I bet."

"Probably, but we had to release him."

"Anything on the car?"

"Stolen."

"You wouldn't think a sculptor would know how to hot-wire a car."

"No, you wouldn't. That's why I wasn't too surprised when I ran his name, and he had an arrest for car theft when he was nineteen, no conviction."

"Celia was right about the guy; I should have listened to her. What's his address?"

"What, you're going down there?"

"No, Dino. What's the address?"

Dino wrote it on a slip of paper and put it on the bedside table. "You up for dinner this evening?"

"As long as the pills last."

"See you then." He walked out of the room.

Stone sat and stewed for a few minutes, then he called Bob Cantor.

"Cantor."

"You're back."

"How'd you guess?"

"Have you heard from Herbie?"

"No."

"I took him to Finger's law office for a deposition yesterday, stashed him in an office, and he ran the moment I left him alone. Dattila's two goons may have followed him out."

"Uh-oh. Did he say where they had held him the first time?"

"Herbie said an attic, downtown. Probably someplace near Dattila's coffeehouse, near a subway station."

"I'll do a missing persons report and get them looking for him again."

"Another thing: Herbie said that before he jumped out the window, Dattila showed up and told Cheech and Gus—that's the two guys who dragged him out of Elaine's—to kill him slowly."

"That doesn't sound good."

"It sounds like we should find him soon, but I'm laid up in bed today. I was hit by a car yesterday."

"An accident?"

"Nope, and I want to talk to you about that."

"Who done it?"

"A guy named Devlin Daltry, a sculptor, who lives at . . ." He looked at the paper on the bedside table and gave Cantor the address.

"You're sure he's the guy?"

"Yes."

"Is he going to be arrested?"

"No. He has an alibi from two retired cops, no names."

"You want something to happen to him?"

"Yes, but the two cops may be hanging around him as bodyguards."

"You care what happens to them?"

"Let's not spread this around. I'd like Daltry found alone and pain inflicted upon him, but not anything even nearly like death."

"Any message you want delivered?"

"The pain will be the message. Oh, and I want his left wrist broken."

"That's an odd request."

"It's what he did to me."

"I know somebody who can handle this discreetly."

"I thought you would."

"When?"

"I'll be at Elaine's this evening with Dino, from about eight-thirty."

"I'll see what can be done."

"If it's not done this evening, call me beforehand, so I can have an alibi."

"Sure."

"Thanks, Bob. I hope Herbie gets found before . . ."

"Yeah." Cantor hung up.

"Before he's too dead," Stone said to himself.

3I

S tone was finishing his lunch when Joan buzzed. "Eliza Larkin
on line one," she said.
  "Who?"
"Emergency room doctor."
"Oh, yes!" He punched the button. "Hello."
"Mr. Barrington, it's Dr. Larkin. I wanted to see how you are
feeling."
"Well, when I take the pills, I feel better than I should."
"Nice and warm and fuzzy?"
"How did you know?"
"I sprained my ankle once."
"I hope you have fully recovered."
"I have, thank you. I don't think you will need any further med-
ical attention."
"Oh, but I will. In fact, I think I will need medical attention at
dinner this evening. Would you like to join Lieutenant Bacchetti and
me at Elaine's at eight-thirty?"
"And just what sort of medical attention do you think you will
need?"
"Well, the Heimlich maneuver, perhaps. I eat too quickly."
She chuckled.

"Or CPR, maybe?"

"I'm sure Lieutenant Bacchetti can handle that."

"Lieutenant Bacchetti can be curiously inept at times, and I want only the best professional assistance."

"Where is Elaine's?"

"Second Avenue, between Eighty-eighth and Eighty-ninth, west side of the street. You'll see the yellow awning."

"Eight-thirty, you said?"

"That would be perfect."

"How does one dress at Elaine's?"

"In clothes; there are no other requirements."

"You are a typical male. What should I wear?"

"A tight skirt with a deep slit and a pushup bra. Or better, no bra at all."

"Big help."

"Anything but scrubs."

"See you then." She hung up.

Stone was feeling rosy, not only from the pill but also from the thought of seeing Dr. Larkin again. Then the phone rang.

"Hello?"

"It's Celia. Can you talk?"

Stone felt unaccountably guilty, as if by having dinner with Eliza Larkin, he was jilting Celia. "Sure, how are you?"

"There was someone outside last night."

"Did you call nine-one-one?"

"No, I went out with your gun, looking for the bastard."

Stone groaned. "Tell me you didn't shoot anybody."

"I didn't shoot anybody."

"For future reference, if you hear troubling noises, you call nine-one-one. You'll probably get somebody out of bed up there, but that's better than your getting hurt. You do not, repeat *not,* go outside with a gun. Is that perfectly clear?"

"I miss you," she said.

"I miss you, too." This was not a lie.

"Why don't you come up here tonight?"

"I was hit by a car yesterday."

"Oh, God!" she said. "He tried to do that once before."

"Devlin?"

"Yes. He thought I had talked too much to some guy in a bar, and he tried to run him down in the street, but he missed."

"Well, he has since perfected his technique."

"Are you all right?"

"I hurt a lot, and my left wrist is broken."

"Oh, shit, I wish I were there to give you a massage. Can I come down there?"

"No, you may not; I think it's still too dangerous. Anyway, that car I rented for you at the gas station probably wouldn't make it to the city."

"So I have to stay here by myself?"

"I'll come up this weekend."

"I'll give you a massage. All over."

"I'll come twice."

"When can I expect you?"

"Book us a table at the Mayflower for eight on Friday."

"Will do."

"I have to get some sleep now."

"See you Friday."

"Bye." He hung up and tried to forget that he had an erection.

A t eight-fifteen he took the elevator downstairs and limped toward the front door. He had a pill in his pocket, but it was too soon to take it, so he snagged a cane that had belonged to his father from the hall umbrella stand and left the house in search of a cab. He looked carefully up and down the street for threats and suddenly wished he had worn a gun.

He was at Elaine's the usual five minutes ahead of Dino, who joined him and accepted a Scotch from the waiter.

"How are the various affected parts of your body?"

"Responding well to drugs." He looked at his watch. "Another half hour before I can take another pill." He took a big swig of his bourbon. "This should help."

"It usually does," Dino agreed, sipping his own drink.

"Oh, a lady is joining us."

"You found me a girl? Oh, Stone, that's swell of you."

"I found *me* a girl."

"What about the lovely Celia?"

"She's in lovely Washington, Connecticut, remember?"

"So who's this one?"

Stone nodded toward the door. "You've met." He struggled to his feet to greet Eliza Larkin. "Good evening."

She shook his hand.

"You remember Lieutenant Bacchetti."

"Of course." She shook his hand and accepted a chair.

"I'm known as Dino, off duty," Dino said.

"And I'm known as Eliza, off duty."

"What would you like to drink?" Stone asked.

"I think a very dry martini with two olives," she replied.

Stone waved at a waiter and ordered.

"So this is Elaine's?" Eliza said.

"It is indeed. Unpretentious, isn't it?"

"Cozy. I like it."

"The food is a lot better than it gets credit for. Restaurant critics don't like it because they can't get a good table, not being regulars."

Eliza noticed the cane hanging on the spare chair. "Are you using that?"

"Yes, the painkiller is wearing off, but I have another twenty-five minutes before I can take another pill."

The martini was placed before her, and she sipped. "You can't take another pill."

"Why not?"

"Because you're drinking," she said, pointing at the nearly empty glass of bourbon. "Those pills don't mix with alcohol. You might run amok."

"I never run amok."

"Have you ever taken those pills with alcohol?"

"No."

"If you do, it will be your first experience with running amok, and Lieutenant Bacchetti will have to arrest you."

"But I'll be in pain."

"My prescription is, have another of whatever you're drinking, and I predict you'll feel very little pain."

"And that woman is a *doctor*," he said to Dino. He waved at a waiter for a refill, then he glanced toward the front of the restaurant and saw Elaine walk in, right on time. But he was distracted by a face in the front window.

"Excuse me a moment," Stone said, grabbing his cane and hobbling toward the door. He let two other people enter, then went outside. A couple of smokers were standing on the sidewalk, to his left, shivering and nursing their drug addiction; Stone turned to his right and saw Devlin Daltry standing there, smiling insolently at him.

32

D altry turned to face him, stepping away from the window. "Oh, I see you're using a cane these days," he said,
still smiling. "When I finish with you, you'll be in a
wheelchair."

Stone glanced to his right, through the restaurant window and
into the bar. A man was standing there, staring at them, a camera in
his hands.

Stone flashed his badge. "You're under arrest for making terroristic threats," he said. "Don't move." He flipped open his cell phone
and punched the speed-dial number for Dino.

"Bacchetti."

"I've just arrested Devlin Daltry for making terroristic threats.
Come out here and take him off my hands, will you?"

"Sure thing."

Stone snapped the cell phone shut. "You thought I would hit you
and your buddy in there would get a picture, right?"

Daltry looked around him.

"If you run, you'll add fleeing arrest to the charges."

Dino came out the door, and, simultaneously, a squad car
screeched to a halt in front of the restaurant, its lights flashing, and
two cops got out of the car.

"Careful," Stone said, "there's a guy in the bar with a camera."

"Lieutenant," one of the cops said. "What do you need?"

"Make sure that guy doesn't go anywhere for a minute," Dino said. He turned and walked back into the restaurant and Stone could see him at the bar, flashing his badge at the photographer. Then Dino took the camera from him and came back outside. "Okay," he said to Daltry, "you're under arrest for . . ." He looked at Stone questioningly.

"Making terroristic threats," Stone said. "He said when he got through with me, I'd be in a wheelchair."

"For making terroristic threats," Dino said to Daltry. "Cuff him," he said to the car, "and take him back to the station house and book him."

"You haven't got any witnesses," Daltry said.

"I have the testimony of a retired police hero," Dino replied. He turned to the cops. "You got a complaint form in the car?" The cop went to the squad car and returned with a sheet of paper. "Make sure this guy doesn't stub his toe. Come on, Stone." He turned and led the way back into the restaurant. Once inside he tossed the camera to the photographer. "Let's see some I.D.," he said.

The man produced a wallet.

"Who do you work for?"

"I'm freelance, but this job is for *The Sheet*," he said, naming a gossip rag.

"I ought to arrest you for entrapment," Dino said.

"Hey, wait a minute, I haven't entrapped anybody. Daltry just asked me to stand inside and take pictures; I didn't know what was going to happen."

"If you'll testify to that, I'll let you go," Dino said.

"Sure, I'll testify." He handed Dino a card.

"Beat it," Dino said. "I'll be in touch."

The man beat it, and Dino and Stone returned to their table and Eliza Larkin. "Retired police *hero*?" Stone asked Dino.

"Well, I stretched that a little bit."

"What was that all about?" Eliza asked.

"That was about the man who drove the car that hit me trying to lure me into taking a swing at him, so he could have me photographed doing it. It didn't work."

"Are all your evenings like this?" Eliza asked.

"No, thank God. Usually I have a drink, eat some dinner and go home. We arranged this evening's entertainment just for you."

Dino handed Stone the complaint form. "I expect you remember how to fill out this thing."

Stone whipped out a pen and began writing. "Doing your work for you," he said, writing rapidly, then signing the document. He handed it back to Dino.

"I'll drop by the precinct on the way home and file this," he said, folding it and tucking it into a pocket.

"I'll have to arrange some ER entertainment for you fellows some evening soon," Eliza said.

"You don't want to do that," Dino said. "Stone can't stand the sight of blood."

"I can so, as long as it's not mine," Stone retorted, "but I'd just as soon not watch people suffer, unless you can get Devlin Daltry admitted for grievous wounds. That I'd like to watch."

"Devlin Daltry, the sculptor?" she asked.

"One and the same."

"He was the one you just had arrested?"

"For making terroristic threats," Dino said. "He threatened to put Stone in a wheelchair."

"I know a woman who went out with him a couple of times," Eliza said.

"With what result?"

"She broke it off, and he stalked her for weeks. Her name is Genevieve James; she works at the hospital."

"How long ago was this?" Stone asked.

"Late last year, between Thanksgiving and Christmas. She had to leave town for the holidays in order to have any peace."

"I'd like to talk to her," Dino said. "Do you think she'd testify to all this in court?"

"I doubt it," Eliza said. "She was pretty shaken up by the whole business. But I'll ask her."

"I'd appreciate that," Stone said. "I'm representing another woman who's had major problems with Daltry. She fears for her life, and I had to get her out of town."

"Well, I hope you can put the creep away," Eliza said, returning to her drink.

Stone returned to his second bourbon.

"How are you feeling?" she asked.

"A whole lot better," Stone said, raising his glass. "Ah, the wonders of medical science."

"So you're a lawyer?" she asked.

"That's debatable," Dino said. "'Disreputable lawyer' would be more like it."

"That's a dirty Communist lie," Stone said. "I mean, you've got to have a disreputable client or two to make a living. After all, they're the ones who need lawyers."

"Are you telling me you can't make a living representing reputable people?" Eliza asked.

"Well, reputable people occasionally sue or get sued, or get divorced, but that's not likely to lead to a protracted trial, the kind that runs up billable hours."

"When was the last time you had a protracted trial?" Dino asked.

"That's beside the point," Stone replied. "I'm simply replying to your baseless charge of disrepute by using an illustration."

"It says Woodman and Weld on your card," Eliza pointed out. "That's a very reputable firm."

"Yeah," Dino said, "and they stay that way by handing off the disreputable clients to Stone."

"It's a mutually convenient solution to both our problems," Stone said. "For instance, at the insistence of Woodman and Weld, I'm currently suing a big-time mafioso on behalf of a client they would *never* represent."

"Which big-time mafioso?" she asked.

"One Carmine Dattila."

"Dattila the Hun?" she asked, wide-eyed.

"You clearly need to be reading a better newspaper," Stone said. "Try the *Times*."

"Oh, I read the *Times*," she said, "but not for fun. I like the *Post* and the *News* for that."

"You sound like my secretary," Stone said.

L ater, when they had finished dinner, they left the restaurant. "Can I offer you a nightcap at my house?" Stone said.

"No, you can put me in a cab and send me home."

"Where do you live?"

"Not far, but you're in no condition to walk."

"I didn't have all that much to drink."

She pointed at the cane.

"Oh, that. The pain has temporarily subsided."

"Not enough for you to walk me home. I'll accept the drink offer when I'm not looking at an early shift on the morrow."

Stone stepped into the street and flagged down a cab, then opened the door for her.

She stood on her tiptoes and kissed him on the cheek. "Thanks for dinner. I liked Elaine's."

"Another time soon?"

"I'm around this weekend."

"Alas, I'm out of town. Early next week?"

"Call me." She got into the cab, and it drove away.

Stone sighed and started looking for his own cab.

33

S tone opened the door and got into the cab, and as he did, someone pushed him across the seat and got in behind him. Stone drew back his right arm, ready to smash an elbow into his assailant's face.

"Hey, Stone, don't hit me!" a plaintive voice yelled.

Stone looked over his elbow. "Herbie, where the hell have you been?"

"Don't yell at me, Stone."

The driver piped up. "Where to?"

Stone gave him his address. "I'm not yelling," he said to Herbie. "Now why did you bail out of your deposition?"

"It was those two guys, Stone; they were after me."

"Did they drag you out of the building?"

"Well, no, not exactly."

"You left of your own accord, then?"

"Kind of. But they followed me out, and I had to outrun them again."

"Herbie, if you hadn't left, they wouldn't have followed you out."

"Well, maybe. I was just uncomfortable with them sitting out there, so I hit the elevator."

"And where have you been since then?"

"Around."

"And why didn't you call me?"

"I was embarrassed."

"I didn't know that was possible," Stone said.

"Huh?"

"What do you want, Herbie?"

"I need some money."

"What for?"

"I've gotta get a room somewhere, and I'm broke. I don't even have subway money. I was waiting for you outside Elaine's, but when I saw the cops come, I ran."

"Why? Are the cops looking for you?"

"No. It was just instinct, I guess."

"Are you dropping the lawsuit?" Stone prayed for a yes.

"Oh, no, I still want to sue the bastard. Can we reschedule the deposition?"

"That won't be necessary. Luckily for you, Dattila's lawyer decided not to depose you. I guess his client had already told him what to expect. We'll get a trial date soon."

"Great! I'm looking forward to the trial!"

"I can't imagine why," Stone replied.

"Because I want to see Dattila squirm."

"Dattila doesn't squirm," Stone said, "and certainly not from anything you could say to him."

"Just wait till I get on the stand."

"It's your word against his, Herbie. That is, unless there's a videotape of Dattila telling his goons to kill you slow."

Herbie reached into his inside coat pocket, pulled out a small dictating machine and pressed a button. There was what sounded like a chair scraping across the floor, then a male voice. "What do we do with him, Mr. Dattila?"

"Kill him slow," Dattila replied.

Stone snatched the dictator from Herbie's hands. "Why didn't you tell me you had this?"

"I was going to spring it in my deposition and make Dattila shit in his pants."

"I don't think that would have been Dattila's response," Stone said, "but his lawyer might have done that. Herbie, I almost hate to say this, but the recording might actually give us a chance of winning this thing."

Herbie beamed. "I thought so."

"And if you'd given it to me immediately, instead of playing games, we might have already settled your suit."

"I don't want it settled, I want to win it."

"Is that what they taught you at your Internet law school, Herbie? Never settle? Settling is a good thing, Herbie; you get money, maybe an apology, and Dattila doesn't put a contract out on you, if you're lucky. Hasn't it ever crossed your mind that, even if you do win the suit and get a judgment, and humiliate Dattila in open court, that you'll have a target on your back for the rest of your days? Or the rest of Dattila's days, whichever comes first."

Herbie looked sober for a moment. "I hadn't thought about that," he said.

"It's time for some thinking, Herbie. Listen, can you get back into your apartment without anyone seeing you?"

"Yeah, I guess."

"Well, then, go home, let yourself in, don't turn on any lights or the TV, and don't make any noise, and don't answer the phone unless it rings once, then stops, then rings again a minute later. If it does that, it will be me."

Herbie muttered these instructions to himself. "But what am I gonna eat?"

Stone pressed some bills into his hand. "Whatever you do, don't order in. Stop at a deli and pick up enough groceries for a few days."

"Okay."

"And, Herbie, draw all the curtains. Don't even let the light in the refrigerator be seen."

"Okay."

"And don't leave the apartment, except late at night, and only then to get more food."

"You said I can't run the TV?"

"No, you can't."

"Well, what am I gonna do?"

"All right, you can run the TV in the daytime, but not at night. They'll see the flickering light."

"Okay."

The cab stopped at Stone's corner. "Herbie," Stone said, "please don't get yourself killed. At least, not yet."

"Okay," Herbie said.

Stone got out of the cab and watched Herbie disappear into the night.

34

S tone worked through the morning, clearing his desk so that he could leave early to meet Celia in Connecticut and avoid weekend rush-hour traffic. Joan came into his office.

"We haven't heard anything from Bernard Finger's office about his financial statement, have we?"

"I haven't," Stone said. "Call Sam Teich over there and tell him I expect the accounting today. I want to get the settlement paid and the money in the bank."

"Okay." She left and came back. "Sam Teich has already left the office for the weekend; won't be back until Monday. Mr. Finger has left, too, for Las Vegas, expected back on Monday."

"Damn it," Stone said, "I forgot to hound them about the accounting. Well, I guess we'll just have to wait until Monday morning. Call Sam Teich first thing. I may wait until Monday morning to come back to town."

"Well," Joan said, "don't wear yourself out up there."

S tone was upstairs packing a bag when Dino called.
"Hey."
"Good morning."
"Afternoon."

"Oh, all right, good afternoon. What's up? I'm trying to get out of here for Connecticut before the rush-hour traffic starts."

"Big news: It's already started."

Stone looked at his watch: two P.M. "Shit," he said.

"I just called to let you know Devlin Daltry made bail at night court. Apparently, he had a lawyer standing by."

"Swell, so he's loose on the town again."

"Yeah, watch your ass."

"I hope he tries to follow me; I'll lose him in the wilds of Connecticut. He'll never find his way home again."

"That fast car of yours is gonna get you killed yet."

"What kind of car does Daltry drive? I mean, apart from the stolen Taurus he used to run over me."

"A white BMW M6, the sports coupe. That was the first thing we checked after your bump-and-run experience."

"It wasn't a bump-and-run experience; it was a *hit*-and-run experience."

"Whatever."

"It was an experience I hope you never have, being hit and runned."

"How's the leg?"

"Several colors of black, blue and yellow, thank you, each indicative of a level of pain."

"Take your pills."

"Don't worry; the minute I'm through driving for the day."

"See you Sunday night at Elaine's?"

"If I don't stay until Monday morning."

"Don't wear yourself out up there."

"You're as bad as Joan. Bye." Stone hung up, grabbed his duffel and headed for the garage. Halfway out of the room he stopped, went back to his dressing room, opened the safe and took out his little Colt Government .380 auto, a holster and two magazines. He put the holster on his belt, slapped in a magazine, racked the slide, flipped on the safety, holstered the pistol and put the spare magazine in his pocket. He checked his wallet to be sure he had his Connecticut carry license, then headed for the garage again.

Third Avenue was jammed with cars headed uptown for the bridge, so he turned west and fought his way across town toward the West Side Highway. By the time he reached it it was after three o'clock, but at least traffic was moving pretty well, at least until he encountered a backup because of a fender-bender. Once past that he zoomed along for all of two minutes before the backup at the turn for the George Washington Bridge slowed him down again, but once past that he was driving at speed again. Farther north, on the Saw Mill River Parkway, he switched on the illegal-in-New-York-State fore-and-aft radar detector and let the Mercedes E55 out a little on the winding road, enjoying the 5.5-liter turbocharged engine and the superb suspension and brakes. Then he remembered the white BMW M6 coupe and started checking his rearview mirror.

Once he thought he caught sight of such a car, but he quickly left it behind. After he joined I-684 north, the fun was over for a while—too many New York State troopers. The radar detector constantly beeped, and he was glad he'd slowed down.

He took I-84 east to the turnoff for Route 7 north and to its end. From there, he was on country roads again, and that was when he found the white M6 in his mirror, staying well back but there.

Once free of some local traffic, he accelerated up a fairly straight stretch of Connecticut roadway, across a bridge, past an old mill, then right on Wewaka Brook Road. Half a mile later, he turned into a friend's driveway, drove up a hill, flew into his friend's garage, then got out of the car and peeped at the road. The M6 passed in a white blur with a howl. Stone got back into his car, reversed his route and drove into Bridgewater.

He parked in front of the local shop and bakery, went in, bought a double espresso, drank it, then got back into his car and made his way to Washington without further sightings of the BMW. He pulled into the driveway of his little cottage, parked behind the hedge, grabbed his duffel and let himself into the house.

"Hello!" he called out. No response. He looked into the kitchen, found it empty, then walked upstairs to the bedroom, the .380 in his hand. At the foot of the bed was a massage table, all set up and draped with sheets. "Celia!" he called out, but there was no answer. Then he felt something hard poking into his back.

"Stick 'em up," an odd, deep voice said.

Stone raised his hands and was greeted with a girlish giggle. He turned around to find Celia, dressed in a short robe, her hand formed into a gun, laughing uncontrollably.

"You thought I had you, didn't you?"

He put his arms around her, lifted the hem of the robe with one hand and slapped her hard on the ass with the other. "Bad girl!"

She laughed and kissed him. "Put the gun away. You have time for a drink while you're getting out of your clothes," she said. "Then I'm going to give you the best massage you ever had." She went to the dresser, where a glass, an ice bucket and a bottle of Knob Creek awaited and poured them both a drink.

Stone was already naked when she turned around. She handed him his drink.

"Take a big swallow, then lie facedown on the table."

"I don't know if facedown is physically possible at the moment," he said, pushing against her to show her why.

"Oh, deal with it," she said, taking his drink and shoving him toward the table. She set the drink on a little shelf, meant for resting his elbows.

Stone climbed onto the table, did some anatomical shifting for the sake of comfort, then settled onto the sheet and put his face into the cradle. Celia had put a straw in his drink, so he was able to sip without lifting his head. She pottered around for a moment, then came toward him.

He felt a trickle of hot oil down his back.

"Too hot?"

"No, just right." He took another sip of the bourbon from his straw.

She began to work on him, rubbing the hot oil into his back and buttocks and the back of his thighs, paying particular and tender attention to his bruised leg. He had forgotten how strong she was and what good hands she had. She spent three-quarters of an hour kneading every available muscle, then told him to turn over. He took the last sip of the bourbon and followed instructions.

"Well," she said, "if I had put a sheet over you, you would have supplied the tent pole."

"All your fault," he breathed, as she began massaging his neck and shoulders and scalp. She continued down his body for another half hour, until he thought he would explode, then she gently cupped his testicles in her hand and, with the other hand and the hot oil and, occasionally, her mouth, she rendered him limp and helpless.

"Sleep for a while," she said, spreading a blanket over him.

His leg was throbbing where she had massaged it. "There's a bottle of pills in the left-hand pocket of my trousers," he said. "Give me one, please."

She gave him the pill with a little water. "I know it's sore, but it will feel better tomorrow. I'll wake you in time for dinner."

Stone drifted into a soft, fuzzy sleep.

35

S tone and Celia arrived at the Mayflower Inn for dinner. He loved the place, and always looked forward to the perfume of wood-burning fireplaces as he entered. The inn had originally been designed as a school by Erich Rossiter, the same architect who designed Stone's house, and had been expensively converted to its new use by a local couple with deep pockets. It was handsome, gracious, welcoming, and the food was good.

They were seated in the dining room and ordered drinks. Stone was still feeling the glow from the massage, augmented by the warmth of the painkiller, when he ordered a cosmopolitan for Celia and his second bourbon of the evening.

The room was full, not unusual on a Friday evening, when the overflow spilled into the adjacent bar, where a pianist could be heard tinkling away.

"Gosh, I feel good." Stone sighed.

"Thank you," Celia said. "I will take that as a compliment."

"As well you should," Stone replied, smiling and waving at a neighbor couple a few tables away. "I'm ready to supply a written recommendation, should you ever need one."

"For the massage or the sex?" she asked, stroking the inside of his thigh under the table.

"Both."

They ordered, and their first course arrived. When they had finished it, Celia excused herself and departed for the ladies' room. Stone sat sipping his wine, happy in his cocoon of well-being. Then Celia returned to the table and sat down, looking flustered.

"Something wrong?" Stone asked.

"Devlin Daltry is in the bar," she said. "I saw him as I passed the door."

A flush of anger swept through Stone. "Did he see you?"

"No, I'm sure he didn't."

"I'll be right back," Stone said.

She tugged at his sleeve. "Don't make a scene," she said. "He revels in that sort of public misbehavior."

"Don't worry," Stone said. He walked to the men's room and paused at the door for a glimpse into the bar. Daltry was sitting on a stool, talking to a pretty girl next to him. Stone used the men's room, then paused again on leaving. Daltry was still there, and he hadn't seen Stone.

Stone walked to the front door and out into the night. A car had just pulled up, and its occupants were walking into the inn as the valet parker drove away their car. Stone found himself alone on the porch. A few cars to his left, he saw the white BMW M6 parked. He looked around once again to be sure he was alone, then he walked down to the car and quickly unscrewed the valve covers from the two tires facing away from the inn's front door, found a twig and let the air out of both tires. He stood up and looked around. He was still alone. He started back toward the door, when suddenly his anger overwhelmed him. The parking lot was lined with a row of stones the size of soccer balls. He walked to the front of the BMW, picked up one of the stones and, with some effort, heaved it through the windshield of the car. The crash was surprisingly muted, and Stone walked back into the inn, leaving the rock in the driver's seat. He encountered no one, and he glanced into the bar again. Daltry had his back to the door. Stone rejoined Celia.

"What did you do?" she asked.

"Nothing. I saw him but thought better of speaking to him." He was giddy with elation at what he had done.

They finished their main course and coffee, and Stone gave his parking ticket to the waiter as the check arrived. "Please give this to the valet," he said. "We'll be there in a moment."

When they departed the inn, the valet was there with Stone's car. They got in and drove slowly back to the house. By the time they were inside, Stone's elation had swung the other way. What had he done? Letting the air out of the man's tires was a stupid, juvenile prank, but heaving the rock through the windshield was insane. If anyone had seen him, he'd have been arrested. What had he been thinking?

They went upstairs, and as Stone was emptying his pockets, he came up with the bottle of painkillers and looked at the label. "Do not take in conjunction with alcohol," it read.

Good God, he thought. Eliza was right; he had run amok! And Daltry was going to go nuts when he saw his car. It would be easy enough for him to learn that Stone and Celia had had dinner at the inn, and he would certainly put two and two together. He would react badly.

Stone fell into bed, exhausted, and Celia was miffed at his inattention.

Stone was awakened early the following morning by the doorbell. By the time he got into a robe, it was ringing again. He slipped the little .380 out of its holder and into the pocket of his robe, then went downstairs to confront Devlin Daltry.

Instead, he found a state trooper on his doorstep, a man he knew, who served as the local constable. He opened the door. "Good morning, Harry," he said.

"Good morning, Stone," the trooper replied. "Sorry to get you up, but I have to ask you something."

"Go right ahead."

"Did you have dinner at the Mayflower last evening?"

"Yes, I did."

"Did you encounter a man named Devlin Daltry?"

"No, I did not."

"Do you know Mr. Daltry?"

"I'm afraid I do."

"Did you do something to Mr. Devlin's car, a white BMW?"

"No, I didn't. I wasn't even aware of such a car."

"It was parked in front of the inn, and someone let the air out of two tires and threw a large rock through the windshield."

"That's unfortunate," Stone said. "There was a parking attendant; didn't he see anything?"

"No. He was parking another car."

"And you suspect me of doing this?"

"Mr. Daltry suspects you. He made a report, so I had to look into it."

"I understand, Harry. You should know that Mr. Daltry is unbalanced. He has been stalking the woman who is my house guest at the moment; she's had to take out a TRO against him. He's behaved in the same way with other women, and on one occasion, I'm told, tried to run down a man who was with one of them."

"I'm very interested to know that, Stone," the trooper said. "Would you say he was unbalanced enough to damage his own car and blame you?"

"I would. The NYPD suspects him of being the man who struck me with a car earlier this week, a hit-and-run that put me in the hospital and did this." He held up the blue cast.

"I'm sorry to hear that, Stone. Are you feeling all right now?"

"Yes, except for this," Stone said. He pulled back the robe to reveal his bruised leg.

"You're lucky it wasn't broken," the trooper said. "I'm sorry to have disturbed you with this, Stone. You leave Mr. Daltry to me. He's ordered a flatbed truck to take his car back to New York; I'll see that he leaves with it."

"Thank you, Harry. I'd appreciate that."

"Does he know where your house is?"

"I don't know, but it wouldn't be awfully hard for him to find out."

"You might just be on alert for the next couple of hours; it'll take that long for the truck to pick him up." The trooper gave him a little salute, got back into his car and left.

Stone went back into the house and found Celia in the kitchen, making breakfast.

"What was that all about?" she asked.

"That was our local constable, a state trooper. Someone damaged Daltry's car at the Mayflower last night, and he blamed me."

"Is everything all right?"

"Yes. I know the man. He's seeing Daltry out of town."

"He'll come back," she said.

"After breakfast, we'll go back to New York. It would be too easy for him to find you."

"All right."

After breakfast Stone called the trooper and arranged to hire an off-duty officer to watch the house for the weekend; then they packed up and left for New York.

They were back on I-684 south when Stone pointed ahead of them. "Look," he said. "That's Daltry's car on the flatbed; he'll be in the truck." He pulled her head into his lap. "Stay down until we're out of sight."

He caught a glimpse of Daltry sitting next to the truck driver as they passed. A glance in the rearview mirror detected no reaction from the man as they passed. He kept Celia's head in his lap until they had exited the interstate onto the Saw Mill River Parkway.

They spent the remainder of their weekend cloistered in Stone's house, cooking, massaging and making love.

36

Stone was sitting up in bed reading the *Times* when Celia came in with a breakfast tray and set it on his lap.

"Thank you," he said.

"I've got to leave."

"We've got to keep you under wraps for a while longer," Stone said. "You're welcome to stay here."

"I have a friend in New Jersey who's agreed to put me up. What's more, I can see some clients out there for a while."

"When do you want to go?"

"She's expecting me for lunch."

"I'll get a car to take you out there as soon as Joan comes in. Leave me the address and number, and I'll keep you posted on events as they happen."

She slipped out of her robe. "I'm going to take a shower."

Stone was tempted to ditch his breakfast and join her, but he calmed himself. He finished his breakfast and was doing the *Times* crossword when Joan buzzed him.

"Good morning."

"Good morning. Did you have a good weekend in Connecticut?"

"It was cut short; we spent most of it here. Could you call the car service and get a car and driver to take Celia to New Jersey?"

"What time?"

"About an hour."

"Will do. I've already called Bernard Finger's office, but Sam Teich isn't in yet, and Finger isn't back from Las Vegas."

"Please call Mrs. Finger and tell them we're still waiting for the final accounting and expect to have it today."

"Okay. Anything else?"

"That'll do it for now."

She hung up. Celia came out of the bathroom fully dressed.

"The car will be here in an hour," Stone said.

"I'll get packed."

The phone buzzed again, and Stone picked it up.

"Mrs. Finger isn't in," Joan said. "The maid said she's expected back from Las Vegas later today."

Stone was taken aback. "Las Vegas?"

"That's what the maid said. Are you thinking what I'm thinking?"

"Nah, it's got to be a coincidence."

"Maybe it's a farewell dirty weekend," Joan said.

"No, I think she's too pissed off at Bernie for that. It's got to be a coincidence."

"Anyway, I left a message for her to call."

"You know what to tell her if I'm not here."

"Sure. Bye." Joan hung up.

S tone checked the block for signs of Devlin Daltry or his two ex-cops, then took Celia's bags out to the car. She handed him a slip of paper.

"Here's how to reach me," she said.

"And you have my numbers."

She kissed him. "Thanks for taking such good care of me."

He laughed. "I think you took better care of me." He waved her off, then went back into the house and his office.

Joan buzzed him.

"Yes?"

"Sam Teich for you on line one."

Stone picked up the phone. "Good morning, Sam. Where's the accounting?"

"Good morning, Stone. I'm happy to tell you that an accounting won't be necessary."

"Oh, yes it will," Stone said.

"You don't understand."

"What don't I understand?"

"Mr. and Mrs. Finger have reconciled; there won't be a divorce."

Stone was stunned. Visions of stacks of money blowing away in the wind raced through his mind.

"They spent a long weekend in Las Vegas and put their marriage back together."

"I'll believe that when I hear it from Mrs. Finger," Stone said.

"I'm sure you will hear from her as soon as she returns to New York later today," Teich said. "I know this must be a great disappointment to you, Stone," Teich said drily. "I'm sure you were looking forward to a large fee."

"If it's true, then I'm very happy for them both," Stone said. "Good-bye, Sam." He hung up. Joan was standing in the doorway.

"What's going on?" she asked.

"Worst fears realized," Stone said.

Her face fell. "They're in Las Vegas *together*?"

Stone nodded. "Teich says they've reconciled."

"She can't do that!" Joan cried. "We need that fee!"

"Bernie is smarter than I thought," Stone said. "He did the arithmetic and made a decision. Now let's see if he's smart enough to dump the girlfriend and get rid of the penthouse."

"If he doesn't, Mrs. Finger will be back," Joan said.

"Get me Bob Cantor."

Joan left, then buzzed him a moment later.

Stone picked up the phone. "Bob?"

"One and the same."

"Bernie Finger has pulled his fat out of the fire, at least temporarily."

"How so?"

"He's reconciled with his wife."

"Oh, shit, and after all my hard work."

"Bob, I want to know if he really gets rid of the girlfriend and the apartment. Give it a day or two, then nose around and see what you can find out."

"You want more intimate snapshots?"

"First, find out if they're still sharing the penthouse, then we'll see how to proceed."

"Will do," Cantor said and hung up.

At dinner at Elaine's, Dino was outraged. "He went back to his wife? The son of a bitch should be taken out and shot!"

Elaine piped up. "Yeah, that's a terrible thing to do, isn't it? Go back to the woman who loves him?"

"But the other one loves him, too," Dino pointed out, "or at least his money."

"Hey, hey," Stone said. "Don't get upset; this can't last. Bernie will be back with his masseuse before we know it, and when he goes, I'll pounce."

"Jesus, what a way to make a living," Elaine said. She got up and left the table.

"The lady came to me!" Stone called after her.

37

Stone had just gotten in from Elaine's when the phone rang. He picked it up. "Hello?"

"It's Cantor."

"Hi, Bob. You got something on Bernie Finger already?"

"It's not that. I'm at Herbie's place. You need to come out here right now."

"What's up?"

"I don't want to talk about it on the phone."

"I'll be there in twenty minutes if traffic's good." Stone hung up, went down to the garage and backed his car out. He headed down FDR Drive, crossed the Brooklyn Bridge and was parking in front of Herbie Fisher's building twenty-one minutes later. A light was burning in the basement apartment. "I told him not to show any lights," Stone said aloud, slamming the car door.

Stone went down the short flight of steps and rang the outside doorbell. Bob Cantor answered it quickly. "Follow me," he said. He led the way into the apartment and stopped.

Stone looked around. The place had been torn up yet again.

"Check that out," Cantor said, pointing at the sofa.

Stone followed his finger and saw a line of blood spatter starting on the back cushions of the sofa and continuing up and onto the living room wall. "Oh, Christ," Stone said, "they've killed Herbie."

He felt overwhelmed with guilt; he'd sent Herbie back here, and they'd found him.

"No," Cantor said, shaking his head. "This way." He led the way toward the kitchen. Lying in the hallway was a corpse, and it wasn't Herbie.

"It's Cheech, I think," Stone said. "He and the other guy worked for Dattila or his bookie. They're the ones who beat up Herbie outside Elaine's." The man had a bad cut across the jugular and a butcher knife in his chest.

"Okay," Cantor said, "now I call the cops."

"Right."

Cantor flipped open his cell phone and dialed 911. "My name is Robert Cantor," he said into the phone. "I'm a retired police officer. I want to report a homicide." He gave the operator the address, answered a few questions, then hung up. "I think we should tell them I arrived here when you did."

"Okay, but I just can't see Herbie doing this; he's not the type."

"A cornered rat will fight a pit bull," Cantor said. "You think I should wipe the prints off the knife?"

Stone shook his head. "Herbie's going to get made for this, and we can't cover it up. But given the history, we can make a clear case for self-defense."

"I guess," Cantor said. "I hope they don't send the two bozos who were here last time."

"Me, too."

The bozos were replaced by a detective of about forty, accompanied by an attractive young woman who, Stone guessed, had a very new gold shield.

Stone and Cantor showed their NYPD I.D. "My name is Stone Barrington; this is Bob Cantor. We're both retired homicide detectives."

"My name's Ed Cardoza," the male detective said. "This is my partner, Emily Swift. What's happened here, gentlemen? We heard of a homicide."

"This way." He led the detectives to the corpse. "There's a back-story here," Stone said.

Cardoza knelt and looked closely at the body. "I can't wait to hear it," he said.

"I'm an attorney," Stone said. "I represent the man who lives here, Herbert Fisher."

"Is this Fisher?"

"No. That's a professional gorilla named Cheech, who works for Carmine Dattila. He and a buddy of his, whose name I can't remember, are collectors for a bookie who's owned by Dattila. Fisher owes twenty-four grand, and the two gorillas have beaten him up twice and kidnapped him once. Fisher was hiding out here from them. My theory is that they found him, attacked him, and Fisher somehow got hold of a kitchen knife and defended himself."

"That's a good theory if you're a defense lawyer," Cardoza said.

"It's the only thing that could have happened," Cantor said. "It's not like Herbie would have invited them here, then killed one of them."

"And what's your connection to Mr. Fisher?"

"He's my nephew, my late sister's boy."

"Okay. Let's say your theory is good," Cardoza said. "Where's Herbie Fisher? And while we're at it, where's Cheech's partner in crime? Gorillas tend to travel in pairs."

"Beats me," Cantor said.

"It would be like Herbie to run," Stone said, "if he had the chance. On the other hand, the partner could have gotten the better of Herbie and taken him somewhere else."

"I guess that's a good possibility," Cardoza agreed, "especially since Mr. Fisher left his weapon in Cheech's chest. How about a description of both men?"

"Herbert Fisher is how old, Bob?" Stone asked.

"Twenty-five."

"Five-six, a hundred and fifty, light brown hair."

"Any visible scars?" the detective asked.

"Not unless he got them tonight."

"How about the partner?"

"About thirty-five, six-three, two-seventy, black hair, a nose like a fist."

"That would also fit Cheech here."

"They could be brothers," Stone agreed.

Cardoza turned to his partner. "Call in the descriptions and ask for an APB, then get a scene team over here." The young woman reached for her cell phone, and Cardoza turned back to Stone and Cantor. "I guess you two are too smart to have touched anything here?"

Both men nodded. "It's as we found it," Stone said.

"How long ago?"

"Ten minutes," Stone replied.

"You arrived together?"

Cantor spoke up. "I took a cab over here; Stone arrived in time to go inside with me."

"Why were you here?" Cardoza asked.

"We were looking for Herbie," Stone said. "He's been on the run from these two guys, and we were worried about him."

"You said he's your client," Cardoza pointed out. "Why does he need a lawyer?"

"He's suing Carmine Dattila."

Cardoza burst out laughing. "For what?" he asked when he'd gotten control of himself.

"Battery, kidnaping, attempted murder. I have a recording of Dattila ordering his death."

"I'm gonna want that," Cardoza said.

"It's evidence in a lawsuit, but I'll get you a copy tomorrow morning."

"I'm gonna need the original."

"Not yet. When I can, or when a judge orders it."

Cardoza shrugged. "That'll do for the moment, I guess."

"How else can we help?" Stone asked.

"You guys wait in the hall while my partner and I go through this place."

Stone and Cantor walked into the hallway and leaned against the wall.

"That went well, I thought," Cantor said.

"As well as could be expected," Stone agreed.

S tone spent the morning working and had a sandwich at his
     desk. He'd just finished a cup of coffee when Joan buzzed
     him.

"Dierdre Monahan from the D.A.'s office is on line one."

Stone started to pick up the phone, but he gave himself a moment to review his history with Dierdre Monahan: They had met a
couple of years ago at a Christmas party in the D.A.'s office. He had
been trying a case downtown, and the opposing counsel had invited
him to the party. After a couple of hours of eggnog and flirtation, he
and Dierdre, who was an up-and-coming assistant D.A., had found
themselves in a conference room, on the long table, wearing few
clothes and exploring each other's nether regions—this at a moment
when the chief deputy D.A. had walked into the room with another
woman, apparently with the same activity in mind.

Dierdre had taken a lot of guff from her coworkers about the incident, to the point where she had threatened to file a sexual harass-
ment complaint, which had resulted in a promotion and a better
office. Last year she had been assigned to prosecute Herbie Fisher
for a DUI and attacking a police officer, who happened to be one of
her four brothers on the force.

Stone took a deep breath, picked up the phone and punched the
button. "Dierdre!" he nearly shouted. "How the hell are you?"

"Oh, I'm just dandy, Stone," she replied, "and I'm sure you are, too. I just called to make your day a little worse."

A trickle of anxiety ran down through Stone's bowels. "Oh, I'm sure you wouldn't do a thing like that," he replied. "What's up?"

"Well, the Brooklyn D.A.'s office is a little backed up, so I took the murder one charge against Herbert Fisher off their hands."

"*Murder one*? Are you nuts, Dierdre? That was a clear case of self-defense!"

"That's not how I read it, buddy. If it was self-defense, why is Mr. Fisher on the run?"

"He's been hiding from Carmine Dattila's goons for a couple of weeks. He owes money to a bookie, and they've already beaten him up and tried to kill him."

"I haven't been able to locate the criminal charges on that," she said.

"We're treating it as a civil matter for the moment, but I've no doubt that criminal charges will result."

"Oh, yeah, the detective told me you were suing Carmine. We all got a great laugh out of that."

"Well, Dattila isn't laughing; he sent those guys to Herbie's apartment to kill him, and Herbie got lucky. That's all this is."

"Tell you what, why don't you bring Mr. Fisher down here tomorrow morning, and we'll talk about it."

"I think that's a good idea, but I don't know where the hell he is. He contacts me from time to time, so when he does, I'll give you a call, and we'll get together."

"You're aware that there's an APB out for him, aren't you?"

"Yeah, but that's purely for his protection, isn't it?"

"Sure. I'm positive he'd be safe in a cell at Rikers."

"Dierdre, he wouldn't last a day at Rikers; Dattila has a long reach, and Herbie's a little guy."

"He's big enough to take out a big chunk of Dattila's muscle guy with a butcher knife."

"A cornered rat will fight a pit bull," Stone said, "as a friend of mine likes to say."

"Well, 'rat' certainly describes the little shit," she said.

"Now, Dierdre, if you're referring to the unfortunate incident with your brother the cop . . ."

"Oh, he's got more than that on his sheet," she said. "There's another DUI and that business when he crashed through the skylight while taking dirty pictures and fell on some poor guy who died as a result."

"Dierdre, you know as well as I that it has been positively determined that the guy was already dead when Herbie fell on him. He was just trying to make a buck."

"Stone, why do you keep getting involved with this little creep? He's nothing but trouble, and one of these days he's going to get *you* in trouble."

"Circumstances beyond my control," Stone said, "but everything I've told you is true."

"Well, maybe so, but I hope you can find your client in time to get him in my office at ten tomorrow morning, because at that time, I'm going to start getting a lot harder to convince. Bye-bye, sweetie. Oh, by the way, bring that tape of Dattila committing a crime, or I'll have your balls." She hung up.

Stone called Bob Cantor.

"Cantor."

"Bob, have you heard anything at all from Herbie?"

"Yeah, he called just a minute ago. He wants me to bring him some money."

"Where?"

"He said he'd call me when he finds a safe place."

"Bob, when you see him you've got to collar him and take him home with you. I've got to have him in the D.A.'s office tomorrow at ten A.M. to keep him from getting a murder charge slapped on him."

"Are you serious?"

"Dead serious. Somehow, the case got assigned to Manhattan, and the A.D.A. in charge is the one whose brother Herbie kicked in the balls last year."

"Oh, shit."

"My sentiments exactly. Hang on to him, Bob. Have him at the D.A.'s office at ten tomorrow, or everything is going to get a lot worse."

"I read you, Stone. I'll bring him over here and handcuff him to a radiator." Cantor hung up.

As Stone hung up, Joan buzzed him again. "A Dr. Larkin on two."

Stone punched the button. "Eliza, how are you?"

"I'm very well, Stone. Do you like Italian food?"

"My favorite."

"I'm cooking this evening. Would you like to join me?"

"What's an Irish girl doing cooking Italian?"

"Would you rather I cooked Irish?"

"Italian will be just great. What time?"

"Seven thirty."

"Can I bring the wine?"

"You'd better." She gave him the address.

"See you then." Stone hung up and walked through the ground floor of his house to a room he kept cooled as a wine cellar. He found two bottles of the Masi '91 Amarone and set them on the kitchen counter to settle. "Yum," he said aloud to himself as he wiped the dust from the bottles. He had been saving them for a special occasion, and this was a special occasion.

He went cheerfully back to work.

S hortly before five, Joan came into his office with a large package. "This just arrived by messenger," she said, setting it on his desk.

Stone stood up and looked at the package. "Any return address?"

"Some gallery downtown," she said, picking up the scissors to cut the string holding it together.

"No!" Stone said, holding up a hand. "Come with me." He took her by the arm and led her upstairs.

"What, are you expecting a bomb or something?"

"No, I am not, but that package is from Devlin Daltry's gallery, and nobody is opening it but the bomb squad." He picked up a phone and called Dino.

S tone sat in his living room with Joan and Dino.

"I hope it's a bomb," Dino said.

"Are you nuts?" Stone inquired. "It's sitting on my desk."

"If it's a bomb, then I can charge Daltry with something that'll keep him in jail while he's awaiting trial."

"That office is where I earn my living," Stone said.

"You earn your living in your head. Wouldn't it be worth a little redecorating to get that guy off the street?"

"It might," Stone said.

There were heavy footsteps on the stairs and a man wearing a lot of protective gear stood in the doorway. "Okay," he said, "you can come downstairs now."

The three followed him back to Stone's office, where the box still rested on his desk. Next to it was a bronze head.

"There was no bomb," the officer said. "It's just a sculpture thing."

Stone walked over and picked up the head. "It's Celia," he said.

"Looks like the head was sawed off a statue," Dino pointed out. "What do you think the symbolism is here?"

Stone nodded. "It's a threat," he said, "pure and simple."

"You better call Celia," Dino said.

Stone sat down at his desk and found Celia's number in New Jersey. She answered on the first ring.

"Hello?"

"Hi, it's Stone."

"Oh, hi. I'm glad you called; I'm bored out of my skull out here."

"Is everything all right?"

"So far, so good."

"Celia, is there any way Daltry could make some connection with the friend you're staying with?"

"I don't think so; they've never met."

"Have you ever mentioned her name to him?"

She was quiet for a moment. "Possibly, but there's no reason for him to remember it, and he doesn't know where she lives."

"Is she in the phone book?"

"No, she has an unlisted number."

"You're sure there's no other way he could trace you there?"

"No, there isn't. What's going on, Stone?"

"Did Daltry ever sculpt you?"

"Yes, he did a full-sized nude last year. It's a very good likeness of me, if I do say so."

"Yes, it is."

"You've seen it?"

"Only the head."

"I don't understand."

"Daltry had the head delivered to me. I perceive that as a threat."

"You mean he cut the head off the statue?"

"That's what I mean."

"Holy shit. He told me he expected to get half a million for the thing, from the right buyer."

"Celia, I want you to think about this some more. Think about every mention of your friend you might have made to Daltry or anyone he knows. If you think of some way he might trace you to her house, then I want you to get out of there and check into a hotel, and be sure you aren't followed."

"All right, I'll think about it, but I don't think he could find me."

"Call me on my cell, if you decide to move, so I'll know where you are."

"I miss you."

"Just take care of yourself." He said good-bye and hung up.

"Is she getting out?"

Stone shook his head. "She says there's no way he could find her."

"I hope she's right," Dino said.

L ater, when he was ready to leave the house for dinner, Stone called Eliza. "Is there a garage near you?" he asked.

"Right next door," she said.

"Okay, I may be a few minutes late, but I'll be there."

"Just as well; I got a late start on the sauce."

"See you soon." He hung up and went to the front windows, checking up and down the block for any sight of Devin Daltry or his two ex-cops. Nothing. He went down to the garage and backed quickly out into the street, made the light at Third Avenue and started a series of turns, making his way gradually uptown, checking his mirrors constantly for any sign of a following car. When he was certain he wasn't being followed, he parked in the garage next door to Eliza's building and, after checking the block once again, rang her bell and took the elevator upstairs.

She met him at the door, still wearing her scrubs, and a delicious smell wafted through the apartment. "What was that about a garage? Did you drive up here?"

"Yes. Didn't you have time to change after work?"

"I'm only wearing the top half of the scrubs; makes a great apron. There's something a little more alluring underneath."

"I can't wait to see it. Something smells great, besides you."

"That's dinner. Why did you drive instead of taking a cab?"

"I wanted to be sure I wasn't followed."

"Don't worry; I don't have an angry ex-boyfriend."

"Why do you mention that?"

"What I meant was, nobody will be following you because you're seeing me."

"I'm glad to hear it, because I have a client who has an angry ex-boyfriend, and that's who I thought might be following me."

"I've never understood this stalker thing," she said, "though it seems to be common enough."

"I'm afraid so."

"Come into the kitchen, and I'll get you a drink."

He followed her through a handsomely furnished apartment to a surprisingly large kitchen, where several pots were bubbling away on a big stove. She seated him at a counter and handed him a bottle of Knob Creek to open. "From what I've seen, you don't drink anything else. I can't seem to get it open."

Stone set down the two bottles of the Masi Amarone, then pulled the string that cut the wax seal and opened the bourbon bottle. "One for you, too?"

"I've already made myself a martini," she said, pouring one from a silver shaker into a frosted glass.

They touched glasses and sipped.

"I'm impressed that you'd tackle such a big meal after a hard day at the hospital."

"I had the day off," she said. "I work twelve-hour shifts four days a week."

"That's still a forty-eight-hour week."

"Don't worry, I get paid for it."

"How long have you worked the ER?" he asked.

"Always. My specialty is emergency medicine. I'm deputy head of emergency services now."

"You must like the work."

"I love it. It's different every day, and I like its decisiveness. You either save a patient or lose him; it all happens fast. I don't have to watch patients die a lingering death, and we save most of them."

"I see your point."

"We'll be ready to eat in just a few minutes," she said. She busied herself with setting a table on the other side of the kitchen, while Stone opened the first bottle of wine and tasted it.

"You approve?"

"I certainly do," he said, offering her a sip.

"*Mmmmmm.* Big wine!"

"I like wines you can't see through." Stone's cell phone vibrated on his belt. He let it go to voice mail.

She untied a string and slipped out of the scrubs, revealing a red dress with considerable cleavage.

"You look gorgeous," he said, taking her by the waist and kissing her lightly. The cell phone vibrated again.

"Answer that," she said. "I can't stand an unanswered phone."

Stone flipped open the phone. "Hello?"

"Is this Stone Barrington?"

"Yes. Who's this?"

"Did you once work homicide at the one-nine with Dino Bacchetti?"

"Yes, I did."

"This is Charley Sample. I worked robbery out of the one-nine for two years."

"I remember you, Charley. What's up?"

"I run the detective squad out in Morristown, New Jersey, now, been out here for six years. We got a situation here."

"Tell me." Stone had a very bad feeling.

40

S tone closed the phone and put his notebook away. "Eliza, I'm sorry, but I have to leave."

"What's wrong?"

"An emergency—the client I told you about."

"I do emergencies for a living," she said, turning off the stove. "This will keep. I'm coming with you."

"All right," he said, glad of the company.

I n the car, he entered the Morristown address into the dashboard GPS navigator and left the garage. "Turn right," the navigator said in a soft female voice. Stone turned right. He was instructed to turn left on Eleventh Avenue, and he followed the voice's orders to the Lincoln Tunnel.

"I've never seen one of these things work," she said.

"It's really quite amazing. It's especially good when there's a hard-to-find address in a place you've never been."

F orty minutes later, Stone stopped across the street from a neat white bungalow, a few steps up from street level. He showed his badge to a questioning cop. "Where's Charley Sample?" he asked the man.

The cop nodded toward the house. "In the living room," he said.

Stone and Eliza walked up the front walk and up the steps to the porch. As they got to the front door, he gave a passing glance to something in a porch chair, covered with a sheet of plastic. They stepped into the front hall, and Stone spotted Sample standing to his right, in the living room. He also spotted a pair of bare female feet, protruding from behind a chair.

"Stone," Sample said, walking toward him, extending his hand, which was clad in a latex glove.

"Charley, it's good to see you again. This is Dr. Eliza Larkin. She might be helpful with preliminary forensics, if you need her."

Sample shook Eliza's hand. "We may," he said. "I'm sorry to get you all the way out here, and I'm sorry for the circumstances."

Stone stepped past the chair, expecting to see Celia's body on the floor. The woman was a stranger to him; her throat had been cut. "Who is she?"

"Helen Gable, the woman who owns the house."

"This has got to be the guy I told you about," Stone said, "and he's probably still in the neighborhood. He'd get a thrill out of watching all the activity."

"Description?"

"Five-nine; a hundred and sixty pounds; longish dark hair; artsy looking. He drives a white BMW M6 coupe. It's possible he had this done, though."

"Come out on the porch," Sample said.

Stone and Eliza followed the detective onto the porch, where Sample paused by the sheet-covered object. "This isn't going to be pretty," he said, reaching for the sheet. He took it in both hands and lifted it away.

Stone took a quick breath. She sat, naked, in the porch chair; her head was gone. Given the size of the headless corpse, it could only be Celia.

Eliza stepped forward and examined the corpse without touching it. "Very tall female, twenty-five to thirty-five. Her assailant used a sharp knife, probably a hunting knife with a partly serrated blade; he wasn't delicate about it. The condition of the neck indicates that he was very angry, probably in a killing frenzy." She looked around. "She was probably killed inside, then undressed and brought out here."

Sample nodded. "We found a lot of blood upstairs and a trail descending the stairs. We think he encountered the other woman first, killed her immediately, before she had time to cry out, then went upstairs after Celia."

"Did you find the head?" Stone asked.

"No. It's not in the house or on the grounds."

"He took it as a trophy," Eliza said. "I'd be willing to bet he brought the means for preserving it with him, maybe a container of ice or dry ice."

Sample produced two plastic bags: one held a sheet of notepaper with Stone's cell number written on it, the other a semiautomatic pistol. "We found these in her hands," he said.

"The gun is mine, Charley," Stone said. "I loaned it to her for protection, when she was at my house in Connecticut. I didn't know she brought it with her. I know she has my cell number."

"I'll see that you get the gun back in due course," Sample said. "Let's go sit down in the dining room." He pulled the plastic sheet back over the corpse and led the way inside, where they took chairs at the table.

"Tell me everything you know about her, from the beginning," Sample said.

Stone related the story in as much detail as he could muster, omitting the sexual nature of their relationship but including the trips to Connecticut and the incident with Daltry's car at the Mayflower Inn, while Sample both recorded the interview on a dictator and took notes, asking an occasional question. Stone told him about the delivery of the bronze head, as well.

"Did you ever meet Celia?" he asked Eliza.

"Not until tonight," she replied.

"Daltry found her very quickly," Stone said. "She didn't even know she was coming out here until this morning. I talked to her around six o'clock, after the bronze head was delivered to my office, and she was certain he wouldn't be able to learn where she was."

Sample's cell phone rang, and he talked for a moment, then closed it. "The NYPD found Daltry at an opening for another artist in downtown Manhattan. Witnesses put him there from six o'clock onward. There were no grounds for an arrest."

"Then he has an accomplice," Stone said. "He had me run down by a car last week when he had established an alibi elsewhere."

"We'll run down all his contacts and see if we can isolate a suspect who doesn't have an alibi. I don't think we need keep you any longer, Stone. Thanks for coming out here. You, too, Dr. Larkin."

"I'm sorry I couldn't be of more help," she said.

They left the dining room and walked outside. The corpse had been removed from the front porch, and an ambulance was driving away from the house.

"A neighborhood kid spotted it," Sample said. "The porch light was on." They had started down the steps, but Sample pulled Stone back, out of Eliza's earshot. "Stone, were you fucking her?"

"Yes, but we'd only known each other a short time."

"I'll try to keep that out of the record, since it doesn't seem relevant."

"Thanks, Charley," Stone said. The two men shook hands, and Stone and Eliza walked back to his car.

No one spoke for another ten minutes, then Eliza said, "You don't lead a dull life, do you?"

"Sometimes it's not dull enough," Stone replied.

———

They went back to Eliza's apartment, and she warmed up dinner.

"The wine is delicious," she said.

"Everything is delicious," he replied.

When they had finished, he helped with the dishes, then made to leave, but she held him back.

"Stay with me tonight," she said. "You're still in shock; you shouldn't be alone." She led him into the bedroom, undressed them both and pulled him into bed.

They lay there in each other's arms, hardly moving, until they finally fell asleep.

The following morning she made them breakfast, then walked Stone to the door.

"We can't see each other for a while," he said.

"Why not?"

"Because this Daltry thing isn't over. If he learned about you, you might become a target, and I don't want that to happen. I took a lot of precautions to see that I wasn't followed here tonight, but I can't go on doing that; it's too dangerous."

"I understand," she said, standing on her tiptoes and kissing him. "I'll wait for you to call me when this is over."

"I hope it's soon," Stone said.

"So do I," she replied.

41

That morning Stone headed for the district attorney's office in a cab, but they were stopped dead by a huge traffic jam going downtown. Stone called Bob Cantor's cell number.

"Cantor."

"Bob, it's Stone. Have you got Herbie?"

"Yep, we're sitting in the D.A.'s waiting room."

"I'm stuck in a huge traffic jam. Just know that I'll be there at the earliest possible moment."

"Do the best you can."

"And you hang on to Herbie."

"Don't worry about that."

Stone sweated his way through the jam and arrived at the D.A.'s office twenty minutes late. Cantor and Herbie were not in the waiting room.

"They're in with Dierdre Monahan," the receptionist said. "You can go in."

The idea of Herbie in Dierdre's office without an attorney to keep him quiet horrified Stone, and he practically ran down the hallway toward Dierdre's office.

Dierdre and Cantor seemed to be having a nice conversation without any participation by Herbie. "Good afternoon, Stone," she said pointedly.

"I'm sorry, Dierdre," he said, shaking her hand. "I've been stuck in a traffic jam for half an hour."

"Of course you have," she said, pointing at a chair.

"Didn't you tell her, Bob?"

"Of course I did."

"Dierdre, I hope you haven't been talking to my client without his attorney present."

"I haven't said a word to him," she said innocently.

"That's right, she hasn't," Cantor confirmed.

"Now, Stone, what do you propose we do about this charge of first-degree murder?"

"Now, wait a minute . . ." Herbie began to say.

"Shut up, Herbie," Stone said, "and don't open your mouth again until I tell you to." He turned to the A.D.A. "Now, Dierdre, as I explained on the phone, these two goons have been after Herbie for a couple of weeks, seeking payment of illegal gambling debts. They've beaten him on the street, kidnapped him and held him under the threat of death. Obviously, they found him at home in his own apartment, and Herbie had to defend himself. Anyone would have done the same in the circumstances. I want the charges dropped immediately and my client released."

"I didn't kill anybody," Herbie said.

Stone rounded on him. "Herbie, don't open your mouth . . ." Stone stared at him dumbly. "What did you say?"

"I said, 'I didn't kill anybody.'"

Stone was flabbergasted. He had been at the point of having the charges dismissed, and suddenly Herbie was off on some other tangent.

"I want to hear this," Dierdre said. "Go on, Mr. Fisher."

"Don't say a word, Herbie," Stone said.

"But I'm innocent."

"Your client says he's innocent, Stone," Dierdre said. "I'd like to know why he feels that way."

"I'd like to speak to my client alone for a few minutes," Stone said.

Dierdre turned to Herbie. "Now, Mr. Fisher, your attorney has told you not to speak, but you have the right to ignore his advice, if you want to."

"Great," Herbie said. "I'm innocent. Gus killed Cheech."

"You want to speak against the advice of your attorney?" she asked.

"Yes, I do."

Stone was half out of his seat.

"Go right ahead. Stone, you sit down and shut up."

"I was at my place, watching television and eating a pizza," Herbie said. "I know, Stone, you told me not to watch TV, because they could see it outside, but there was a rerun of *The Sopranos* on, and I pulled the curtains and everything. Anyway, I heard somebody fooling with the lock on my door, so I hid in the closet in the living room. A second later, Cheech and Gus came through the front door and looked around.

"Then they got into an argument. Gus said they should have covered the back door, and it was Cheech's fault that I ran. Of course, I didn't run at all, I was in the closet, and I could see them through a crack in the door.

"They argued some more, and then Cheech slapped Gus, and I mean slapped him *hard*. Gus just stood there for a moment, while Cheech called him a lot of names, then he went down the hall toward the kitchen, and when he came back, he swung his fist at Cheech, only it turned out he had one of my kitchen knives in his fist, and blood spattered all over the wall, and Cheech and Gus started to wrestle around. They fell on the floor where I couldn't see anything but their legs, and I heard this sound like somebody being punched, then I heard this gurgling sound and a lot of heavy breathing. Then Gus stood up, and I could still see Cheech's legs stretched out.

"Gus stood there, looking down for a minute, and then he said, 'Fuck you, Cheech,' and he turned around and walked out of the apartment. When I heard the door close, I came out of the closet and looked at Cheech. I was going to call nine-one-one for an ambulance, but then I saw Cheech die. It was like he just deflated, and he was just this dead lump on the floor. I felt for a pulse, and I couldn't find one, so then I picked up the pizza box and got the hell out of there by the back way."

Stone stared at Herbie, speechless.

"Okay," Dierdre said, "I'll buy that. The charge of murder in the first degree is dropped. You're free to go, Mr. Fisher, but I'll need you to testify against Gus at his trial, if he doesn't roll."

"Yes, ma'am," Herbie said, getting to his feet. "Uncle Bob, can you give me a ride home?"

"Sure, Herbie," Cantor said. The two men left the room.

"Stone," Dierdre said, "I've never seen you at a loss for words."

"What just happened?" Stone asked.

"Well, your client told me what happened at his apartment, and I believed him, so I dropped the murder charge. I'll send you a letter confirming that he's not a target of our investigation."

"Let me get this straight: you *hate* Herbie Fisher, because he kicked your little brother, the cop, in the balls, and yet you dropped the murder charge against him, because you liked his story?"

"That's about it," she said.

"I'm going nuts," Stone said. "I'm dreaming."

"Of course," she added, "there was the fact that we found Gus Castiglione's prints on the butcher knife, and when we arrested him early this morning, Cheech's blood was on his shoes."

Stone stared at her in disbelief. "Why didn't you tell me that to begin with?"

"Because it was so much more fun watching your face while Herbie told his story," she said. "Can I buy you lunch?"

S tone got out of a cab at the Tribeca Grill and waited for Dierdre Monahan to arrive in her own cab. She had suggested this
place, which was way off the beaten path of the courthouse
legal fraternity, because she didn't want to be seen having lunch
with him. At least, that was what he figured.

He was not thrilled about this meeting, since he thought he knew
what she had in mind, but he didn't want to make an enemy of a
woman who had become an important A.D.A. and with whom he
would certainly have dealings in the future.

Dierdre arrived five minutes later, gave him a smile and waved
him inside. As they were seated at their table, Stone noticed that she
had changed from her A.D.A. standard-issue business suit to a tight
dress that showed more than a little cleavage—definitely not your
average courtroom costume.

Dierdre ordered a cosmopolitan and Stone ordered fizzy water.
Somehow, he felt that he needed his wits about him on this occasion.

"You're looking very fetching today," Stone said, sipping his
fizzy water.

"Why, thank you, kind sir," she said, taking a deep swig of her
cosmo. "I thought that went very well this morning, didn't you?"

"Let's just say that I achieved my objective in a surprising manner. I had no idea what Herbie was going to say, and because of the

traffic jam, I didn't have an opportunity to find out before we landed in your office."

"Well, it all turned out all right, didn't it? Your client lives to fuck up another day."

"And fuck up he will," Stone agreed. "I just hope I'm a long way away at the time."

"How'd you get involved in this thing with Dattila the Hun, anyway?"

"I didn't get involved; Woodman and Weld, in the person of Bill Eggers, suddenly decided it was a good idea that I should sue the most murderous goombah thug in the city, maybe the world. I can't tell you what a nightmare it's been."

"I can imagine," she said. A waiter appeared at their table. Dierdre handed him the menu. "I'll have the shrimp pasta dish, no starter, and another cosmo."

"Same for me, hold the cosmo," Stone said.

"So, what have you been doing besides suing the Hun?" she asked.

"Well, I had a client murdered last night."

"This is the one with Devlin Daltry as the suspect." It wasn't a question.

"You're very well informed."

"Was she really . . ." She grimaced.

"Headless? Yes, she was. It was an ugly business, and Daltry has an alibi."

"And I suppose you feel responsible?"

"I thought I had done everything I could do to protect her, but, yes, I can't shake that feeling. I'm not sure I ever will."

The waiter came back with the cosmo. Dierdre polished off her first drink and took a swig of the second. "Okay," she said, when the waiter had gone, "gimme." She held out a hand.

"Give you what?"

"You want me to subpoena you? Get a search warrant for your house?"

"Dierdre, I can't imagine what you're talking about."

"Gimme the Dattila tape, and we'll go back to your house and I'll fuck your brains out."

"That's the nicest thing anybody has said to me this year," Stone said, placing his briefcase on the table and opening it. He handed her a dictator with an earplug and pressed the Play button.

Dierdre listened intently. "I don't believe this," she said, giggling. "That's his voice. I only met him once, but I recognize it."

"And Herbie can put him in the room, along with Cheech and Gus, and swear he said it."

She popped open the dictator, emptied the tape into her palm and tucked it into her very impressive cleavage. "Do you want lunch before I fuck you, or shall we get on with it?"

"I'm hungry," Stone said. He wasn't up for this, and he didn't know how he was going to get out of it. As if on cue, the waiter set down two plates of pasta.

"Okay, but be quick about it," she said, digging in. "I haven't got the whole afternoon; there's a deposition at three."

"Are you that fast these days?"

"I'd love the whole afternoon, but duty calls. What else you working on these days?"

"Well, I had a really juicy divorce case, but it blew up in my face."

"Anybody I know?"

"How about Bernard Finger, Esquire? I was representing his wife."

"What fun!" she giggled. "Nice fee, I'll bet."

"I was doing it on a contingency basis."

"So, you're going to get ten percent of half of everything Bernie has? Wow!"

"Thirty percent."

"You're shitting me!"

"I shit you not. Only thing is, Bernie took her off to Las Vegas for a weekend and they reconciled. And I had the settlement all worked out."

"Oh, poor baby," she said, patting his cheek and sticking her shoeless toe into his crotch.

"I'll live, I guess. Anyway, it can't last; she'll be calling me again as soon as she catches him with some doxie."

"Speaking of that, hurry up with the pasta, okay? I'm getting wet." She had already finished hers.

Stone scraped the last of the pasta from his plate. As he was about to rise, a belt buckle appeared beside his table. He looked up and found it cinching the waist of the district attorney, the Old Man himself, so called because he was a man and very old, but it didn't seem to be slowing him down. He had just been reelected for the umpteenth time.

"Why, hello, Dierdre," he said.

She was obviously flabbergasted to see him so far off the reservation. "Uh, hello, Boss. You know Stone Barrington?"

The Old Man offered his hand. "We've opposed each other once or twice. It's one to one, so far, isn't it?"

"I thought it was two-nil, your favor," Stone said.

"No sucking up," the Old Man said. "Come on, Dierdre, I'll give you a lift back to the office. You've got a deposition, haven't you?"

She was momentarily nonplussed. "Yes sir, I have, and I'd love a lift. It's so hard to get cabs at this time of day." She got up and went with the Old Man, but not before she had turned to Stone and mouthed, "Call me!"

Stone sighed, put away his dictator and dug out a credit card. Saved from a fate worse than death by the district attorney. And he had done himself some good, too: He had Dierdre interested not just in Carmine Dattila but in Devlin Daltry, and that could come in useful.

43

S tone arrived back at his house to find Herbie Fisher waiting in his office.

"Hey, Stone!" Herbie cried, as if they hadn't seen each other in years.

"What are you doing here, Herbie?"

"I didn't know where else to go, unless you think it's safe for me to go back to my apartment. I mean, Cheech is dead and Gus is in jail, isn't he?"

"You think those two guys are the only muscle working for Dattila?"

"Well, I . . ."

"Exactly." He pressed a button and Joan answered. "Have we got a thousand dollars in the safe?"

"Yes, I guess so."

"Bring me that much in an envelope." He regarded Herbie. "Do you have any relatives besides your uncle Bob?"

"Well, there's my mom's sister, Gladys. She lives out on the Island. Her husband's a plumber out there, does really well."

"Is she speaking to you?"

"Are you kidding? I'm her favorite!"

"When did you last see her?"

"I don't know, maybe a year ago."

"If you turned up on her doorstep, would she take you in?"

"Sure, I guess so."

"Then why aren't you out there? You've been on the run for a while now."

"She's in East Hampton, and that's too far out. I don't like being away from the action, and that's in Manhattan."

"Herbie, has it occurred to you yet that just being in Manhattan could get you killed?"

"Well, I guess that after all that's happened . . ."

"Exactly." Joan came into his office and handed him the envelope. Stone handed it to Herbie. "There's a thousand dollars in this envelope," he said. "Here's what I want you to do: go to Third Avenue and take a left; there's a cell phone store there, almost on the corner. Buy a throwaway, untraceable cell phone with a couple of hundred minutes on it and be sure to ask the clerk if it has a GPS chip in it; don't buy it if it does. Call Joan and give her the number, then get a cab to Penn Station and take the next train to East Hampton. Throw yourself on your aunt's mercy, and don't do anything to make her or her husband mad at you. Call Joan every morning at ten and let her know you're okay."

"Gee, East Hampton . . . I don't know, Stone."

"Herbie, the Hamptons are full of beautiful girls, *very rich* beautiful girls. Be nice to them, and they'll be nice to you."

Herbie brightened. "Good point, Stone. I'll need some clothes."

"Then sneak into your place and pack a bag, and get out of town. The D.A. is going to want you to testify to back up what's on the tape."

"In court?"

"That's where testifying gets done, Herbie. You've been to court; you know about that. And you're a lawyer, remember?"

"Oh, yeah."

"The courtroom experience will be good for you."

"What's this going to do to our civil suit, Stone?"

"If Dattila is convicted it will improve our chances of getting a judgment against him a lot."

Herbie managed a smile.

"But I've got to be able to get in touch with you on a moment's notice, so you keep that phone on you at all times, and don't use up all the minutes."

"Okay, Stone."

"Well, get going!"

Herbie shook hands and left the office.

Stone asked Joan to come in. When she had taken a chair he said, "I want you to take a vacation, sort of."

"What's a vacation sort of?" she asked.

"That's where we close the office, and you go somewhere nice, and you have all the office calls forwarded to your cell phone. You can reach me on my cell."

"Where should I go?"

"Jesus, I don't know. Isn't there somewhere in the country you'd like to be, besides behind that desk?"

"What's going on, Stone?"

Stone took a deep breath. "Devlin Daltry, or somebody who works for him, murdered Celia last night."

Joan turned white.

"Now don't faint on me."

She took a couple of deep breaths. "I'm okay. What happened?"

"He somehow tracked her down in New Jersey and, well, it wasn't pretty."

Joan put a hand to her mouth. "Her head. That's what he did, didn't he? Like the sculpture."

Stone nodded. "You don't want more details, believe me."

"So, I'm running from Devlin Daltry?"

"I think anybody connected with me might have problems."

"When can I go?"

"Why aren't you already gone?"

She got up and headed for her office. "Herbie's going to call you every day, so we'll know he's alive!" he shouted after her. "I think."

Joan had her bag and was letting herself out the front door. "Bye!" She waved and was gone.

Stone ran to the front door and checked the block while she got into a cab. He waved her off, then he went inside and up to his bedroom. He opened the safe in his dressing room and took out his favorite little .45 and a holster.

He would be going armed for the duration.

S tone left the house by the rear door and walked into Turtle Bay Gardens, the common area behind all the Turtle Bay houses. The paths were lighted, so finding his way in the dark was not a problem. He walked across the garden and used his garden key to open the door leading to Second Avenue. He looked both ways for a full minute, then stepped out into the street and hailed a cab.

Fifteen minutes later he was seated at Elaine's with a Knob Creek on the rocks before him, and Dino was working his way toward him from the front door, table by table, greeting acquaintances. Finally he plopped himself down and accepted a Scotch from a waiter.

"So, how was your day?" Dino asked.

"I hardly know where to begin," Stone said.

"Just begin, and don't be a pain in the ass."

"Okay, Herbie's off the hook for Cheech's murder; they've arrested his buddy, Gus, whose fingerprints are on the knife. Herbie's gone to his aunt's in East Hampton, I hope to God."

"And?"

"And Joan's on vacation, sort of, to keep Devlin Daltry from killing her."

"And?"

"And that's about it."

"That's funny, you seem to be forgetting the part about why Devlin Daltry might want to kill Joan."

"Oh, that."

"I know it's probably of little consequence to you, but when a beautiful woman gets her head cut off, I would have thought that that would have been the first thing on your mind. Charley Sample called me."

"Oh, and Dierdre Monahan almost got me into bed, but I was saved by the D.A., the Old Man himself."

"See? You did it again?"

"I don't want to even think about it," Stone said, taking a large pull on his bourbon.

"Stone, if you don't talk about it, get it off your chest, you're gonna have nightmares for a year."

"Do I have to?"

"It's for your own good, pal."

"Dino, I want to hunt down Devlin Daltry and kill him slow, to quote Carmine Dattila."

"I know you do."

"I mean, I really, really want to do that. At lunch today, I was actually thinking about fucking Dierdre Monahan, after she asked me. I was desperate for something to think about besides Celia sitting in that porch chair without a head."

"Well, fucking Dierdre Monahan is something you've done before, and when in your right mind, something you'd do again in a heartbeat, right?"

"Well, sure, I guess so, but how could I think about that when I was fucking Celia only a couple of days ago? I must be a terrible excuse for a human being."

"Stone, nothing is more human than sex, expecially with women as beautiful as Celia and Dierdre. Thinking about sex with either of them is a great defense against having to think about Celia with no head." Dino mopped his brow. "Jesus, I want to kill Daltry myself. Maybe if we go down to his studio he'll give us an excuse."

"I'd love to do that, I really would," Stone said.

"Yeah, but it's my job *not* to do that, and not to let you do it, either."

"I know."

Stone looked up to see Dierdre Monahan coming through the front door. She gave him a little wave, then stopped and said something to Gianni, the headwaiter, who picked up a remote control and changed the TV channel to New York 1, a 24/7 local news channel, then cranked up the volume.

Dierdre came over and sat down. "Well, hi, guys," she said. "Who does a girl have to fuck to get a drink around here?"

Stone waved at Gianni, who came over and took an order for a cosmo. Dierdra was still wearing the dress she'd worn at lunch, Stone was pleased to see. He stopped thinking about Celia.

"How was your limo ride back to work?" he asked.

"The Old Man was really sweet, wasn't he? Either that, or he figured out what you and I were about to do and saved me from a fate worse than death."

"Probably that one," Stone said.

"Stone and I were having lunch, Dino, and . . ."

"He already told me," Dino replied.

"Oh, oh, here we go," Dierdre said, pointing at the TV. "Listen up."

Dierdre's face popped onto the screen, over a copse of microphones. "The district attorney's office is pleased to announce that we have indicted and arrested Carmine Dattila on multiple charges of murder, attempted murder, extortion, abetting prostitution and abetting gambling." TV Dierdre went on, but the real Dierdre was yelling at Gianni to change the channel back. She turned back to Stone. "I just wanted you to see that, so you'll know I'm not lying."

"Well, that's great, Dierdre," Stone said. "All this because of Herbie's little tape?"

"Herbie's little tape and the fact that Gus Castiglione rolled over this afternoon."

"You're kidding!"

"Nope. Turns out Cheech was his younger brother, and he was feeling just terrible about stabbing him repeatedly with a butcher knife. We had to get the poor thing a priest, and when that was done, he spilled his guts into a VCR and gave us names, dates, places and anything else we wanted. Believe me, this time Dattila is *nailed*."

"If you can keep Gus alive," Dino pointed out.

"And Herbie, too," Stone mentioned.

"Gus is already in the safest house you ever saw, but that reminds me, where's Herbie? We've got to put him on ice."

"My best guess is he's in East Hampton at an aunt's house or, more likely, at the first singles' bar he could find."

"What's the aunt's name?"

"I don't know. She's married to a very successful plumber, though, if that helps."

"Let's see, this means that the aunt is Bob Cantor's sister?"

"Very possibly."

Dierdre dug a cell phone out of her purse and pressed a speed-dial number. "Hank? Get hold of Bob Cantor. Young Herbie is at Cantor's sister's house in East Hampton. Get the address from Cantor, find Herbie and ice him down good; I've already got the material witness warrant. The office will give you a copy. Right, see ya." She put away the phone.

"It may not be as easy as that," Stone said, "given my experience with Herbie, but it's a start."

She leaned into his ear and whispered, "After you've bought me a huge steak, we're going back to your place, and I'm going to do to you everything you always dreamed about—every orifice, every position, as many times as you're good for, kiddo."

"Is a porterhouse big enough?"

"Why, Stone, I've never heard you call your dick a porterhouse, but I like the reference."

Stone waved for a waiter.

45

They were sipping double espressos over the remains of the porterhouse and the cognacs that Elaine had sent over. Stone spoke up. "Before you and I leave here I have to offer a disclaimer."

"Offer away," Dierdre said, sipping her cognac.

"Being in any way associated with me, at the moment, may be dangerous to your health. That's why I didn't call you after lunch."

"Why, Stone, don't tell me you've contracted a social disease."

Dino broke in. "You'd better pay attention, Dierdre."

"All right, be specific," she said.

"A client of mine who had been hiding from a jealous boyfriend was killed last night."

"The boyfriend was jealous of you?"

"Not just me, everybody. He's nuts. His name is Devlin Daltry."

"The sculptor?"

"Jesus, why is it that everybody knows about this guy, and I'd never heard of him until a couple of weeks ago?"

"He's a very well-known artist," Dierdre said.

"I am the son of two well-known artists," Stone said, "and I have more than a passing interest in the arts, but somehow Devlin Daltry had escaped my notice until he started trying to kill me."

"I thought it was your client he killed."

"It was, but he ran me down with a car on Third Avenue last week. My body has many bruises, and this . . ." He held up his left hand to display the blue plastic cast. ". . . is a result of that incident."

"My goodness, that's a cast? And I thought it was a sex toy!"

"My point is, Dierdre, that this guy has been known to follow me around, and if he spots us together, you may very well be in danger."

"I can handle myself," Dierdre said.

"Are you packing?"

"Always. How did he kill your client?"

"After cutting the throat of the woman she was staying with in New Jersey, he decapitated my client. And she was the kind of woman who could take care of herself, too. She was six feet, three inches tall and no shrinking violet."

"Was she packing?"

"She was. I loaned her one of my own weapons."

Dierdre regarded him calmly. "I'd rather it were a social disease than a crazed killer," she said, "but if he messes with me, I'll shoot him, and as soon as I'm sure he's dead, I'll arrest him and prosecute him. Are the police looking for him?"

"They found him shortly after the killing at an art gallery opening in SoHo; witnesses put him there when the killing took place."

"So he hired somebody?"

"Apparently."

Dino spoke up. "It's gotta be tough to hire somebody to cut off the head of a six-foot, three-inch woman with a gun."

"Yeah, and a doctor on the scene said that the killer did it in a fit of rage," Stone pointed out. "Professional killers don't do rage."

"Now that you mention it," Dierdre said, "I've never heard of rage in the case of a pro who was prosecuted. Those guys just walk up to you, put two in your head and walk away. Cold is their trademark."

"Give us the benefit of your experience, Dierdre," Dino said. "What does it mean when a guy kills by proxy and there's rage involved?"

"Well, Daltry has to be enraged in order to go far enough to arrange her death."

"Yeah, but what about the hiree?"

"I suppose he could have hired a crazy person to do it, somebody who hates women, maybe."

"He hired somebody to run me down, too," Stone said. "He had another airtight alibi."

"An enraged serial killer using a surrogate?" Dierdre asked.

"Seems unlikely, doesn't it?" Dino said. "Serials may be enraged, but they do their own killing."

"Dino," Dierdre said, "go to the men's room and take your time."

"Okay," Dino replied. He got up and walked away.

Dierdre leaned into Stone. "Okay, I've heard your disclaimer, and I still want you. I have a disclaimer, too."

"Okay, shoot."

"This isn't love, it's sex. When I get horny, I do something about it, and I'm not talking about using my hand."

"Okay."

"I'm not going to cling to you, stalk you or make your life miserable. All I want from this relationship is an occasional drink or steak and a spectacular roll in the hay. We clear on that?"

"Perfectly clear."

"Then let's get out of here." She stood up and started for the door.

Stone was right behind her. "Dino will get the check," he said to Gianni. He kissed Elaine on the cheek as he passed her, and by the time he got outside, she was in a cab with the door open, waiting. Stone took a second to check out the block, then he got in.

"Anybody following us?" she asked, as they drove down Second Avenue.

"We seem to be alone," Stone replied.

Dierdre undressed him slowly, kissing him here and there, then she shucked off her own clothes, revealing a body that had everything her dress had promised. She ran her fingers over his bruises. "That's the worst bruising I've ever seen on anybody who wasn't a corpse," she said. "Poor baby." She pushed him back onto the bed and began kissing him more purposefully.

Stone was delighted to find that he couldn't think of anything but what was happening at that moment. He was tumescent and oblivious.

Dierdre helped with that, bringing him to full attention with her lips and tongue. "God, I love porterhouse," she said.

Stone could make noises, but he couldn't form words. He put his hands under her ass and lifted her onto him. She supplied the only lubrication necessary.

By the time they allowed themselves to fall asleep, Dierdre had kept every word of the promise she had made at the dinner table.

In the middle of the night, Stone got up to go to the john, and on the way back he walked to the front windows and looked down into the street. A black sedan sat, idling, a couple of doors up the block. The reflection from a street lamp on the windshield made it impossible to see who was inside.

"Stoooone," Dierdre cooed from the bed.

"Coming," he said, returning to her.

"Soon," she said, holding the sheet back for him.

He settled into her as if she were a bear rug, and they started all over again.

After daybreak, he checked the street again. The black sedan was gone.

46

S tone sat in his office, his cheek pressed against the smooth, walnut desktop, snoring slightly. A voice came from afar.

"Rough night, huh?"

"Mmmmff," he replied.

The voice came close to his ear. "Here's coffee, very strong."

"Blllfff," he replied.

"Wake up!" Joan shouted.

Stone sat straight up, blinking. Joan nudged the steaming cup of coffee closer.

"Either drink this and start making money, or go upstairs and go back to bed. You're no good to me asleep at your desk," she said.

"Right," Stone said. He picked up the coffee cup and sipped it, burning his tongue. Down the hall the doorbell rang, the outside office door.

"I'm awake," he said.

"We'll see. Drink more coffee."

Stone blew on it and sipped again. "I swear I'm awake. See who's at the door."

Joan sauntered down the hall toward the outside door. She was back in a flash. "Call Dino," she said.

"Why?"

"There's a box on the doorstep and nobody outside."

"What kind of box?"

"Pretty big box," she said, holding out her arms to indicate the size. "No return address or shipping form that I can see. Looks like it was hand delivered."

Stone picked up the phone and pressed a speed-dial button.

"Bacchetti."

"Good morning."

"Good morning, rough night?"

"Why do you ask?"

"Everything I heard from you and Dierdre last night leads me to believe that you both had a rough night. Or was that just a lot of talk?"

"Rough night," Stone said, "but maybe not as rough as this morning."

"Clear that up for me," Dino replied.

"There's a box on my doorstep, no return address or shipping label, probably hand delivered."

"How big?"

"Bigger than a bread box."

"Don't touch it."

"You think you have to tell me that?"

"I'll get our people over there pronto."

"If it goes up in the street, people could get hurt."

"I'll tell them to finish their doughnuts quickly."

"Thank you."

"And you and Joan go upstairs."

"Okay."

"Right now."

"All right!" He hung up. "We're going upstairs," he said to Joan, but she was already headed that way. Then, as he started up the stairs, he had an awful thought.

Dino sat with them, sipping his coffee. Nobody was saying much. "You don't think it's a bomb, do you?" he asked.

"Probably not," Stone replied. "I think murder by car or hunting knife is more his style."

A heavily equipped cop appeared in the doorway. "It's not a bomb," he said.

"Dino," Stone said, "I think you'd better get a forensics team over here."

"What's in the box?" Dino asked the man.

"An aluminum case," the man said, "the kind you carry camera equipment in."

"How do you know it doesn't contain a bomb?"

"I X-rayed it, then I opened it."

"What did the case contain?"

"I think you'd better get a forensics team over here," the cop said, then he left the room.

Dino opened his cell phone and pressed a button. "This is Bacchetti; it's not a bomb. I want a forensics team and the medical examiner over here pronto." He closed the phone. "You want to go see it?"

"I've already seen it," Stone said. "I liked it where it was before."

They all got up and went downstairs. The bomb squad had moved the box and the aluminum case into Stone's office hall-way. The cop stood in the door. "I don't think we're needed here anymore. Good luck." He closed the door, and a moment later, the squad's truck pulled away from its position in front of a fire plug.

The three of them stood and gazed at the aluminum case.

"There's got to be fingerprints on that, right?" Joan asked.

"I wouldn't count on it," Stone said. "I wouldn't expect fibers or DNA, either."

Dino shook his head. "Right. At least, no DNA that would be of any use to us."

"I need a drink," Joan said.

"It's eleven thirty in the morning," Stone pointed out.

"If I don't have a drink, I'll faint," she said.

"You know where the bar is."

Joan disappeared upstairs.

"Funny thing is, I feel pretty much the same way," Stone said.

"Me, too," Dino echoed.

"I'm not going to have one, though."

"Me, neither."

"And I'm not going to faint."

"Me, neither."

"I may throw up, though," Stone added.

"It's your rug."

Stone sat down in one of the waiting-room chairs and put his head between his legs.

A moment later, the doorbell rang, and Dino went to answer it. He came back with four people wearing latex gloves.

"This it?" a man in a green lab coat asked.

"Yeah. You other guys start with the box outside."

"You stay," the M.E. said to the one who had cameras.

"Don't touch the case any more than you have to," Dino said.

"No kidding?" the M.E. said sarcastically.

"Sorry."

The M.E. took out a pocket dictator and switched it on. He knelt beside the aluminum case and used a tape measure. "The object is inside an aluminum camera case with the trade name Halliburton affixed to it." He recited the measurements of the container, then he flipped open the securing catches and opened the case. A small cloud of some sort was released.

He continued to dictate. "The case contains the human head of a female Caucasian; the hair is dark brown. The head is frozen and is packed in dry ice." There was a rattling noise. "On lifting the head from the case I observe that it is wearing cosmetic makeup and the hair is neatly coiffed." There was the rattling noise again. "I am returning the head to the case and closing it," he said, snapping the case shut.

The M.E. stood up. "As soon as they've processed the exterior of the case I'll take it to the morgue, and we'll try to get a cause of death for you."

"I think you'll find," Stone said, "that the cause of death is exsanguination as the result of a severed carotid artery and jugular vein, and that the implement used was a large, partly serrated hunting knife wielded by an enraged male unsub."

"That's pretty good," the M.E. said.

"I'm quoting another doctor," Stone replied. "The rest of her is in the custody of the M.E. of Morris County, New Jersey. The detective in charge is Lieutenant Charles Sample of Morristown."

A tech came in and went to work on the aluminum case.

"Come on," Dino said to Stone, "I'll buy you some lunch."

Stone stood up. "I'll watch you eat," he said.

47

S tone sat at a table in the back room of P. J. Clarke's and
watched Dino devour a steak. His own lunch was a single
beer, which he sipped occasionally. "I don't know how you
can eat that," he said.

Dino carved a chunk off the steak and stuffed it in his mouth.
"Why? It's a decent piece of meat. Not as good as the strip steak
they used to serve, though; I don't know why they took that off
the menu."

"I'm not talking about the quality of the steak."

"Oh, come on, Stone. You and I have attended a passel of corpses
and autopsies over the years; what's the big deal with a head in
a box?"

"I knew her, that's the big deal. You knew her, too."

"You're like most people, I guess: You confuse the remains with
the person. A corpse—or part of a corpse—is a shell, a husk that
once contained a human being. It deserves respect but not senti-
mentality."

"You're getting awfully philosophical in your old age," Stone said.

"That's always been my philosophy. Haven't we talked about
this before?"

"No."

"I'm sorry it took so long; you need this information."

"Now that I have it I don't feel any better."

"That's because you haven't eaten anything. Have a bacon cheeseburger; that always improves your morale." Dino waved at a waiter. "Bring my friend a bacon cheeseburger, medium, and tell the chef if it arrives well done I'll take it back there and make *him* eat it; I don't care about his product liability policy." The waiter left. "Have you noticed that you can't get a burger anything but well done these days? It's not like Clarke's ever gave anybody food poisoning. Drives me nuts." He waved at the waiter again. "Bring him some fries, too; he needs the grease."

"I had a thought," Stone said.

"Well, that's an improvement."

"I thought I might go and see Eduardo." Eduardo Bianco was Dino's former father-in-law, before his divorce from Eduardo's daughter, Mary Ann. Although a distinguished elder statesman of the city, he retained discreet connections to his Mafia past.

"Why? You want somebody capped?" Dino chuckled.

Stone said nothing.

Dino looked more serious. "Oh, I get it: You want to get Eduardo to get somebody to get somebody else to knock off Devlin Daltry, right?"

"It crossed my mind."

"Would that solve all your problems?"

"Pretty much."

"That would never work, Stone."

"Why not?"

"Because you have a conscience, and you take lawyering seriously. You believe in the system, and you won't violate that."

"I've violated it before; so have you."

"My ethical system is based on something older than the law," Dino said, "and besides, maybe I've done some things, but all you did was watch and keep your mouth shut."

"That's abetting, isn't it?"

"Sure. You're not above abetting if you don't have to get your hands dirty. That's why you want Eduardo to get somebody to get somebody else to whack Daltry, instead of doing it yourself. Of course, you'd be just as legally guilty and as morally reprehensible if you did that, instead of actually doing it yourself."

"I guess." The bacon cheeseburger arrived, and Stone took a big bite and chewed thoughtfully.

Dino inspected the burger and found it properly cooked. "Look, if you really want him dead, it would be a lot more fun to do it yourself."

Stone swallowed and took a sip of his beer. "I grant you that, but there's always the messy part about getting caught and arrested and tried and imprisoned and spending the rest of my life appealing a death sentence. It's funny, but Celia told me once that she wanted Daltry dead, and I lectured her about the personal dangers involved in doing that, and now here I am giving myself the same lecture, instead of throwing caution to the wind and hunting the guy down and blowing his head off."

"Well, if that's what you want to do," Dino said, "I'd advise against throwing caution to the wind."

"You mean I should plan the perfect murder?"

"It doesn't have to be perfect," Dino pointed out, "at least, not if you do it in my precinct. A friend on the force is better than a perfect plan. You know, witness statements get changed, evidence gets lost. Like that."

"You'd do that for me?"

"Sure. I'd even work the case myself, to make sure it gets done right."

"And risk your career?"

"I don't care about promotion, and, thanks to my divorce settlement, I don't need my pension anymore."

"The pension comes in handy, believe me. There are times when I would have gone belly up without mine." Stone, having been involuntarily retired from the NYPD for medical reasons after taking a bullet in the knee, got seventy-five percent of his detective's salary, tax free.

Dino shrugged. "I'll do whatever you want. What do you *really* want?"

Stone thought about that for a minute, while wolfing down half a dozen fries. "What I really want is to see him caught, convicted and imprisoned forever."

"Then let's do that," Dino said. "You call Charley Sample and get him to call me and make a formal request for NYPD assistance. That'll give me an excuse to put some people on Daltry. We'll see what we come up with."

"I like that, Dino," Stone said, brightening.

"You know what the best possible thing would be?"

"What?"

"If you could get Daltry to make a serious pass at killing you. Then we could catch him in the act and send him up for ten-to-twenty while we keep working on Celia's death."

"You mean, like, if I just go stand in the street he might try to run me down again?"

"Yeah, like that. I don't think there's any doubt that Daltry would like to kill you; let's just give the guy a chance."

"And hope he misses?"

"Preferably. After all, we'd need you as a witness."

"Well, Dino, as appealing as your idea is, I have a better one."

"Stone, it's been a long, long time since you had a better idea than I did. Maybe never."

"How's this? Let's find out who the accomplice is, then we can bust him and turn him and fry Daltry."

Dino nodded. "Well, it's not a very original idea, but it has its points."

"It keeps me out of the traffic, for one."

"There is that."

"I've got an idea about how to go about it, too."

"I'm all ears."

"I'll bet Daltry already has another girlfriend. Get your people to find out who she is, then let's turn her."

Dino shook his head. "That's asking an amateur to do undercover work. It could blow up in your face, might even get her killed. I've got a better idea."

"What's that?"

"Let's get him a new girlfriend who's trained for the work." Dino smiled a secret smile. "You get Charley Sample to call me."

Stone got out his cell phone and made the call. "Charley? It's Stone. Give Dino a call, will you? He needs an official request for help with nailing Devlin Daltry." He hung up.

A moment later, Dino's cell phone rang. Dino flipped it open. "Why, Lieutenant Sample, how can the NYPD be of service today?"

S tone was back at his desk in time to catch a call.

"Herbert Fisher, Esquire, is on the phone," Joan said drily.

Stone didn't want to take the call, but he was curious as to Herbie's whereabouts. He punched the button. "Hello."

"Stone!"

"Where are you, Herbie?"

"I'm calling from the backseat of a police car, that's where I am."

"I didn't know they had phones in the backs of police cars these days. What'll they think of next?"

"No, no, they let me use my cell phone."

"That was very nice of them."

"Don't you get it, Stone? I've been arrested!"

Stone heard another voice from the car. "You haven't been arrested; you're in protective custody."

"You haven't been arrested, Herbie," Stone said. "You're in protective custody."

"What the hell does that mean? Am I in the witness protection program or something?"

"No, Herbie, it's just that the D.A. wants you to remain alive at least long enough for you to testify against Carmine Dattila."

"Testify against Carmine Dattila? Is the D.A. nuts?"

"Herbie, you have a lawsuit against Dattila, remember? That means you'll have to testify against him in civil court. What's the difference if you testify in criminal court, too? If he's convicted, it strengthens your lawsuit."

"So I have to sit in jail until he goes to trial?"

The other voice came again. "You're not going to jail; you'll be in a nice hotel room with a big TV and room service."

"Wouldn't you like a nice hotel with a big TV and room service, Herbie?" Stone asked.

"Well, sure, but I'd like to get laid now and then."

"We don't provide that service," the other voice said. "You'll have to talk to a bellhop about that."

"Herbie," Stone said soothingly, "there's nothing you can't get sent to a hotel room. You can order Chinese or pizza; you can order a girl with her own donkey."

"Donkey? Why would she want a donkey?"

"Herbie, it's just an illustration of the wide world that's available to you from a hotel room. Tell you what, I'll call the D.A. and see if I can get you a suite."

"Well, that would be better," Herbie said, but he still sounded doubtful. "Can my girlfriend visit me?"

"Do you have a girlfriend, Herbie?"

"Not at the moment."

"Well, then, whether she can visit you is kind of a moot point, isn't it? You remember *moot,* from law school?"

"Uh, yeah, sure. What about my clothes?"

"I'm sure the nice policeman would be happy to stop by your apartment and let you pick up some essentials. My advice is, take lots of pajamas. Pajamas are good to wear when you're swanning around a hotel suite."

"Sort of like Hef, huh?"

"Exactly like Hef, Herbie. Look at it this way: You'll be safe, you'll be comfortable and you can have anything you want to eat, and the D.A. pays the bills. All that and cable with pay-per-view movies."

"Will the D.A. pay for the movies, too?"

"Just charge it to the room, Herbie. And when you're all settled in, you might give me a call and let me know what hotel you're in."

"Okay."

"But Herbie, it's very, very important that you don't tell anyone else but me what hotel you're in. You see that, don't you?"

"Yeah, okay."

"Enjoy, Herbie." Stone hung up and called Dierdre Monahan. "Dierdre, your men have located Herbie Fisher."

"I heard, Stone; they work for me, remember?"

"Of course. Listen, kiddo, the boy is going to need a suite."

"A *suite*? Are you kidding me? We're not springing for a suite."

"Dierdre, the kind of hotel you stash witnesses in doesn't charge much more for a suite than for a room, and you're going to have to have a couple of cops on duty there, and they'll want someplace to hang out. You don't want to trap them in one room with Herbie Fisher; they'll blow their brains out."

She was silent for a moment. "You have a point there."

"And I'm sure the D.A.'s office can get a really good rate from the hotel."

"I guess."

"And Dierdre, don't take the kid's cell phone away from him. It's a throwaway and untraceable, so Dattila can't find him that way."

"I got Dattila held without bail," she said.

Stone could hear her grinning. "That's great, kiddo!"

"When are we going to, you know, again?"

"Whenever you say; just call."

"Will do."

"And be nice to my client."

"Yeah, yeah, yeah." She hung up.

Joan buzzed him. "I've got Bob Cantor holding on two."

Stone pressed the button. "Bob? What's up?"

"I got good news and bad news," Cantor said.

"Bad news first, please."

"Bernie Finger has put the penthouse on the market."

"That is bad news," Stone agreed. "You think he's really going to give up the girlfriend and go back to his wife?"

"You haven't heard the good news. The girlfriend is shopping for a new apartment with the same agent who's listing the penthouse."

"Well, I guess she's got to live somewhere. How is that good news?"

"She's looking at apartments she could never afford, that's how. Bernie can afford them, though."

"That *is* good news. Keep on her, okay?"

"Oh, yeah." Cantor hung up.

Stone toyed with the idea of calling Mrs. Finger and telling her about the masseuse's search for shelter. No, he thought, not yet; not while Bernie is still being sweet to her. Wait until the girl finds a place and moves in; then Bernie will suddenly start working nights again. Stone would be patient.

49

Dino walked through the detectives' squad room at the 19th Precinct, tapped one of his people on the shoulder and motioned toward his office. He settled behind his desk and watched the new detective walk toward him.

"Have a seat," he said. "How tall are you?"

"Six foot, two, Boss."

"How long you had the gold shield?"

"Three weeks, Boss."

"You don't have to call me 'Boss' all the time, just sometimes. Try Dino."

"Three weeks, Dino."

"How would you like to do a little undercover work?"

The detective's eyes brightened. "I'd love it, Boss. Uh, Dino."

"You know why I picked you for this assignment?"

The detective looked thoughtful for a moment. "Does it have something to do with how tall I am?"

"That, and how beautiful you are," Dino said. "And I don't mean that in a sexual harrassment way. What's your first name, Detective?"

"Willa."

"As in Willa she or won'ta she?"

"Gee, I hadn't heard that one before, Dino. Uh, Boss. What kind of undercover are we talking about?"

"The dangerous kind."

"Goes with the territory, I guess."

"Let me explain, Willa. There's a corpse out in New Jersey, a very beautiful, six-foot, three-inch woman, and it has only recently been reunited with its head. It's very likely that she was murdered by someone sent by a man named Devlin Daltry."

"The sculptor?"

"If you've heard of the guy you're a lot more artsy-fartsy than I am. Yeah, the sculptor. The guy has a history of obsessing over women, stalking them and doing violence to other men who are interested in them. He's not a very big guy, but he seems to have a thing for tall women who are also beautiful."

"I get the picture," Willa said.

"I want you to study up on him, then place yourself in his way and see what happens."

Willa straightened her skirt and looked uncomfortable. "Do I have to fuck him?"

"Of course not. Do you think I would order a detective to fuck somebody in the line of duty?"

She thought about it for a moment. "I guess not."

"That would be very unprofessional, even if it was a good idea in the context of the thing."

"Are you saying, unofficially, that it might be a good idea for me to fuck him?"

"Are you wearing a wire or something?"

"No, Boss."

"That sounds like the kind of question somebody who was wearing a wire would ask."

"I'm not. You want to search me?"

"We're not going there, Detective. All I'm saying is that you have a certain amount of personal discretion in how you handle this. Suffice it to say, if you're ever asked in court whether you fucked him, the answer had better be an emphatic no. Never mind what Daltry says."

"I think I get the picture."

"Good. Just remember that I ordered you never to fuck him."

"You did? I missed that."

"Well, I'm ordering you now, just in case you're ever asked about that in court."

"Got it."

"You're going to need to wear a wire."

"All right."

"The new equipment is very good: hard to detect and it works like a charm."

"I'm glad to hear it."

"You can actually wear the microphone in your hair, in a whatayacallit."

"A barrette?"

"Yeah, that. Or even glued to your scalp, under your hair."

"So, even if I took all my clothes off, I would still be wired?"

"That's an extreme example, but yes."

"What is it we want to learn about Daltry? Whether he had the woman killed?"

"Somehow I don't think he's going to confess to you. What we want to know is who he got to do it. The guy cut off this woman's head in a fit of rage, and that doesn't square with a hired pro. Maybe it's somebody who's Daltry's friend, or something. We're looking for suspects so we can work their alibis and see who was available to run out to New Jersey and commit this heinous act."

"How soon do I start?"

"Just as soon as you've researched Daltry."

"I can do that in a few minutes, on the Internet."

"Okay, this evening, then."

"What am I going to have for backup?"

"I'm putting four detectives on this. Who's your partner? I forget."

"Bernstein."

"And what's your last name again?"

"Bernstein."

"You're not married to your partner, are you?"

"Nope. No relation."

"Okay, Bernstein and four other detectives."

"Do I get to choose?"

"I get to choose."

"Who do you choose, Boss?"

"You get started on the Internet thing, and I'll see who doesn't have enough work to do."

"Can I make a request?"

"Maybe."

"Can I have another woman as one of the four?"

"Why?"

"Because I think a woman who was listening to me on a wire might understand better what I'm thinking than a bunch of guys. She could also cover me in, say, a bar without attracting attention. Cops have a way of looking like cops."

"You've got a point. Okay, pick one of the other women in the squad."

"Shelly Pointer."

"Okay, you've got Pointer; you can have her partner, too. Go tell her."

"Thanks, Boss." Detective Willa Bernstein got up and left.

S he found Detective Shelly Pointer in the ladies' room. Pointer was an attractive, cafe-au-lait black woman of average height with a better-than-average body. "Hey, Shelly."

"Hey, Willa."

"You and I have got an assignment."

"What, together?"

"Yeah."

"What about my partner?"

"He's on it, too."

"What's the assignment?"

"You ever heard of Devlin Daltry?"

"The sculptor?"

"Right."

"Sure."

"He's suspected of persuading somebody to cut off a girl's head. Bacchetti wants me to find out who he got to do it."

"Do you have to fuck him?"

"I don't think Bacchetti cares one way or the other, but if I do, I'm supposed to deny it. I'll be wearing a wire, and I want you on the other end of it, not just a bunch of guys."

"When do we start?"

"Right now. Let's get on the Internet and see what we can find out about Daltry."

"Lead the way."

The two women headed toward Willa's desk and her computer.

"Willa," Pointer said, "are you going to fuck him?"

"Shelly, I don't even know if he's nice yet."

50

G us Castiglione sat quietly in his cell on Rikers Island, reading the *Daily News* sports section. A bell rang, and there was the sound of a hundred cells being electronically unlocked. What surprised Gus was that his cell door opened as well.

He had been in protective custody since arriving at Rikers, and his meals had been brought to him. He got an hour's exercise daily in an empty yard, and he showered alone daily while a guard watched. He sat and stared at the open cell door, uncertain what to do.

A guard walked by. "Get your ass to lunch, Castiglione," he said as he passed.

"But . . ." Gus started to say.

The guard banged his nightstick on the bars. "I said, get your ass to lunch!"

Gus sighed, folded his newspaper, tossed it on his bunk and joined the line of prisoners shuffling past his cell. It would make a nice change, having somebody to talk to over a meal. The line stopped moving while the barred door that led to the dining hall was opened. Gus heard a slight commotion behind him and started to turn to see what was happening. Before he could move he felt a searing pain in his back, near his spine. He managed to make half a turn, and he saw a small, wiry man he knew holding a bloody homemade shiv.

238 | STUART WOODS

"Skinny?" he managed to say, before the man shoved the knife into his chest. His legs turned to water, and he hit the floor hard. Something warm and wet flowed past his cheek on the concrete floor. It got very noisy, then the sound went away.

D ierdre Monahan was in the chief deputy D.A.'s office when his phone rang and he picked it up. "It's for you," he said, handing her the receiver.

"Monahan," she said. She listened to what the voice on the other end of the line was saying, and she felt herself turning white. She asked some questions, then hung up.

"Dierdre," her boss said, "you look weird. You're not going to faint, are you?"

"I hope not."

"What's wrong?"

"Gus Castiglione is dead."

"What?"

"He got knifed at Rikers."

"Didn't you put him into protective custody?"

"Yes, but for some reason his cell opened at lunch call, and he went to the dining hall, or at least he started out for the dining hall. Somebody put a shiv into him twice. They've got a suspect, a little rat named Skinny diSalvo, who's awaiting trial on a gambling charge, but, of course, nobody saw anything."

"I want an investigation of how that cell door got opened," the chief said.

"Somebody got bought," Dierdre replied, "and I don't think we're going to find out who."

"You've still got that other witness, what's his name?"

"Fisher, Herbert Fisher."

"Is he in Rikers?"

"No, I've got him in a safe house, a hotel."

"You'd better make sure nothing happens to him."

"Right," she said. "I have to go make some calls."

Herbie had been in the hotel for nearly a whole day, now, and he didn't like it. The bed was hard, the food from room service was lousy, the TV in the bedroom was too small, and the two cops who were always with him hogged the bigger one in the sitting room.

One of the cops opened the door. "You okay, Herbie?"

"Yeah, I'm okay. I'm gonna take a shower."

"Good idea," the cop said. "I was gonna mention it to you."

Herbie got out of his pajamas, went into the bathroom and turned on the shower. Then he started getting dressed.

There was a knock on the sitting room door, and the two cops looked at each other. "Yeah?" one of them yelled.

"Room service," a muffled voice said from the other side of the door.

"Jesus, is that kid eating again? It's only been an hour since the cheeseburger." He got to his feet and went to the door. As he turned the knob, somebody kicked it wide open, and something hit him in the chest. There had been no sound. He tried to yell to his partner, but somebody was stepping over him. He heard his partner yell, "Oh, shit!" followed by a tiny *pfffft*.

The man with the silenced semiautomatic pistol put one extra shot into the head of each cop, then he moved quietly to the door to the bedroom. He put his ear to the door and listened: The TV was playing, sounded like a soap opera. He pushed the door open and stepped into the room, the gun held out before him. Nobody in sight. Then he heard the shower running.

He walked quickly to the bathroom door, which was ajar, allowing steam from the shower to escape. He pushed the door open and stepped inside. There was so much fog, it was difficult to see, but after a moment, he made out the shower curtain. He reached over with his left hand and snatched it open, ready to fire. Nobody. He checked behind the door. Still nobody. Where was the kid?

Herbie hadn't wanted his guards to see him dressed, so when he heard the cop yell, he ducked into the bedroom closet and watched as the man with the gun went into the bathroom. He didn't hesitate but ran into the living room, looking for the cops, who were both on the floor with holes in their heads. Once again, Herbie didn't hesitate. He went into the pockets of the cop lying by the door and found a roll of bills, then took the cop's gun and ran like a deer down the hallway to the fire stairs, then ran all eleven floors to the lobby. There was a cab waiting in front of the hotel, and he dived into it.

"Just drive," he said to the driver.

"That don't do it, pal," the driver replied. "Where you want to go?"

"Brooklyn. I'll give you directions."

Stone had left his office for the day and was in the basement exercise room, running on the treadmill, when the phone rang. He paused the treadmill and went to the phone on the wall.

"Stone Barrington."

"It's Dierdre."

Dierdre was horny, that was it. Okay, he had a couple of hours before he had to meet Dino at Elaine's. "Well, hi there," he said, panting from his exertion.

"Did I interrupt you in bed?"

"No, I was on the treadmill. You want to come over?"

"I'm not in the mood right now."

Stone was disappointed. "Whatever you say."

"That's not why I called."

"What's up?"

"Gus Castiglione got shivved at Rikers today; he's dead."

"Oh, no, there goes most of your case. I mean, Herbie can testify to the kidnapping and the murder threat, but it was Gus who could really have put Dattila away, wasn't it?"

"That isn't all the news," Dierdre said. "The two cops who were guarding Herbie at the hotel are both dead, small-caliber handgun, two each."

"Oh, shit," Stone said, dreading what might come next.

"One of the cops' guns and the expense money in his pocket are missing."

"And Herbie?"

"Herbie's missing, too."

51

S tone sat at Elaine's, staring into his bourbon.

Dino sat down. "All right, what fresh disaster has visited you now?"

"A cascade of them," Stone said. "First of all, Gus Castiglione got shivved at Rikers while on his way to the dining hall. You probably heard about that."

"No. Although the NYPD's grasp of technology is improving, I don't yet get a daily e-mail about who got shivved at Rikers on his way to the dining hall. What else?"

"The two cops guarding Herbie at a hotel got capped, and Herbie's missing."

"All right, let's start with Gus. I thought the D.A. had him on ice. What's he doing going to the dining hall?"

"Nobody knows. He was supposed to eat in his cell, but the door was unlocked with all the rest, and he started for the dining hall."

"That means Dattila has somebody inside who could work that."

"Right."

"With regard to Herbie, I thought he was in a safe hotel."

"So did everybody else."

"That means Dattila has somebody in the D.A.'s office, too. Jesus, New York law enforcement is turning into a sieve. You think Herbie's dead?"

"Probably not. Why would they kidnap him again? Who would spend ten minutes with him who didn't have to? Dattila's already on tape saying he wants Herbie dead, so the hit man was obviously sent there to shoot him. Also, some expense money was missing from one of the cops' pockets, and his gun was gone, too. That doesn't sound like a pro."

"So Herbie's on the loose with some cash, and he's armed. Has Bob Cantor heard from him?"

"Nope."

"And Herbie hasn't called you, either?"

"Nope. I don't know if he even got out of the hotel with his cell phone. We had an arrangement where he'd call in every day. I hope he sticks to it."

"Herbie has more lives than any three cats I know," Dino said.

"Yeah. Gus's death is a big blow, though. I thought Dierdre would send Dattila up for life, and that would bolster Herbie's civil suit. Even if Herbie lives to testify, he can only nail Dattila for kidnapping and attempted murder."

"Dattila's what, fifty? He might get enough time to keep him in the rest of his life."

"I'm not counting on it, and if he gets Herbie, he won't do any time at all. Any news on Devlin Daltry?"

"I've got six people on it, including a knockout blonde detective who's six-feet-one."

"That's encouraging, and I need encouraging."

"I'm expecting to hear more tonight," Dino said.

Detective Willa Bernstein parked her Camaro Z80 across from the Art Scene Gallery. Detective Shelly Pointer, who was in the passenger seat, leaned forward and looked into the gallery. "You think Daltry is in there?"

"A magazine interview I dug up on the Internet said that he

loves other artists' openings, and he goes to all the big ones. This one—a painter named Jason Griggs—is tonight's big one. Why don't we go and find out?"

"Okay."

"Don't go in together," a voice in Willa's ear said.

"Thanks, we figured that out," she replied. All five detectives could hear her and talk to her on the new equipment. "Shelly's going in first to case; I'll wait to hear from her." She nodded at Shelly, who got out of the car, crossed the street and went into the gallery.

Willa took deep breaths to calm herself. Two minutes later, Shelly spoke into her ear. "Bingo," she said.

"On my way." Willa got out of the car and crossed the street. She could see her partner's car ahead of her, and she knew the other car was behind. She walked into the gallery, stopped and looked around. She didn't see Daltry, so she walked to the bar, where a lot of glasses of wine were arrayed, and picked up some white. Then she saw Daltry, standing in a group near a huge painting. She sidled over and stood, staring at the big oil, but nothing happened. From the corner of her eye she could see Daltry still talking with the group.

Willa walked around the knot of people gathered around Daltry and stopped before the next painting, careful not to look at him. She took a sip of the wine and winced.

"Was that expression for the wine or the painting?" a voice asked.

She turned a little to her right and found Daltry at her elbow; he came up to about her collarbone. "Both," she said. "The painting is not so hot, and the wine is even worse."

"Jason has never deserved his reputation, and the wine, well, my guess is it's made in a basement somewhere in Queens."

Willa laughed. "The painting could have been made there, too."

This time Daltry laughed. "Have you seen the rest of the show?"

"No, I just got here."

"Let's take a quick walk through," Daltry said. "By the way, I'm Devlin Daltry. Who are you?"

"I'm Willa Bernstein. Are you the sculptor?"

"Yes."

"I saw your show at the Modern last year." She hadn't, but she'd found that on the Internet, too. "I thought it was brilliant."

"Thank you. I wish you were an art critic." He walked her slowly around the room, not stopping.

"Well, that's that," Willa said. "No reason to spend another minute here."

"Would you like to go somewhere else?"

She nodded. "Somewhere where they have Scotch, instead of this wine, and food, instead of cardboard canapes."

"There's a favorite place of mine just down the street," Daltry said. "Shall we?"

"We shall," she said, taking his arm.

They walked past Shelly on the way out. The moment they hit the sidewalk, she heard her partner, Bernstein, say into her ear, "Good girl."

"You a fast worker, bitch," Shelly said, in a bit of self-caricature.

Willa laughed out loud, in spite of herself.

"What's so funny?" Daltry asked.

"I was just thinking," Willa replied. "Isn't it strange how a semi-talented painter like Jason Griggs can get rich, selling poor work?"

"And a semitalented sculptor like me, as well?"

"You are *extremely* talented, and your work has substance and beauty." She smiled slyly at him. "But I don't need to tell you that, do I?"

This time they both burst out laughing.

"You got him hooked, baby," Shelly said into her ear. "Now all you got to do is reel him in."

The couple walked on toward the restaurant.

52

S tone and Dino had just tucked into their pasta when Dino's cell phone rang. Dino flipped it open.

"Bacchetti."

"It's Bernstein, Lieutenant," a deep male voice said.

"Yeah? Which one?"

"The one with the balls."

"Willa? Is that you?"

"Very funny, Lieutenant."

"I thought so. What's happening?"

"It's going like a dream. I tell you, this girl is *good*."

"Details, please."

"Well, first of all, she did some research on the Internet and nailed where he would be tonight, at a gallery opening. Then she waltzed in there, and inside of five minutes, he's walking her around the gallery, disparaging the artwork. Now they're in a restaurant down the street, and she's in the process of wrapping him around her little finger."

"Good girl!"

"She sure is."

"You think she can handle him, then?"

"I think she could handle Osama bin Laden."

"The equipment working okay?"

"Like a dream; we can hear everything."

"And you're recording?"

"Every word."

"Okay, then, don't hang too close to her. Give her room to work, and keep me posted."

"Will do, Lieutenant."

Dino hung up. "Can I pick 'em, or what? She's already having dinner with Daltry."

"Wow."

"Wow, exactly," Dino said, but he was looking toward the door.

Stone followed his gaze to see two women who had just walked in. One of them was a tall, very beautiful woman in, maybe, her early thirties; the other was Eliza Larkin, M.D. Stone stood up and waved them over.

Eliza gave him a kiss. "Stone, Dino, this is my friend Genevieve James."

Everybody shook hands, and Stone seated them. Dino, he noticed, seemed stunned by Genevieve.

"I'm sorry," Eliza said, "We just wandered in for a drink. I know you and I are not supposed to meet while this thing with Daltry is going on."

"The snake," Genevieve said.

"It's okay, Eliza," Stone said. "As it happens, I know exactly where he is at this moment, and he won't be a concern. I am *very* glad to see you."

Dino leaned toward Genevieve. "And I'm *very* glad to see you."

"You're cute," she said, as a cosmopolitan was set before her. They clinked glasses. "How tall are you?" she asked.

"Not as tall as I look," Dino said.

She laughed. "You're not intimidated; that's good."

"I am not intimidated."

"So many men are. I mean, I'm only six feet; I've known lots of women taller."

"So have I," Dino said. "I'm very pleased to hear that you have a low opinion of Devlin Daltry."

"I certainly do," she said. "He made my life hell for weeks last fall."

"I'll personally see to it that he never does that again," Dino said.

"Oh, I don't want you to get involved with him; he can be dangerous."

Dino flashed his badge. "Allow me to introduce myself; it's Lieutenant Dino."

"Oh, good, then you can shoot him."

"Only if I get the chance."

"Dino has Daltry under surveillance as we speak," Stone said.

"I hope you catch him doing something criminal," Genevieve said.

"I hope so, too," Dino said. "I've already charged him with something minor; now I'm hoping for something major."

Willa Bernstein sat at the bar with Devlin Daltry, sipping single-malt Scotch. "*Mmmm,* this is a lot better than that Queens wine at the gallery."

"Certainly is. Willa seems an odd name for a Jewish girl."

"My mother was reading Willa Cather—*Death Comes for the Archbishop*—when I was born, and I'm not Jewish. My father is, but Jewish identity is passed down through the female line, and my mother is Episcopalian. So am I."

"My mistake."

"Everybody makes it. When are you having another show?"

"I opened one a couple of weeks ago, but it's sold out, so we're closing it."

"Oh, I'm sorry, I didn't know. I'd love to have seen it."

"I have a number of pieces at my studio. Maybe I can show them to you after dinner."

"I'd like that," she said.

The headwaiter came over. "Your usual table is ready, Mr. Daltry. May I take your drinks over?"

"Of course, Eddie. We're right behind you."

They stood up and followed the man toward the table.

"I hope it doesn't bother you that I'm so tall," Willa said. "It bothers a lot of men."

"Not in the least," Daltry replied smoothly. "In fact, I'm rather partial to tall women."

Dino's cell phone rang again. "Excuse me," he said, flipping it open. "Bacchetti."

"It's Bernstein, Lieutenant."

"Update?"

"They've just sat down to dinner. He's already invited her to his studio afterwards, and she's accepted. Do you want us to let her do that?"

Dino thought for a moment. "Yes," he said. "She's doing a great job so far; we have to believe she can take care of herself if she goes back to his place."

"Well, she's half again as big as he is," Bernstein said. "She ought to be able to handle him."

"Joe Dowdell and Hank Ortega are in the other car, right?"

"Yes, sir."

"Well, you just be sure that the four of you—sorry, five, I forgot about Pointer—are ready to go in there pronto if anything happens. She's got a code word if she gets into trouble, right?"

"Yes, Lieutenant. She'll say 'My back hurts' if she needs us."

"As soon as they're inside his building, find a way in; it'll save time if she needs help."

"Will do, Lieutenant."

Dino hung up, and Genevieve was staring at him oddly. "Am I to understand that you have a female police officer who's going to Devlin Daltry's studio?"

"Yes, I do," Dino said.

"Well," Genevieve said, "I think that's a very big mistake."

"What?" Dino asked.

"I went there once, and I almost didn't get out alive. And believe me, *I* know how to take care of myself."

53

Stone's cell phone rang. He didn't recognize the caller I.D. number. "Hello?"

"It's Dierdre."

"Hi."

"Dattila's out of jail."

"*What*?"

"His lawyer got a judge to release him, based on the fact that, since Gus's death and Herbie's disappearance, we have no witnesses against him."

"But there's the tape of Dattila ordering Herbie's death."

"The lawyer claimed they would show at trial that it's fabricated."

"Did Dattila buy a judge or something?"

"I don't think the judge can be faulted. Dattila's lawyer is right, except about the tape. It's not fabricated, is it?"

"No, it's genuine."

"Have you heard from Herbie?"

"Not a word."

"I know I'm not supposed to say this about my witness, but tell him he'd be smart to leave town. Dattila is going to spare no effort to see him dead. We got a tip that word has gone out to his people all over town: There's a hundred grand on Herbie's head."

"There ought to be a hundred grand on Dattila's head."

"This is my third try at getting the guy, and I've never even gone to trial."

"I can imagine how you must feel."

"No, you can't. If you hear from Herbie, tell him to scamper. After what happened at the hotel I'm not at all sure we can protect him."

"I'll give him the message."

"Good night."

"Good night." Stone hung up and turned to Dino. "Dattila is out, and if what Dierdre says is true, Herbie's as good as dead."

Willa watched while Devlin Daltry unlocked three deadbolts on a huge steel door and let them into his building. They were on the ground floor, which was being used as a garage. Daltry pressed a button, and a freight elevator descended.

"That's a very big elevator," Willa said, for the benefit of her colleagues.

"Some of my pieces are of heroic proportions," Daltry said, as they started up. "I couldn't get them out of the studio without this."

She counted three floors as they rose. "You live and work on the top floor?"

"Yes."

"What's on the others?"

"Not much, some office help on one. I'm thinking of converting the other two to lofts and selling them."

They stopped at the fourth floor and stepped into an enormous room.

"My goodness," Willa said, actually overwhelmed. The space was furnished as a living room, and at the other end she could see a professional-style kitchen. "This is fantastic." She pointed at the kitchen. "You must do a lot of cooking."

"I don't cook at all, actually, but I need the kitchen for parties. The caterers love it. Come, I'll show you my studio."

They walked for perhaps half a block and passed through huge double doors into an artist's studio that she could not have imagined. First of all, contrary to her notion of what an artist's studio was like, it was spotlessly clean and extremely neat. Double-height windows rose to receive the north light, and scattered around the space were pieces of Daltry's work, some already cast, some still in clay.

"You are obsessively neat, aren't you?" Willa said.

Daltry seemed to take umbrage at the characterization. "I am not obsessive about anything," he said defensively. "I simply like to live in an orderly world."

Willa's attention was riveted on a bronze of a very tall woman, missing its head. "What is that?"

"Oh, I was unhappy with the way the head turned out, so I'm going to redo it."

"After it's already cast?"

"It can be done. Would you like to see the rest of my home?"

"Yes, thank you. Is there still another level?"

"Yes. The elevator only goes to the fourth floor, but the stairs lead one more flight up."

"Don't go to his bedroom," Bernstein said into her ear.

"Is that where your bedroom is?"

"Yes, but there's more. I don't need the sort of living spaces that occupy this floor; they're just for work and entertaining. There's another complete apartment upstairs."

"Don't do it," Bernstein said.

"I'd love to see it," she said to Daltry.

D ino's cell phone rang. "Bacchetti."

"Boss, it's Bernstein. She's inside Daltry's place, and against my advice, she's going up to the level where his bedroom is."

"Are you inside yet?"

"We're having hell's own time getting in. There are three Assa locks in a steel door, and we haven't been able to pick even one of them. A crowbar didn't work, either."

"Then break a goddamned window or something," Dino said. "Be a burglar! His alarm system probably isn't on while he's home."

"Yes, Boss."

Dino hung up. "She's locked inside Daltry's building with him, and my people are having a hard time getting in."

"Oh, my God," Genevieve said. "I hope she's armed."

"I hope she is, too," Dino said. "Since she's undercover, she may not be."

Stone's cell phone rang. "Hello?"

"Stone, it's me."

"Herbie! Where the hell are you? Are you all right?"

"No, I'm not, and I'm not about to tell you where I am. The last time I told you where I was I nearly got killed."

"Herbie, I didn't tell anybody where you were. In fact, you never told me, remember?"

"Well, somebody knew, and he told Dattila."

"What happened there, Herbie?"

"I didn't like the food and stuff, so I was going to sneak out for something, so I turned on the shower and got dressed. I heard somebody yell in the next room, so I hid in a closet, and I saw this guy come into the bedroom with a gun. While he was in the bathroom, I got the hell out of there."

"It's good that you did. Now, listen. I talked to the D.A. a few minutes ago, and she says that you should get out of town, that she's not sure she can protect you."

"Well, that's pretty clear, isn't it?" Herbie yelled. "You said I'd be safe in the hotel; not even the two cops were safe."

"It gets worse, Herbie. Dattila is out of jail, and word is he's put out a very large contract on you. He's probably got a couple of hundred people on the street looking for you right now. You've got money, haven't you?"

"I've got about twelve hundred dollars."

"My advice is take a cab to New Jersey—don't go to the Port Authority Terminal or to Grand Central or Penn Station—just get to Jersey and get a bus out of there to anywhere."

"Your advice hasn't been very good so far, Stone."

"What are you talking about? If you'd taken my advice and not sued Dattila none of this would have happened!"

But Herbie had already hung up.

54

Willa walked up the curving staircase with Daltry holding her hand.

"I think you'll like my living quarters," he was saying. They emerged into a handsomely furnished living room with cream-colored paneled walls, crown moldings and many pictures and sculptures.

He led her to the bar and was pouring them a drink when the phone rang. Daltry looked at the instrument on the bar and muttered something under his breath. "Excuse me," he said, "I've got to take this call." He picked up the phone. "What is it?" he said without preamble, then he listened for a moment. "Jerry, I've told you repeatedly how important it is for you to stay where you are and not go out for a while. You've got enough groceries to last a month, and enough to drink, too." He listened some more. "I don't care. I want you to do as I say, or I won't be able to protect you. Don't you understand?" More listening. "Jerry, do you want to go to prison? I didn't think so. Well, that's the alternative to doing as I say, at least for a little while. Look, I've got somebody here at the moment. I'll come up there tomorrow morning, and we'll work something out. I promise." He hung up.

"Some people never listen," Willa said.

"You're right about that. I have this friend who's gotten himself into a jam, and I'm trying to help him, but he just won't be helped. Will you pour us a drink? I need the powder room."

"Of course." Willa filled two glasses with ice and made to pour. The moment Daltry was out of sight she checked the many buttons on the phone and found one that read "Log." She pressed it. "Bernstein, did you hear that conversation?" she whispered.

"Every word."

"Write down this number." She read it out to him. "It appears four other times today in his phone log."

"I'll check it out."

She pressed the button again, and the log disappeared, then she poured the drinks.

Daltry came back from the john and picked up his drink. "To an interesting future," he said. They drank, and he snaked an arm around her waist.

She let him kiss her, helping out a bit. "What time is it?" she asked, when they broke.

"Who cares? The night is young."

She looked at her watch. "I'm afraid it's not all that young, and I have an eight o'clock meeting tomorrow morning that I have to do some reading for." She danced lightly away from his grasp. "Can we continue this another evening soon?"

He grabbed her wrist and not gently. "Now is soon enough for me," he said. "I'll send you home with my driver in the morning; you'll be in plenty of time for your meeting."

"Not tonight, I'm afraid," she said, breaking free.

"You're just a little cock teaser, aren't you," he said, advancing toward her.

"No, I'm a *big* cock teaser, and I'm going home now."

He reached into a pocket and came out with a small spray canister. "I've got something for you," he said, spraying her in the face.

Her eyes were on fire, and she was having trouble speaking. "My . . ."

Then he hit her in the midriff hard, with his fist, and she went down. "I knew you'd like it rough," Daltry was saying, as he knelt beside her, ran his fingers into her cleaveage and yanked half her dress off, baring her breasts.

"My back hurts," she managed to say.

"Don't worry, sweetie, I'm going to make it all better," Daltry said. He had produced a switchblade knife and quickly cut the rest of her dress and underwear off.

She got in one punch, aiming for his nose, but caught him on the cheekbone when he turned his head. "My back hurts, goddammit!" she screamed.

He backhanded her, bouncing her head hard off the wooden floor.

He flipped her over on her belly and got a knee between her legs. "Well, let's give you something else to think about," he said. He put the knife against the back of her neck. "And if you move, I'll cut your fucking head off!"

Willa went limp and began to lose consciousness. She tried to think of something pleasant and failed.

They were on coffee at Elaine's. Dino's phone rang. "Bacchetti."

"Lieutenant, it's Bernstein. Willa got something, I think: a phone number. Joe Dowdell is running it right now. It's up north of here, at Sneden's Landing, on the Hudson."

"What's so great about this number, Bernstein? We're not shopping for real estate."

"Daltry got a call, and I could hear his half of it. It sounds like he's got somebody called Jerry stashed in a house up there, and he told him if he left the house, he could end up back in prison."

"That sounds promising."

"Wait a minute, Dowdell's got it. The phone is in Daltry's name; must be a country house."

"That's a start. You got an address?"

"Just a minute. Yeah, here it is." He read off the address.

Dino jotted it down on the tablecloth. "Okay, I'll get some people up there to talk to whoever the guy is."

"Wait a minute, we got a Mayday from Willa!" The connection was broken.

"Holy shit," Dino said, "Willa's in trouble, and I don't even know if they're in the building yet." He snatched Stone's phone and dialed a number. "I've gotta keep my line clear." He waited impatiently for the number to answer. "This is Bacchetti," he said finally. "I want you to get hold of the state police at the nearest station to Sneden's Landing, then meet them at this address and hold whoever is in the house until you hear from me." He read off the address. "You got that? Also, I want backup at Devlin Daltry's address in SoHo right now! Officer needs assistance. They may need battering rams!" He hung up.

"I told you she shouldn't go into that building," Genevieve said. "He raped me."

Eliza looked shocked. "You never told me."

"I never told anybody," she said.

Dino patted her hand. "I'm sorry, Genevieve. Don't you worry, I'm going to make him pay for that."

"Why don't you call Bernstein back?" Stone said.

"He'll call me," Dino said. "He's got enough on his hands right now without having to take my phone calls. His partner is in trouble; I shouldn't have let him send her in there," he said. "This is my fault all the way."

"It was her call, Dino; she was on the spot, and you have to back her decision. Nothing is your fault."

"Shit," Dino said, banging on the table.

55

Bernstein screamed, "Mayday, Mayday," and pulled out his gun, intending to shoot at the locks. He didn't know if it would do any good. Then he heard Willa scream.

"My back is killing me, goddammit!"

Joe Dowdell came running with the crowbar. "I'll try again!" he yelled.

"Not this door, the garage door!" Bernstein shouted.

Dowdell ran toward the garage door and ran the tip of the crowbar under it until it stopped where the door latched into the pavement. He worked it to no avail, then he stood on the end of the bar and put his whole weight on it. There was a metallic snap, and the door came unanchored from the concrete. All four cops got their fingers under it and managed to raise it about eighteen inches. Then the flying form of Shelly Pointer scooted under the door.

Shelly ran for the elevator. "It's five floors!" she yelled back. "It's faster to wait for the elevator."

Bernstein, who was in the best shape of the four men, ignored her and ran for the stairs.

The elevator seemed to take forever.

"I don't like the noises I'm hearing," Pointer said. There were grunting sounds coming from their equipment. "And I don't hear Willa at all."

The elevator finally came, and the other three cops boarded it. As they passed the third floor they could hear Bernstein's feet pounding on the steel stairs. He reached the fourth floor just as they did and was banging on the steel fire door.

Somebody let him in, and the five cops ran through the apartment to the curving staircase and, with Pointer in the lead, ran up the last flight.

As Pointer reached the top of the stairs she could see across the living room to the bar. Willa was on the floor, naked, and Daltry was behind and on top of her, oblivious to the five cops rushing across the room. Pointer got there first, and swung her gun at his head. There was a flash of blood, and Daltry fell sideways, clutching at his scalp and screaming. The four men fell on him.

Pointer shucked off her raincoat, went to Willa and covered her. "Oh, Willa, baby," she crooned, stroking her hair. "What did that bastard do to you?" She turned back toward the cops. "Don't kill him, for Christ's sake! Get on the horn and get an ambulance down here, and tell them to send a fucking doctor, not just an EMT. Willa is unconscious!"

B ack at Elaine's, Dino answered his cell phone again. "What?" Bernstein was breathing hard. "He's hurt Willa," he shouted into the phone. "We got him, but he's hurt her."

"Have you called for an ambulance?"

"Yeah, it's on the way. We'll probably end up at Bellevue; I'll call you."

"I'll meet you there," Dino said. He snapped the phone shut and turned to Stone. "You take care of the ladies," he said. "I'll call you when I know more." His cell phone rang again, and he flipped it open. "Bacchetti." He listened for a moment. "Great! Get him into the city pronto. I'm going to Bellevue, and when I know what's going on there, I'll come back to the precinct." He snapped the phone shut again. "The state cops have arrested one Jerome Daltry at Devlin Daltry's house in Sneden's Landing on a parole violation. They're bringing him down here. I gotta go. I'll call you later." Dino ran for his car.

Willa Bernstein slowly came to in a dimly lit room. Somebody was holding her hand.

"Willa? It's Shelly, baby, can you hear me?"

Willa nodded. "My head hurts," she said. "And that's not all. What happened?"

"Don't you worry, baby, we got Daltry; everything's going to be all right."

"What happened to me?" Willa asked. "We were fighting; that's all I remember."

"Don't you worry about that," Shelly said. "You just get some rest."

Willa's voice got stronger. "Goddammit, Shelly, tell me what happened!"

Shelly took a deep breath. "He raped you, honey. He knocked you unconscious, and then he raped you."

Willa involuntarily moved her hand to her crotch.

"Not there, Willa."

"Oh, shit."

"You're all right. The doctor already checked you out, and you're all right. You just be quiet now."

"I want some aspirin," Willa said. "I have a hell of a headache, and my eyes are burning, too."

Shelly reached over and pressed the bedside buzzer. A moment later, a nurse appeared. "She has a headache," Shelly said to the woman. "Get her something, will you?"

"He sprayed me with something, mace or pepper spray; I need my eyes flushed out."

"I'll see to it," the nurse said, then disappeared. She was back in a moment with two Tylenol, some eye solution and a syringe. In another moment she was dabbing the excess away with a tissue.

"That's better," Willa said. "Crank the bed up a little, will you?"

Shelly grabbed the bed control and sat her up. "The guys are all outside. So's Bacchetti. They're beside themselves. Can I bring them in?"

"Sure, go ahead, but let's not discuss my . . . condition with them, all right?"

Shelly nodded. "I'll get them."

Bernstein led the way into the room. He took Willa's hand. "I'm sorry it took us so long to get in," he said to her. "The place was a fortress."

"Where's Daltry?"

"He's downstairs being treated for his injuries. We'll run him uptown when they're done with him."

"What injuries?"

Bernstein glanced at his lieutenant. "Well, before you passed out, you must have gotten in a few good punches."

Willa managed a chuckle. "Yeah, I'll bet I beat the shit out of him."

Dino spoke up. "Whatever he got, he deserved. Listen, kiddo, that phone number you got us paid off. It was for Daltry's country house in Sneden's Landing, up the Hudson, and we found his younger brother there, freshly paroled from Attica, after doing seven years for a collection of violent crimes. They're bringing him down to the precinct, so now that I know you're okay, I'm going to go up there and interrogate him myself."

"You think he did the girl in New Jersey?" she asked.

"I'd bet on it," Dino replied. "We'll collect some DNA from him, then get the Jersey cops on it. With a little luck we'll put them both away forever. At the very least we've got Daltry on the two rapes."

Dino looked immediately annoyed with himself. "I'm sorry, I didn't mean . . ."

"There was another rape?"

"A nurse at a hospital uptown named Genevieve James. Nice girl; she'll testify."

"I want him for the murder," Willa said.

"Don't worry about it. Leave it to me."

"Done. Now can I get some sleep, guys? And thanks for rescuing me."

The men filed out of the room.

"You want me to stay, baby?" Shelly asked. "I'll stay all night, if you want."

"Just until I fall asleep," Willa said.

She didn't take long.

56

S tone was awoken from a sound sleep by the ringing of the phone. He tried to move but seemed to be pinned in place. He opened his eyes to a close-up of Eliza Larkin that was very close up, since they were wrapped around each other.

He freed an arm and reached for the phone. "Yeah?" he croaked.

"Rise and shine, pal," Dino said. "It's five-thirty in the morning. Greet the new day!"

"You sound alarmingly happy for this time of day," Stone said. "Why are you up?"

"I never went to bed," Dino said. "Never needed to. I never had so much fun in my life!"

"How did you spend your night, Dino?"

"Questioning Jerome Daltry," Dino said. "Charley Sample brought a D.A. over here from Jersey, and he did a deal with little Jerry, who, I might add, is a straight-out, honest-to-God psychopath."

"What's the deal?"

"Jerome gets twenty to life in a New Jersey joint for the crimi-nally insane, and, in return, he confessed to running you down with the car and killing Celia. We got it all on videotape, and we got it in writing, too—signed, sealed and delivered! He even told us he delivered Celia's head to Devlin, put it right in his hands! Can you imagine how that's going to play in court?"

"What did Devlin have to say for himself?"

"Oh, he was having a little trouble talking, what with his broken jaw and all, but he did manage to speak the word *lawyer* a number of times. Doesn't matter, though, we've got him sewed up for Celia's murder and for the two rapes, too!"

"There was somebody besides Genevieve?"

"Yeah, he got over on my detective before the cavalry could get there. Couldn't be helped. She's taking it like a champ, though, and she'll be great in court. So will Genevieve, come to that. She's pissed off enough to kill him, if we'd let her."

"You did have a good night, didn't you?"

"Sometimes I just love this job!" Dino crowed. "I'm going home and get some sleep. We'll talk later." He hung up.

Stone put the phone down and turned back to Eliza, who was wide awake. "That was Dino; he . . ."

"I could hear him shouting," she said. "I got it all. He's right about Genevieve; when she gets her day in court she'll nail the guy."

Stone kissed her. "You're very nice to wake up to," he said.

She shortened the distance between them. "You, too," she said. She ran her hand down his belly. "I sense that something is going on down there."

"You're a perceptive woman," Stone said, rolling her over on top of him.

"I'll think of something to do with it," she said, kissing him again and slipping him inside her. "It's my day off, too, so we're going to be here for a while."

The phone rang again. "Fuck it," Stone said.

"It's probably more good news," Eliza said. "I can wait another few seconds."

Stone grabbed the phone. "What?"

"Well, don't bite my head off," Herbie said.

"Jesus, Herbie, do you know what time it is?"

"I've got five-forty. You really ought to invest in a watch, Stone."

"What do you want, Herbie?"

"I just wanted to let you know that I'm taking your advice," Herbie said. "I took a cab to Jersey, and I'm on a bus, headed south."

"Great news, Herbie. Good-bye and good luck."

"Oh, will you tell Uncle Bob good-bye for me?"

"Sure, I will. Good-bye."

"And say good-bye to that nice D.A., too. You know, if I'd been able to hang around, I would have taken a shot at that. She's cute!"

"I'll tell her you said so, Herbie; I'm sure she'll be devastated to lose the chance. Good-bye."

"Hey, you think she'll really be devastated? Maybe I'll hang around and . . ."

"Good-bye, Herbie," Stone said and hung up. He turned back to Eliza. "That was Herbie."

"I heard. Do you think you've seen the last of him?"

"Dear God, I hope so," Stone said, turning his full attention to her again.

"You know, you went down a bit when you were talking to Herbie, but now . . ."

Stone made a little thrust.

"You're back," she said, helping him.

57

Herbie got off the subway downtown and began looking for a place to have breakfast. He passed a newsstand and picked up a *Daily News*. He reflected that he was going to have to start reading the *Times*, now that he was a lawyer. It looked better.

He found an early-opening restaurant and ordered eggs, bacon and pancakes. He had lost weight in that lousy hotel, and now he was going to gain it back. He ate slowly and turned to the paper. There was a front-page story: Carmine Dattila released from jail. That pissed him off all over again. He checked his watch frequently; he didn't want to be too early.

At nine o'clock he paid for his breakfast and took a walk. He found a street vendor selling cheap raincoats, and he bought one, along with a rain hat and some sunglasses. It did look like rain after all, and he could use a disguise of sorts. Dattila's people were still out there, looking for him.

He walked slowly downtown, window-shopping and looking at the career girls on their way to work. He was going to specialize in career girls after he got his law office open. He stopped and looked for a long time in the window of an expensive men's store. He was going to buy good suits like that and get a better haircut, too. Also shoes. A lot of men who were trying to look good stinted on the shoes. He hated cheap shoes; they made the whole outfit look cheap.

He continued downtown, checking his watch from time to time. Just after ten would be perfect, he reckoned, and this had been confirmed by what he had read in the paper.

He reached Mott Street and increased his pace a bit. He turned and walked quickly down to where he could see the sign for the La Boheme coffeehouse. A black Cadillac sedan sat at the curb, its engine idling.

He had it all worked out; he knew exactly what to do, from start to finish. He opened the door to the coffeehouse and walked quickly in; the door closed itself behind him. He kept walking at the same pace, not hurrying, heading for the table at the rear. He walked straight up to it, raised his hand and fired two shots at Carmine Dattila's head, then he spun around, waving the cop's pistol he had borrowed at people who were half out of their chairs. He was surprised not to see any weapons; he had half expected to be shot himself. He went quickly to the door and backed out into the street, still holding the gun out before him.

Half a dozen men fell on him from different directions. He dropped the gun and offered no resistance. A moment later he was handcuffed and in the back of a police car. "Hey, where did you guys come from?" he asked the driver.

"We're all over town, pal," the driver replied.

S tone lay on his back, breathing deeply, emptied of the ability to do anything about his desire for Eliza Larkin. She sat up in bed, naked, eating a piece of toast from a tray and reading the newspaper.

"How many times was that?" Stone asked.

"I don't know exactly," she replied, "but you will astonish me if you have anything left."

"But you do?"

"I don't have to get an erection," she explained. "And I'm in pretty good shape, so I expect I could go all morning, if you have any interest."

"Interest, yes; strength, no."

"Interest is good," she said, patting his belly.

Joan's voice came from the intercom. "Assistant District Attorney Monahan is on line one," she said, articulating the title carefully. Good Joan.

Stone held a finger to his lips for Eliza to see, and she nodded. He picked up the phone. "Hello?"

"Stone," Dierdre said, "I hardly know what to say to you. I would have thought, just thought, that you would have been able to keep Herbert Fisher out of trouble, after his close call at the hotel."

"Herbie is on a bus to Florida," Stone replied, careful not to use her name. "He called me from the road early this morning."

"Maybe from the road," Dierdre said, "but not the road to Florida. Try the road to Little Italy."

"What on earth are you talking about?"

"You should be hearing from Herbie again soon," she said, "when it finally dawns on him that he needs a lawyer."

"You're not making any sense," Stone said. "What was Herbie doing in Little Italy?"

"Killing Carmine Dattila."

"*What?*" He couldn't think of anything else to say.

"At ten minutes past ten this morning, Herbie walked into the La Boheme coffeehouse and shot Dattila the Hun twice in the head, and actually got out of the place alive, because half an hour before, the police had gone in there and arrested everybody who had a gun. We still had a whole bunch of people hanging around the block in plain clothes, and they managed to disarm and handcuff Herbie before he could hurt himself."

"Where is he now?"

"In the lockup downstairs. Frankly, we're a little undecided as to what to do with him: charge him with first-degree murder or give him a medal for his service to the community. Could you get your ass down here as quickly as possible, please?"

"I'll be there in an hour," Stone said. He hung up.

"I couldn't hear that one," Eliza said. "I guess nobody was shouting."

"It's just as well; you wouldn't have believed it. I certainly don't."

A n hour and ten minutes later Stone presented himself at the district attorney's office and was ushered into a conference room where Dierdre Monahan and the chief deputy D.A. were already seated. Simultaneously, Herbie was brought in through another door, wearing shackles, his hands cuffed to a chain around his waist.

"Hey, Stone," he said. "I . . ."

"Shut up, Herbie, and don't say another word, or I'll borrow a gun and shoot you."

"I'll loan you a gun," Dierdre said.

Stone sat down opposite her and her boss, while Herbie was pressed into a chair at the end of the table. A uniformed policeman stood behind him, glowering.

Dierdre shoved a sheet of paper across the table. "That's your client's signature at the bottom of a waiver of his right to an attorney," she said. She held up a cassette. "And this is the videotape of his full confession to the murder of Carmine Dattila."

"Well, I don't know why I had to come all the way downtown," Stone said. "Why don't you just electrocute him and get it over with?"

"Hey!" Herbie said.

"Shut up, Herbie, or I'll have your mouth duct-taped."

Herbie muttered something about free speech.

"Do you have any duct tape?" Stone asked Dierdre.

"I'll send out for some," she replied. "Stone, as I mentioned on the phone, we're in a bit of a quandary here. We'd like your views on how to handle this."

Stone looked back and forth between the two prosecutors. He had time to reflect that no D.A. had ever asked his advice about prosecuting a client of his. Then he got the picture. "Oh," he said. "Right. My client, Mr. Fisher, has been hounded and abused by Carmine Dattila and his employees for weeks. They have beaten him, kidnapped him and his murder has been ordered by Mr. Dattila, a tape of which statement is in your possession. Additionally, after the only other witness against Mr. Dattila was murdered in jail, Dattila sent a hired assassin to the hotel where Mr. Fisher was being held in protective custody, where he murdered the two police officers guarding him and would have murdered Mr. Fisher, had he not had the presence of mind to escape the hotel suite before the assassin found him.

"These events convinced Mr. Fisher that the District Attorney and the police could not *ever* protect him, so, while the balance of his mind . . . may have been disturbed by these events, he found himself in the presence of Mr. Dattila and did the only thing he could do to protect himself in the circumstances and entirely in self-defense." Stone stopped and took a breath. "That's what I'd say to a jury, and I'd get an acquittal."

Dierdre nodded. She looked at her boss questioningly, and he nodded. "All right," she said. "You understand we can't have people walking around the city armed and shooting people. How about he pleads to one count of illegal possession of a weapon and gets a year, suspended?"

"Done," Stone said.

"A year?" Herbie asked, sounding horrified.

"Suspended, Herbie. Shut up."

"There's a judge waiting for us in his chambers," Dierdre said, getting to her feet.

———

Half an hour later, Stone and Herbie stood on the steps of the courthouse in the sunshine. Herbie was examining the contents of an envelope that had been handed to him on the way out of the judge's chambers.

"Do you have any money, Herbie?" Stone asked.

"Yeah, all my stuff is in here, except the cop's gun. I guess they kept that."

"Well, yes, they would have," Stone said. "Do I have to explain to you that there are friends and employees of Carmine Dattila out there who would still like to squash you like a bug, even though the contract on your head may have expired with Dattila? And that you should go back to your aunt's in East Hampton or any other place you like and lie very low for as long as possible, and that you should never again go near a bookie or a loan shark or Little Italy? Did I explain that to you?"

"I think you just did," Herbie said.

"Then get your ass into a cab," Stone said, clapping Herbie on the back. "And don't ever, ever call me again."

"Wait a minute," Herbie said. "What about my civil action against Dattila? We could go for his estate."

"Estate? You think Dattila had an estate? Like on paper? If he did, the IRS would get there first, believe me, and you'd find yourself in small claims court."

"Oh," Herbie replied.

"Get lost, Herbie." Stone ran down the steps, waving at a taxi, and he did not look back.

58

S tone got out of the cab and ran up the stairs into the house, avoiding the office door. Eliza was upstairs, still in bed, waiting. Before he could get into the elevator, he heard Joan's voice calling to him over the phone's intercom.

"Stone," she said, "there's a client here to see you. I think you're going to want to take this meeting."

"I'll be back as soon as humanly possible," he said to Eliza.

"Sooner than that," she said.

Stone sighed and started down the stairs. If Herbie had beat him here, well, there was a gun in his office safe. He walked into his office and found Bernice Finger sitting on his leather sofa.

"Why, Mrs. Finger," he said, extending his hand. "How nice to see you." It really was very nice to see her; she had obviously come to her senses. He sat down next to her. "How can I help you?"

"Well," she began, then stopped. "First, I have something to give you," she said, opening her handbag.

Stone watched her, baffled, as she came up with a gold-plated .38 Detective Special with a snub-nosed barrel.

"Could you do something with this, please?" she asked, pointing it at him, as if to shoot.

Stone grabbed the weapon. "Bernice," he said, "please don't tell me you . . ." He flipped open the cylinder of the gun and found it fully loaded. Two of the cartridges had been fired. "Oh, no," he said, half to himself.

"I shot them both," she said, dabbing at her eyes with a handkerchief.

"Oh, no," he said, this time aloud.

"But I missed," she said. "I scared the shit out of them, though." She smiled.

Stone let go the breath he had been holding. "I expect you did," he said. "Did Bernie call the police?"

"I don't think so," she said. "That was a couple of hours ago, and nobody's tried to arrest me."

Stone nodded. "And what are your intentions now?"

"I believe I'm ready to proceed with the divorce."

"Really? No backing out this time?"

"I give you my word."

Stone looked at his watch. "Just a moment." He rose, went to his desk and picked up the phone. "Get me Sam Teich at Bernie Finger's office," he said to Joan. A long moment passed, then Joan came back. "He's on line one," she said.

Stone picked up the phone and pushed the button. "Good afternoon, Sam."

"Good afternoon, Stone. I've been expecting your call; Bernie's here with me. I want you to know, up front, that Bernie has no intention of pressing criminal charges."

"That's awfully sweet of Bernie," Stone said.

"Are the figures we talked about before still acceptable?"

"Hardly," Stone said, "but I'll tell you what I'll do: Add fifty percent to the cash amounts in the agreement, have it retyped, have Bernie sign it before a notary, send the signed deeds for the real estate and a cashier's check for the money over here by close of business, and we're done."

"Just a minute." He covered the phone with his hand for a minute, then came back. "We'll need a nondisclosure agreement," he said. "Bernie doesn't want to read about this on Page Six of the *Post*."

"That's acceptable," Stone said.

"I already have everything but the cashier's check and the re-typed agreement. You'll have it all in two hours."

"Thank you, Sam. Best to Bernie." He hung up and turned to Bernice Finger. "We have a firm agreement," he said. "Everything will be here in a couple of hours. We'll process the check, deduct our fee, according to our agreement, and issue you a cashier's check from my account first thing tomorrow morning. All we need do then is present the signed agreement to a judge with a joint petition for a decree. And remember, you can't tell a soul what you got in the agreement. It's big trouble if you do."

Bernice Finger pressed a hand to her ample bosom. "Oh, that's such a relief," she said. She stood up. "Well, I'll look forward to receiving my check in the morning."

Stone walked her to the front door. "Bernice, I hope I don't have to put you under armed guard to prevent another trip to Vegas."

She laughed aloud. "Fat chance!" she said, then walked to her waiting car, where the chauffeur was braced with the door open, got in and was driven away.

Stone went back inside. "Were you listening on the phone?"

"Oh, yes," Joan said. "That was thrilling."

"Call the bank and tell them we're making a late deposit, a cashier's check, and we want the funds cleared immediately. When it clears, deduct our fee and messenger Mrs. Finger a cashier's check for the balance, along with the property deeds, then write yourself a bonus check for ten thousand dollars."

Joan came to attention and saluted. "Yes, *sir*!"

Stone walked back through his office, up the stairs and into the elevator. A moment later, he was walking into his bedroom, where Eliza was sitting up in bed, doing the *Times* crossword puzzle.

"Hello, sailor," she said. "How are you feeling?"

"Revitalized," he replied, working on his buttons.

AUTHOR'S NOTE

I am happy to hear from readers, but you should know that if you write to me in care of my publisher, three to six months will pass before I receive your letter, and when it finally arrives it will be one among many, and I will not be able to reply.

However, if you have access to the Internet, you may visit my Web site at www.stuartwoods.com, where there is a button for sending me e-mail. So far, I have been able to reply to all of my e-mail, and I will continue to try to do so.

If you send me an e-mail and do not receive a reply, it is because you are among an alarming number of people who have entered their e-mail address incorrectly in their mail software. I have many of my replies returned as undeliverable.

Remember: e-mail, reply; snail mail, no reply.

When you e-mail, please do not send attachments, as I *never* open these. They can take twenty minutes to download, and they often contain viruses.

Please do not place me on your mailing lists for funny stories, prayers, political causes, charitable fund-raising, petitions or sentimental claptrap. I get enough of that from people I already know. Generally speaking, when I get e-mail addressed to a large number of people, I immediately delete it without reading it.

Please do not send me your ideas for a book, as I have a policy of writing only what I myself invent. If you send me story ideas, I will immediately delete them without reading them. If you have a good idea for a book, write it yourself, but I will not be able to advise you on how to get it published. Buy a copy of *Writer's Market* at any bookstore; that will tell you how.

Anyone with a request concerning events or appearances may e-mail it to me or send it to: Publicity Department, Penguin Group (USA) Inc., 375 Hudson Street, New York, NY 10014.

Those ambitious folk who wish to buy film, dramatic or television rights to my books should contact Matthew Snyder, Creative Artists Agency, 9830 Wilshire Boulevard, Beverly Hills, CA 90212-1825.

Those who wish to make offers for rights of a literary nature should contact Anne Sibbald, Janklow & Nesbit, 445 Park Avenue, New York, NY 10022. (Note: This is not an invitation for you to send her your manuscript or to solicit her to be your agent.)

If you want to know if I will be signing books in your city, please visit my Web site, www.stuartwoods.com, where the tour schedule will be published a month or so in advance. If you wish me to do a book signing in your locality, ask your favorite bookseller to contact his Penguin representative or the Penguin publicity department with the request.

If you find typographical or editorial errors in my book and feel an irresistible urge to tell someone, please write to Rachel Kahan at Penguin's address above. Do not e-mail your discoveries to me, as I will already have learned about them from others.

A list of my published works appears in the front of this book and on my Web site. All the novels are still in print in paperback and can be found at or ordered from any bookstore. If you wish to obtain hardcover copies of earlier novels or of the two nonfiction books, a good used bookstore or one of the online bookstores can help you find them. Otherwise, you will have to go to a great many garage sales.

Stone Barrington
and Holly Barker
team up again in

SHOOT HIM
IF HE RUNS

In stores September 2007

To read the first chapter, go
to **www.stuartwoods.com**.

PUTNAM | A member of
Penguin Group (USA) Inc.
www.penguin.com